ANCHORS AWAY AND MURDER

Book Seven: The Fiona Fleming Cozy Mysteries

PATTI LARSEN

Cover design by Christina Gaudet
www.castlekeepcreations.com

Thanks, Kirstin!

ISBN-13: 978-1-988700-91-5

CHAPTER ONE

Ready for More in Reading

It's not hard to see the massive changes happening to our town, nor is it difficult to lay equal amounts of kudos and blame on those in power who have led us here. Namely, and I have no qualms naming names, our own mayor, Olivia Walker, and her never-flagging energetic promotion of Reading to the rest of the known world. I'm not the first to benefit from the clever and sometimes overzealous attempts she's made to draw in tourist dollars, and I'm sure I won't be the last. However, it's become increasingly apparent that those who reap the rewards of her consistent attention to the details of Reading's increasing popularity have joined the vanguard of those choosing to oppose her continuing guidance and position as our fearless leader.

Inexplicable? Or deception fed by years of control by one

particular family who can't stand to see change come in such a dramatic way?

I sat back from the keyboard of my laptop and sighed. The kind of heavy, weighted sigh that left me sagging and my back aching from poor posture. The deep and draining kind of exhale that told me, yet again, I'd be deleting this start to the column I'd been trying to write for a couple of months now.

Literally months. When Pamela Shard, the seemingly fearless and somewhat jaded local newspaperwoman approached me to create said column for our paper in all its local glory and authority, I'd initially been tickled and rather nervous about the prospect. After all, I wasn't a writer, per se. I'd been a college student, a barista, a waitress, a retail saleswoman among other countless small, frustrating jobs that got me nowhere during my time living in New York City. But, most recently, drawing on my stint as the owner/operator of Petunia's Bed and Breakfast—and the brand new and still shiny annex next door—I figured I had enough life experience to at least jot down the kinds of thoughts others might want to read. After all, this wasn't the *Boston Globe* or the *New York Times*. It was the *Reading Reader Gazette* for heaven's sake.

Yeah, so I hadn't factored in a number of things, apparently. Like my creeping doubt and self-judgment that every word I wrote came out trite, contrived and painful. Or that my particular writing style—train of thought, run on from one mixed metaphor to the other—might not appeal to everyone.

Sure, I had, as yet, to test said writing skills on a real-life audience. I was fully aware my pressing sense of sadly missing skill came from my own lack of confidence that I could do what Pamela asked of me. After my first attempt to write something coherent, I'd quickly deleted the mess of not only jumbled thoughts but clearly opinionated ramblings about my town and the people who had been pissing me off lately and stepped away from the computer.

Did I want the entire town to hate me? Did Pamela? Horror shudders at my snarky near-societal death still gave me stomach cramps. I had no idea why I kept trying, either. This latest stab at a column, while an opinion piece, was so far from what I wanted to write I cringed before selecting all and hitting the kill button on my words.

I closed my laptop and sat back, head resting on the cushion of my sofa, the sunlight beaming in the basement windows lighting the center of my kitchen island and making it visually apparent no matter how much I cleaned the fine, pale hairs from the snoring creature at my side made it to all the nooks and crannies of my life, including the places I ate. I paused to stroke Petunia's fur, shedding some said bits into the fabric of my couch, before heaving my feet off the coffee table and setting aside my computer, waking the sleeping fawn creature in a snorting, farting and hilariously familiar alert awareness that triggered a giggle from me and the immediate wiggle of her cinnamon bun tail. Small black ears perked as my phone buzzed, my attention drawn to the familiar face that appeared, Crew Turner's handsome avatar smiling back at me. I grinned in response to the memory of taking that picture the night of Aundrea and Pamela's wedding, the easy smile on his face, the crinkle around his blue eyes, the way his tanned skin looked so delicious against the open white collar of his dress shirt.

Meow.

I hit answer and heard the smile reach my voice. "Good morning, Sheriff. How's Montpelier?" He and Jill were at a conference in the state capital, gone since last Sunday night. He'd been great to keep in touch, calling when he knew I'd be alone, usually about this time of day and again late enough at night we had lots of time to talk. Did he really know me that well, my schedule? Apparently. Made me feel a happy little bubble of joy like we were really a couple. Weren't we?

"Good morning, Miss Fleming," he said in that deep gravel voice of his that made me shiver and grin all over again. "I'm bored silly, ready to come home tomorrow and wishing you'd come with me instead of Jill." Well, growl, Sheriff Turner.

"Did you learn lots and lots?" I giggled. He'd complained previously about going at all, though Olivia insisted. Something to do with making our presence obvious and our competence clear.

Crew's heavy sigh told me he'd had enough. "It's been okay," he said, though he sounded tired. "And I got a chance to talk to some of my old friends from the Bureau." I wasn't sure that made me so happy, selfish as that thought was. I wanted him here in Reading with me, not gallivanting off to rejoin the FBI. He'd reassured me he had no intentions of doing such a thing, but who knew what the future held? He'd had enough of a rocky road here as sheriff, if the opportunity came up would he take it?

We'd deal with it if that time ever came. Because I had a say in what he did, right?

Doubt, you suck.

"I can't wait to see you." His own tone held nothing of worry or anxiety and helped calm me down. Wow, I really had trust issues. No shocker there, but still. This was Crew. Time to dump the nerves. "Can you get the night off tomorrow? I want to make you dinner."

Yum. In more ways than one. "I'll ask Daisy." She'd have my back, no doubt about it. The way she looked at me and the delicious sheriff when we were together? She had us married already, the brat. "Sorry, Crew, I have to go." I'd already been down here long enough. "Have a great weekend," I said. "I'll talk to you tonight?"

I heard a faint knock on the other end of the line, heard Crew call out for the person to wait. "Perfect. Talk tonight," he said and hung up.

I hated that he was gone, just like that, and stared at his picture for a long moment, one finger tracing over his happy expression before I sighed deeply one last time and looked down at Petunia. "Time to get back to work," I said.

The pug grunted her agreement, snorfling at my pant leg in a hopeful search for food crumbs. Which reminded me I'd meant to have some breakfast when I came downstairs for a quick quiet moment between morning setup and the breakfast rush, not waste the entire twenty minutes I'd set aside for some personal time on a column I wasn't even going to keep.

Great. Well, at least skipping a meal was good for my waistline, though I'd be drinking enough coffee in the next few hours I'd make up the calories in sugar and the real cream Mom stocked in the fridge upstairs.

I left my laptop on the coffee table and pushed the column from my mind. I'd either come up with something I could live with, or I'd just tell Pamela I couldn't do it. Thing was, I really needed to tell her one way or the other. Funny, she hadn't been pushing me for an entry. Did she know I struggled internally with creating something I could be proud of? Could be. She'd been reporting for years, after all. If anyone understood, it would be her. And it had been a request, hadn't it? Not some kind of edict. Which meant there would be no hard feelings if I told her I was out.

So why then did I continue to come back to the blank, white page and keep trying to write something that felt like the most wicked and painful torture of my life?

Grunt. Sucker for punishment, anyone? Or did I really, honestly think I had something important to say? So, pride before the fall...?

I emerged from my basement apartment into the busy and brightly lit foyer of Petunia's to the chattering laughter of visitors, the warmth of the August morning taxing the air conditioning as the front door opened and closed multiple times. I winced at the thought of my electrical bill before shoving that consideration aside. Things had never been busier, with both Petunia's and the annex filled to the brim since the next-door property opened in May, booked straight through to the end of September. I had zero to complain about and plenty of income to pay for the loss of cool air out my front door. Still, I had two partners now, though thanks to Mom's efforts the restaurant was busier than ever, no longer just a breakfast service—belying the B&B description of Petunia's—but a full service, seven-days-a-week location in high demand, both at the main house and across the yard for finer dining. It had been her brilliant idea to split the two dining rooms into more casual and a distinctly upper-crust eating experience that drew tourists and locals alike.

In short, my mother was a genius. And if she ever chose to sell and leave me, I'd be screwed.

Speaking of the culinary and business mogul, I swept through the kitchen door and offered her a big hug, the pug at my feet hunkering down to stare up at the lovely redhead who beamed at me after letting me go from her own enthusiastic grasp.

"Did you have a good break, dear?" Mom spun away from me before I could answer, her matching green eyes and auburn locks giving me an excellent idea of how good I'd look when I was her age. I was going to age very gracefully, it seemed. I joined her at the counter, offering my pug a handful of blueberries Mom stirred into a bowl of batter before helping myself to a few.

"Fine, Mom." No need to tell her I'd skipped eating in favor of writing. She was too busy to take time to force me to sit down and gulp some of her delicious oatmeal or serve me a plate of bacon and eggs. Instead, I stole a mini muffin from the pile she deemed not pretty enough to serve for breakfast and peeled the paper casing, popping it into my mouth where the mix of banana and cinnamon dissolved in sugary perfection. See, who needed to cook when I had my mother around?

"You're still able to help me set up for the yacht club fun day, Fiona?" I had no idea how Mom found the energy or focus to balance this place and her own catering business, but she seemed to be handling it all in stride. Like she saw the challenge as a way to redeem herself for the months she put into feeling sorry for herself when she'd crashed and burned over the TV show episode of *Bake or Break* last winter. I was just happy to have my mother back and better than ever, though I inwardly winced at the reminder of the promise I'd made her—and through her, Olivia—in passing a week ago.

"Sure, Mom," I said, aiming for perky so she wouldn't know I'd rather just stay here. Not that I had anything against the yacht club or Olivia's needy, attention-grabbing events that seemed to come up far too often. Might be a fun chance to get out, except of course it meant lugging and serving and work.

Sigh.

The third slice of our particular pie of awesome swept into the kitchen, brightening my day enough I forgot about being grumpy. Her gray eyes alight, dark blonde hair in artful pigtails that draped in glossy curls over the shoulders of her flowered dress, Daisy Bruce always looked fresh, happy and full of the kind of charismatic charm that made her the perfect front runner for Petunia's. Not to mention the fact she'd finally found her calling after all these years, her adept skills at managing people, logistics and timing making her the perfect partner in all things events held at the two locations.

"We're prepped and ready for guest turnover." She beamed at me, kissed Mom's cheek, then bent to give Petunia a hearty pat before exhaling a sigh that resembled nothing like the depressed one I'd let out myself just a few moments ago. I found myself smiling back at her, feeling the content and excitement of the way things were wash over me. Busy or not, run off my feet or not, I'd never been this happy in my entire life. And, from the way the two women I loved most in the world stopped to grin at each other and me in the perfect synchronization of sisterly adoration, I wasn't the only one.

How lucky was I?

The kitchen door swung open, one of the many girls Daisy hired to keep our businesses running bustling in with dirty dishes, interrupting the moment but not erasing it completely. Nothing could do that. I was positive of it. I stepped out of her way—damn it, was she Molly or Bianca? Argh, I sucked at names—while Daisy adeptly side swept with a soft swish of her pattered skirt, joining me out of the path of the next girl—Darcy? Erin?—who hurried in with lunch plates on their way to the dishwasher.

"You two," Mom pointed at me with her spatula, "out!"

I laughed and headed for the foyer, Daisy at my side, the way things should be.

CHAPTER TWO

The two of us dodged more girls with more platters, hurrying past the dining-room door. I glanced inside, delighted to see a full house, not unusual for a Saturday morning, with a small group waiting for yet another girl to clear a table for them. Part of me itched to help out, but Daisy guided me to the sideboard and the computer in the foyer as if sensing I was about to interfere in her domain. Not that I was a control freak or anything. But she and Mom both had to rather firmly guide me away from trying to do everything and let them handle their parts of the puzzle since they'd signed their contracts in May.

Okay, so I was used to being the numero uno around here. They just had to be patient.

Daisy walked me through the list of pending check-outs and check-ins, our morning devoured by chatting with guests and working out kinks that she'd caught in our lineup. Leave it to her to save our butts time and again. She really was good at this, better than I'd ever been.

And all the while putting the clients first. I beamed at her as she waved at an older couple exiting the front door as we wrapped up our meeting. "So sweet," she said, heart in her voice. "Did you see? They were holding hands."

Leave it to Daisy to catch that particular detail, though thinking about holding hands led me to thinking about Crew Turner all over again and much, much more than just that simple touch. Growl. Down, girl.

Daisy made a soft meu of distress before hugging me quickly. "You must be missing the good sheriff this weekend. Has he texted to say how horribly lonely he is without you?"

I grinned at her, blushing despite myself thanks to the carnal thoughts I'd just been indulging in. While Crew and I had moved past the initial awkwardness of choosing to date, we had, as yet, to commit fully to our relationship. And while kissing him was about as close to the top of my happiest moments list ever, I was ready for so much more.

Seriously, Fee. Wash that mind out with soap.

"We had our usual quick talk this morning," I said, looking down to keep her from seeing the full flush on my cheeks. I was, after all, a redhead.

Freckles and the palest of tans did nothing to hide the deep crimson my face turned when I blushed. I'm sure she noticed, but she kept the temptation to tease me to herself, bless her, while I rushed on. "He's totally bored and can't wait to get home." His question struck and I grinned at her. "Mind taking the desk for the night tomorrow? He offered to cook and I'm *starving*."

She giggled wickedly, blushing herself, eyes a-twinkle. "You bet," she said and sighed. "At least one of us is dating." She pushed on past that comment while I frowned a bit in response. Daisy was gorgeous and hilarious and awesome. She could have anyone she wanted. How had I failed to notice she was alone these days? I really had to stop being so selfish. "I'm still not sure what he was thinking." Daisy tsked softly under her breath, arms crossing over her chest. "I mean, I understand why he took Jill with him, considering his choices." I knew what she meant. That left Robert Carlisle of all people in charge of the sheriff's department.

"Jill's a great deputy," I said, reiterating what he'd said to me the night they'd left, almost a week ago. A long, lonely week ago. Argh. "She deserves the chance to learn." That kind of training would be wasted on my cousin.

"I know," Daisy said, patting my hand with hers as she relented. "I just hate that Robert is parading around Reading these days looking like he's the king of the mountain." She flinched faintly, paling as if she felt bad for what she'd just said. No, guilty. Well, she was the sweetest person I knew, but badmouthing Robert was kind of a pastime for the two of us. She could drop the regret right now.

Besides, she wasn't stretching the truth, not by a long shot. The last time I'd run into him, only yesterday morning when I slipped into Sammy's to get a cup of coffee and a chance for fresh air outside Petunia's, he'd been strutting the street like a puffed-up peacock, his freshly shined badge thrust outward as if everyone in town wasn't aware of the fact he was acting sheriff. It made my jaw ache just at the thought of him in charge of anything, let alone our little town's safety. But the likelihood of anything bad happening in the short week Crew and Jill were out of town was pretty slim. A time that was almost over.

Then again, we'd suffered through a rash of murders over the last two years since I'd moved home, so I held my breath and did my best to trust Crew knew what he was doing leaving Robert behind unsupervised. Considering the council had quieted down about their opposition to Olivia in the face of the success of her corporate retreat initiative, at least I didn't have Geoffrey Jenkins to deal with. The town councilor and husband of one of the local Pattersons still gave me the creeps. The fact he was no longer campaigning so openly to replace Olivia was a mix of nervous relief and anxiety. What I saw out in the open I could at least tackle head-on. But what if more insidious things were happening under the surface of the cutest town in America? The fact there had been zero word about Blackstone

Corporation or their role in the almost loss of the *Zip It!* park my friend Jared Wilkins helped open wasn't lost on me, either. Nice to see my friend no longer so stressed out and stretched thin, to watch tension and anxiety leave his handsome face the more he leaned on his new fiancé, Alicia Conway. The fact the two of them were planning their wedding in the annex, just like his mother, Aundrea, and Pamela just a few short months ago filled me with the kind of happy pride I struggled to keep to myself every time I saw the delighted couple.

Funny how the heart chose to focus on the here and now and the things that could be seen and felt instead of the darker and more mysterious secrets that maybe should have taken priority. Still, it was easy to let all of that slide for the time being, what with being so busy I could barely find time to eat and all.

Maybe I was dropping the ball, but for now, I was happy to focus on Petunia's and the annex and my flowering love life.

"Has he come up with anything new regarding you know what?" Daisy's broad wink and not-so-subtle reference to our shared investigation into the Reading hoard made me giggle. She was so hilarious about the whole thing, her attempts at clandestine chatter when I included her in my talk with Crew after he revealed his past connections to town enough to make this whole search worth it, treasure or no treasure.

While the three of us carefully connected the dots

we had access to, Crew's reveal his grandfather Alistair Markham was the author of the book in question, the very tome my Grandmother Iris directed me to find through the clues of her music box and the various other bits and pieces, did little to help us crack whatever code it was kept us from finding the hoard. Crew's scrap of the map was interesting and connected to mine, but aside from the tattoo he wore on his wrist—the same one his father wore, inked as a tribute to his own dad—and the sheriff's familiarity with the book, he had nothing new to offer.

Not that I cared. Honestly, every step of that particular mystery had led me deeper into the kind of giddy joy that reminded me of being a happy kid waiting for Santa at Christmas. I was more than delighted to let it linger. I guess, in part because a healthy slice of me really didn't think we'd uncover the treasure after all. Doubloon or not, I found it hard to believe we'd find anything after so many treasure hunters debunked the myth.

Still, there was enough of a trail of breadcrumbs I had zero reticence about sharing the curiosity and fun with my bestie and the guy who was well on the way to becoming my boyfriend.

That happy thought in my heart, I found it easy to smother any remaining animosity that might linger as a young brunette with her nose in the air and the kind of attitude that set me off the moment I saw her swept through my front door.

CHAPTER THREE

Now, it wasn't that Rose and I were exactly enemies, per se. Daisy's step-sister was more of an annoying irritant with a slowly growing list of personality traits and emotional attributes that ground my teeth together and made me want to smack her until she stopped being an arrogant twit who really had no reason to treat the world around her like it owed her something.

Yeah, okay, so frenemies. Made worse because she was, after all, Daisy's stepsister.

It was just that attitude she wore like a set of queenly robes, an invisible wrapping of *I'm better than you and don't you know it* that made my teeth ache and my stomach clench. And as far as I could tell there was zero reason for her gloating mightier than thou.

She normally lived at home with her parents in Montpelier, a late twentysomething who didn't hold a permanent job of any kind with the sort of normal looks and overly skinny frame that leaned away from pretty and into emaciated and a complete lacking in social skills and graces that might endear her to the average person.

Judgmental, who, me?

Rose's eyes settled on mine as she paused in the entry, her patterned dress so reminiscent of Daisy's wardrobe I was positive she'd gone shopping in my bestie's closet. Giant gold rim sunglasses perched in her dark brown hair, the flat brown of her gaze, as always, sweeping over me as if she judged every single strand of my auburn hair out of place—messy buns were a thing, right?—every minute stain on the front of my button-up despite my hard work to stay clean, each individual but obvious flaw that she'd rather be caught dead than exhibit in public. I flinched and forced a smile, refusing to allow my traitor hands to rise and touch my mass of red hair, to smooth the front of my shirt or my green eyes to flicker downward to check and see if I had something embarrassing happening elsewhere on my person.

Daisy hurried to her stepsister's side as if sensing the tension, her apologetic smile aimed at Rose as much as me. She hurried the younger woman past me and into the kitchen, ending our happy interaction and reminding me that my relationship with Daisy, while still awesome, had been strained since Rose appeared a week ago.

The longest week of my life, without Crew, and dealing with Miss Awesomepants. I did my best to hide how I was feeling if only to smooth things over with Daisy. But it was hard to pull back on my animosity, aimed at the dull, distasteful expression on the face of the young woman who'd recently shown up daily at my bed and breakfast and set down the kind of roots that made me think she was staying put no matter what I had to say about the matter. The fact that Rose Norton was Daisy's stepsister kind of curtailed my ability to kick her sorry butt out of my place, since said Daisy was now a partner. Still, just the way my bestie reacted every time she set eyes on her sort-of sibling raised my blood pressure and told me in no uncertain terms who it was I had to blame for sowing the seeds of not good enough in Daisy's mind.

I'd always wondered why my best friend was so hard on herself, just who it was in her life prior to my return to Reading had undermined her to the point she could barely hold down a job let alone feel confident enough to do what she now did—run events and staff in our very successful business. But since Rose's appearance less than a week ago, Daisy's steady increase in confidence had visibly paled to the point I hated the sight of her stepsister's brown hair and eyes, her overly thin face and narrow nose, the way she looked down on Daisy and everything else at Petunia's like she was assessing us for value in her world. Where the little pain in my patootie got off carrying around her ego in such a massive bundle of all that and a chocolate chip cookie that rivaled Vivian French's attitude I had no idea. But her sense of entitlement was getting old, fast.

Case in point, I witnessed yet another instance of bossypants behind thinly veiled disdain as I followed the pair into Mom's domain. Rose waved to Daisy with a lazy wrist, fingers flicking in my direction. "Your serving girls left a platter in the dining room." Like she couldn't have brought it into the kitchen with her? "They really need a talking to, Day." I hated she used that beloved nickname like she deserved to let it pass her lips. "Honestly, I don't know how you get along working in such a provincial setup."

Argh, snarl, growl, shriek. Internally, because I loved Daisy. But externally was pending.

Daisy actually twitched but when I glanced at her, hoping for anger, I caught a flare of disappointment and more than enough self-judgment it confirmed my suspicions about Rose's involvement in her undermining all over again. Why Daisy put up with her I had no idea. Her father divorced Rose's mother years ago when Daisy was fifteen. They weren't even technically family anymore. Then again, if Daisy decided you were hers, you were hers for life. That part of her I loved had clearly turned around to bite her in the butt.

"I'll take care of it," Daisy said, turning and hurrying from the kitchen in pursuit of the guilty platter while Rose smiled indulgently after her. When her eyes met mine, I made it clear and apparent just what I thought of her. And from the flat line of her own expression as she absorbed my visible dislike? The feeling was mutual.

Good. We were on the same page. I'd hate to think she'd have any doubts about why I dumped her on the curb when the time came to heave her out my front door.

Mom didn't seem to be troubled by Rose's comment, nor to pay a bit of attention when the young woman's terrible attitude showed up, like just now. Despite the fact Dad was away on a case outside town, my mother had never seemed happier, glowing as she created yet another culinary masterpiece that filled the space with the kinds of smells that made me want to lick the bowl.

I was about to suggest Rose find something to do aside from sit at the kitchen counter and take up space—after all, she was here on the premise she was working for Daisy, right? Sure, she was—when Mom turned on me with that glowing kind of smile that told me no matter what sort of mood I was in now, it was impossible to say no to her. Sigh. Moms.

"Fee, thank goodness." She spun and grasped for a box of tinfoil-wrapped something that smelled like chicken, depositing it into my arms. "The boy we hired is late and I need help running the rest of the food to the club."

And just like that, I was delegated as a delivery girl. Never mind I owned the place or anything, Mom.

CHAPTER FOUR

Despite my best intentions, then, I found myself loading Mom, three boxes of food and two trays of sweets into my car, Petunia firmly ensconced on my mother's lap with her harness tugging against her excited body. Maybe it wasn't a great idea to bring the pug along. She practically drooled on Mom's shoulder as she leaned as far over my mother as she could, big eyes white around the edges while she smacked her lips and panted at her proximity to all of that deliciousness. But she'd been cooped up in the B&B she was named for far too long and a bit of a romp outside would be good for her.

I might have been running again, happy to be back in shape, but the idea of taking her with me for my exercise jaunts was really ludicrous. Besides, I much preferred to share such outings with Crew these days. Something about his handsome, sweaty self pounding the path next to me roused visuals of other kinds of activities we really needed to explore together that might lead to accelerated heart rates.

Inhale. Exhale. Hormones.

The five-minute drive would have been hilarious if we'd had a video camera, Mom wrangling the wriggling pug while I navigated the busy streets of our town on our way to the lakeside. When I finally parked, Petunia's butt on the gearshift as Mom's red cheeks told me she was at the end of her rope with the overexcited creature, I gladly took the surprisingly strong pug in my arms while Mom unclasped her seatbelt.

"Maybe we leave her home next time." That was as close as Mom would ever get to criticizing Petunia. Her narrowed green eyes skimmed over the pug before meeting mine. "Okay, sweetie?"

I grinned, couldn't help it, while Mom got out and started unloading the car. Juggling necessary items kept my hands full, so when my cell buzzed insistently, I tossed it, warm from my pocket, into one of the boxes after a quick message check that had it vibrating. Just a few notes from Daisy on the day, nothing serious, but I had to text her back. The visible disappointment on Petunia's wide, flat face, set me off on a round of giggles that only increased Mom's irritation to the point she didn't say goodbye, huffing off with her arms loaded down with food boxes and my phone, leaving me to take the rest of the items while the pug sagged in dejection.

Crap, I had to get my cell back. I heaved Petunia out of the car and set her down, her solid self about as wieldy as hefting a bag of potatoes. Her good humor returned the instant I set her on the parking lot pavement, her seemingly unending supply of happiness renewing my own good humor, though her eager attempts to saunter off on her own made retrieving and carrying the remainder of Mom's items more difficult than it should have been. Arms overladen with two boxes full of plastic cutlery and enough napkins to soak up Cutter Lake, I let the pug lead the way, following her as she snuffled and snorted her joyful waddle toward the docks and the party already underway.

I grinned at Lily Myers as she looked up from painting a lion on a little girl's face. She waved before getting back to her task. While she might have been helping out today, her usual job was much more challenging. As the local dog trainer, she'd done a great job with Petunia, helping me figure out a healthier diet and exercise for the once portly pug. And while the mistress of my B&B wasn't exactly svelte, she'd come a long way from the truly obese creature I'd taken on with my grandmother's business.

I kept moving, averting my eyes from the sweeping attention of none other than Olivia Walker, knowing she stared at me as I hustled past, but refusing to meet her gaze just now. Hard to miss her glaring attention as it seemed to pierce my back when

I hurried by. At least she didn't chase me down, seeming to prefer the company of Lester Patterson. The red-faced and round-middled president of the Reading Yacht Club with his receding hairline and jolly joviality had his beady eyes on my mother's behind as she settled her burden on the food table and proceeded to set out the catering. I fought the urge to throw something at him, grossed out by his blatant attention in my mother's direction and wished Dad was here to do the defending her honor deed. Instead, knowing Mom was a big girl who could take care of herself, I instead let it go, wondering as I did when I'd forgotten my mother was actually a really beautiful woman. Of course, men would look at her, right? And I had her looks as a prequel to my own future, so I knew I wasn't going to age badly. Still, it creeped me out and made me want to go home and wash my brain out with bleach.

The second thought that crossed my mind as I joined Mom, Petunia instantly wrapping herself around my mother's legs as she twisted and turned until her leash was hopelessly tight, forcing my mother to stop what she was doing and release the pug, was to wonder about the Patterson family dynamic. After all, Geoffrey was married to a Patterson, right? And he'd been hot and heavy after Olivia's job. But here she was making nice with another of the clan if her fake laughter and tolerance of the leering Lester was doing at present was any indication. Then again, was she faking her joviality? For all I knew, the mayor loved his attention, despite his wandering eyes (watch where you're staring, jerkface—that's my mother's cleavage, not yours). So, were there factions inside the founding family of our little town? Or had the Patterson tide turned back in Olivia's favor? Was she purposely pandering to them to keep her job?

So many questions and far too much speculation. Maybe I should have written a column about it.

Heh.

When I turned from tugging Petunia closer to me, Mom's frustration so clear at last I knew if I didn't act to save the pug, she'd be meeting the sad end of Mom's disfavor, I had an answer to at least one of my questions. I looked up at the instant our town's council joined Olivia, Geoffrey in their ranks, and witnessed the utter disdain and revulsion on Lester's face when his eyes met those of the accountant who'd married into the family.

As for the slimy councilman I hadn't trusted from our first meeting, his visible response was just as visceral, making it very clear to me without a word spoken between them just what they thought of each other. And was that a smug grin on Olivia's face in response?

Yup, she was brilliant to a fault. I just hoped she wasn't backing a horse that would founder in the backstretch.

"Lester." Geoffrey's words carried, tone sharper than his usual shark-like subtlety.

"Geoff, old boy." Lester's voice sounded like he'd been smoking two packs a day for the majority of his life with a hearty bit of laughing at the world under it. "Gail kick your sad butt out yet?" He guffawed, an honest-to-goodness knee-slapping laugh that no one else seemed to find funny. Least of all Geoffrey whose strained attempt at a polite smile ended at his thinned lips.

"My wife is very well," the accountant said. "And your fourth marriage? I hear you've been told to pay yet another round of alimony."

Lester took that attack in stride, though his nasty grin soured somewhat. "Tell the family to mind their own business."

"Then you mind yours." Geoffrey was done with any pretense, apparently, the two facing off as Olivia stepped between them.

"Gentlemen," she said, "this is a fun and happy occasion. Please keep your internal conflicts to yourselves."

Lester grunted something obviously impolite while Geoffrey backed off, the burly head of the yacht club instead turning to grin and wink at Mom who forced a smile in return.

"Looking good, Lucy," he said.

"Should be delicious, Lester," she clipped back, all professional while I bit my tongue hard.

"I bet." He had to stop looking at Mom like that. Just. Gross.

At least he didn't come closer, keeping his distance and bending his head to talk in a quieter tone with Olivia. I didn't get to ponder the family dynamics of the Patterson situation further. Because as I turned away, deep in thought, a shadow fell over me, followed instantly by the scent of too much sandalwood barely covering a case of B.O. that made me cringe before I looked up and into the eyes of Robert Carlisle.

CHAPTER FIVE

"Fanny." Yeah, because that nickname was ever funny and hadn't gotten old decades ago. He really needed to come up with some new material to impress me these days. Arse.

I eye-rolled despite myself. "I'm a bit busy, Robert," I said, just keeping my temper in check as Petunia wagged her little tail and looked up at him with the kind of gentle eagerness she reserved for every single person who might or might not offer her food. She wasn't exactly a discerning creature. He ignored her, instead choosing to loom over me—or try to as I straightened up to my full height and challenged his few superior inches with confidence and a particularly prickly need to show him who was boss. Sure, maybe I shouldn't have let him get to me, but honestly, his continuing existence was the sort of irritating thorny bramble that made my particular rose garden lose points for quality.

He didn't move away, typical Robert, doing his awkward, socially inept best to put on a superiority show for whoever might be watching. Made worse, thank you very much, since Crew left town and this disaster of a human being in charge. I was going to have a firm and unhappy talk with the handsome sheriff as soon as I kissed him into submission.

Who was I kidding? The kissing would diffuse me enough I'd let this whole Robert mess drop. I was a sucker for Crew Turner's lips.

My hateful cousin snuffled, wriggling that hideously heavy mustache of his under his nose like a dying caterpillar in its final moments before expiring from sheer ugliness. His beady eyes made my skin crawl, how he hooked his thumbs in his belt and stuck out his rounded potbelly as if planning to use it as a weapon in his war against all things normal and decent. I refused to flinch or back down, keeping a firm grip on Petunia's leash if only as a not-so-subtle trick to restrain myself from smacking the so-called acting sheriff for being publically revolting.

"Going to have to chat about the parking problem outside Petunia's," he said, grinning then, showing his uneven and yellowing teeth, the black bristles of his facial hair making me queasy. I forced myself to stare in his eyes so I wouldn't lose my lunch and crossed both arms over my chest.

"You honestly don't have anything better to do,

Robert?" I raised an eyebrow at him. His gaze flickered over my shoulder, following someone behind me and, when he tipped his hat, I turned, at last, to see Geoffrey looking in our direction. Though, oddly, the accountant was looking at me, not at the man who actually gave a crap he was there. More creepiness. Awesome. Where was Crew when I needed him to clean up this multi-yuck town?

"'Fraid there'll be some tickets issued," Robert said without a hint of regret. If anything, he sounded gleeful, like he could barely contain the joy he felt dinging my business for something out of my control.

"Look," I snapped, "just because my guests sometimes—briefly!—park on the side of the street," recently marked as no parking thanks to newer, tighter laws brought in by the council, "doesn't warrant tickets. I have them move the instant I realize they've broken the law." A ridiculous and asinine and frustrating law. Argh.

Before Robert could comment—and he looked determined to do so, despite the fact I'm sure my intent to stomp him into the ground was written all over my face—Mom spoke up from behind the table.

"Really, Robert," she said, her voice mild and her words light but all the weight of her Momness snapping his head around and flashing shame and guilt briefly over his face, "we're a bit busy here. Maybe you'd like to find something constructive to do and leave Fiona alone." Mom's gaze lifted at last, her small, gloved hands stopping their quick, concise movements where she tucked a pair of stray sandwiches tighter together on the tray in front of her. Her flat, even expression held zero kindness or warmth, the face I associated most with the end of her principal rope when she was still acting in that role at the local high school.

I know she'd used it on Robert in the past when we were kids. I'd witnessed her dressing him down in this very clean and cold manner, had always marveled at her utter control and the slicing surety she wielded despite her small stature and the relatively innocuous delivery of her "request" for obedience. Why it worked I still didn't know, except that despite the fact it wasn't aimed at me I still felt the chill and the tightness in my stomach and was very happy she hadn't aimed that particular weaponized perfection at me.

Instead of responding vocally, Robert tipped his hat to Mom and turned away, one foot stepping on the edge of Petunia's leash. The pressure tugged on her collar, making her yip in surprise and I had to jerk myself under control to keep from yelling at him to be more careful. He seemed genuinely surprised by the hurt he'd caused, though, so I let it go, turning my back on him and bending to pat Petunia on the top of her head while she licked her lips and stared up at me with bemused confusion. A quick nab of a sandwich quarter relieved her stress and she was happily tail wagging and watching me with those adoring and ever-hungry brown eyes all over again.

Mom met my eyes when I straightened, hers

snapping anger. "Seriously," she said, then sighed before turning back to her work. "I really wish we had another set of tablecloths," she fretted then, wringing her gloved hands over the food. "These white ones are going to show every single crumb."

All we had at Petunia's were white, but the yacht club colors were blue and gray, right? I tied my pug's leash to the leg of the table and grinned at Mom. "I'll be right back." I was sure I'd seen some tablecloths at the last event I'd attended, a cocktail party that devolved into too much drinking and Crew busting up three fights between wealthy boat owners who really should have known better.

Mom beamed at me, waving me off when I gestured to Petunia. "She's fine," she said. "Just hurry, Fee! People are hungry." She wasn't wrong. A short line had formed behind the cordon keeping them from the tables and Olivia's unhappy expression told me we were later than she would have liked. Um, it was barely past breakfast, only shortly before 11AM. Considering we had a busy business to run? She was lucky we took this on in the first place.

Grunt. Gratitude was in short supply these days, I guess.

I hurried toward the front doors of the club, the long, squat building's weathered gray shingling looking more old-fashioned than the kind of chic I thought the board should be aiming for. A good coat of paint never hurt anything, as far as I was concerned. Whatever, not my concern, though I would have thought Olivia would be pressuring Lester and his people to upgrade now that business in Reading was booming. After all, every other part of town had seen some kind of facelift or cosmetic improvement in the last few years as funds became more readily available and tourism expanded possibilities. As I stepped into the dim and slightly musty interior of the club's front entry, the old laminate tile under my feet squeaking against my sneakers and the dark paneling screaming the 1970s had been here and done that, I exhaled past the urge to sneeze and wondered why the club of very wealthy and locally prominent boat owners would be the only holdouts.

I turned the corner past the large common room and the bar, heading down the length of the t-shaped building toward the kitchen area, passing the offices on my way to storage. I'd spent enough time here as a kid learning to sail on quiet Cutter Lake, I knew the ins and outs and honestly was continually surprised by the lack of upgrades. Not a single thing had changed, most definitely not since I'd been here and well before, from the light switch covers someone thought were cute because they were anchors but were more suited to a child's room to the carpet under my feet that switched out from the linoleum, likely navy blue a long time ago but now an indiscriminate shade I wasn't about to look closely at, thanks. The whole place felt like time stood still as if the last scraps of Reading's history lived in this building and refused utterly and completely to give up the ghosts of our small town's past.

I was so wrapped up in my mental judgment of the place, wondering if I should write a shaming column about it—was it dragging us down as a whole? Would a refresh bring more status to Reading or was I turning into a snob?—that when I reached for the storage room closet door and jerked it open, I couldn't help the shriek that escaped my lips at the sight of something writhing in the near darkness.

The answering meeps of shock gave me the warning I needed not to strike out at the unknown shapes now untangling themselves from what I quickly assessed was a passionate embrace, and my eyes adjusted enough to the low light I made out the sheepish and nervous faces of the young couple I'd disturbed.

I grinned and giggled, unable to help myself, while Keira Campbell flushed darkly enough, I could see it clearly on her round cheeks, her dark ponytail loose at the nape of her neck, a few curls escaping with static pulling them toward the hand of the young man who was just letting her go.

"Hi, Fee," my former employee, now a barista at Sammy's Coffee, whispered before clearing her throat. Hey! I remembered her name. After she left my employ. Awesome. "This is Luke. Luke Patterson."

The handsome young blond waved weakly in my direction, dimples showing. "Hi, Miss Fleming," he said, voice soft and contrite. "Did you need something?"

I reached past Keira's shoulder and switched on the light, blinding the three of us a bit while I pointed at the shelves and the stack of blue and gray tablecloths inside. I couldn't wipe the grin from my face and barely held in my amusement as they eased past me and into the hallway, looking like they were both ready to bolt.

"Sorry," the nervous girl said, patting at her clothing, tugging the hem of her t-shirt down while Luke did the same. "Can you not tell my dad I was here?"

Hey, Keira was eighteen if I recalled correctly, and Luke looked about her age, so as far as I was concerned, they were old enough to make their own mistakes in dark storage closets without me calling them out to her father. From the brief encounters I'd had with David Campbell, his temper was about as in check as the passion these two clearly had for each other. The boat owner and local hardware store owner wasn't exactly known for his kind-hearted manner. I could only imagine his reaction if he found his daughter with someone he didn't approve of. "I have no idea what you're talking about," I winked before Luke's last name registered. "Patterson?"

He looked distinctly uncomfortable. "My dad's Lester," he said, pale blue eyes flickering to Keira before landing on me again, his about as stressed as hers. "Our fathers don't exactly see eye-to-eye. We'd appreciate it if you didn't say anything."

Far be it for me to crush this little Romeo and Juliet affair. "You two were never here," I said, grabbing a handful of tablecloths and turning off the light, closing the door behind me. "And neither was I."

I walked away without another word, hearing them whispering behind me and feeling, briefly, a bit hurt they didn't trust me. On the other hand, I was an adult, so maybe not to be believed? Huh, since when did I become the responsible and judging type that young people didn't think was cool and hip?

I snorted to myself, hugging the tablecloths to my chest as I made my way back down the hall. Maybe if I wasn't old enough to think terms like "cool" and "hip" were still exactly that, I'd be eligible for instant trust. Sigh. Getting older kind of sucked.

I'd almost reached the corner when my sneaker simultaneously caught on the gross carpet and the stack of cloths in my arms decided to go in the opposite direction of my near fall, sending me almost to my knees. Grunting in irritation, I gathered the fallen fabric, hearing the distant sound of a door closing—the kids leaving, I assumed—and the sudden and harsh but muffled exclamation of someone's voice quite close by.

CHAPTER SIX

Now, I've never been accused of minding my own business, so this moment was no different. I found myself in the somewhat compromising and yet enviable position of crouching beneath the window over the door where the shout had come from. One glance upward and I easily read the black lettering on the crystalized glass. Lester Patterson, Club President. And, even as my mind processed the name, the voice came through loud and clear.

"I'm done with this conversation, Nortz," Lester said, his shadow nearing the door. I gasped, reaching faster for the fallen tablecloths, straining my ears to listen as the knob rattled. Wouldn't do to have them find me eavesdropping when it really was an accidental listen in to their private conversation. But when the door didn't open, the sound of Chris Nortz's voice swelling with anger, I stopped, breathless, all of my goods recovered but unable to move until I knew what he was going to say.

Busybody? Check.

"My cottagers are sick of being treated like second-rate citizens." I only knew Chris because of my father, to be honest. He and Dad played the occasional game of golf and Dad's little cottage/cabin in the woods fell under the cottager association's umbrella of which Chris was the head. "Your boats are a menace and if you don't take steps to keep those noisy, dangerous machines away from our docks, I'll be taking this to town council!"

Interesting. Lester's reply was even more so.

"Stop being such a baby," he laughed like he found Chris's concerns shallow and beneath him. Typical Patterson. My bias was showing, obviously. "Besides, Olivia won't take a single act against me, and you know it. You and your little club want peace and quiet? Go find another lake to live on. This one's mine."

The sound of Chris spluttering was so loud it was impossible to miss. "You'll pay for this, Lester," he snarled. And stomped toward the door. I had a split second between the realization I was about to be uncovered and the knob turning to spin with a gasp and leap for the door opposite, jerking it wide and throwing myself inside before slamming it shut behind me. I leaned against it, hearing the muttering retreat of Chris Nortz, wincing at my obvious escape and looking up with what I'm sure had to be a deer in the headlights on an oncoming tractor-trailer into the startled gaze of Doreen Douglas.

She stood up from behind her full desk, a faint smile warring with concern as she looked down at the bundle of now messy cloth in my arms. Her expression firmed into welcome as she circled toward me, holding out her hands and helping me while the short, round, elderly woman who'd hired Mom in the first place divested me of half of my load.

"Fiona, how shortsighted of me." She ushered me out of her office, closing and locking the door behind her with the full keyring she returned to the pocket of her pale yellow cardigan sweater. "Of course, you need the club's colors. Forgive me for not being out there when you arrived." She hurried me toward the exit and the bright sunlight on the other side, squinting her pale hazel eyes into the sunny day. She waved to Mom, lines wrinkling around her lips and creating folds in her neck, her well-advanced visible age doing nothing to slow her down, it seemed. I followed her at a rapid pace, her shorter legs in hose and practical shoes carrying her faster than I expected across the parking lot to where my mother quickly emptied first one table then the next. With a swift and efficient flick of her hands, Doreen draped the three tables in a trio layer of crisscrossing coverings, diving in to help Mom reassemble the food display just as Olivia, her eyes tight and jaw set, purposely met my eyes while she removed the cordon with an abrupt gesture and let the line of people flood the tables.

You're welcome.

I stepped away, letting Mom handle the influx of people, Doreen at her side.

"You two are darlings for taking this on," the yacht club treasurer happily beamed at Mom. "I know how busy you are these days."

"Our pleasure," Mom said. "Anything for you, Doreen."

Thanks for including me in that particular offering, Mom. Grumble. "I thought this was Olivia's venture?" Way to sound all happy to be there, Fee.

Doreen smiled despite my lack of enthusiasm. "Originally," she said, "but anything at all to bring new faces to the club, and I'm delighted to participate."

Was that the problem? The fact there weren't many new people buying boats and using the moorings? This was a lake, after all. Was the appeal of the yacht club waning despite Olivia's efforts? If only they'd update it, I was sure things would turn around.

But I didn't get to suggest it. Doreen chatted with my mother, the pair old friends while they quickly restocked the vanishing foodstuffs. I retrieved my dog, hearing the women laughing over something they'd shared while working together—Doreen retired from her position as bookkeeper for the school board a decade before my mother. Come to think of it, she'd served in that capacity for most of the town at one point, though I'd held off using her services. Something about having a local know my financial business bothered me, Mom's friend or not. Rather than intrude on their catch-up time and seeing they had things well in hand, I instead led Petunia away from temptation and the bits of dropping food left behind by over-eager kids who grabbed and ran. Her disappointment was audible, a deep, wrenching groan ending in a yelping yawn that made her sound like a petulant three-year-old.

"Oh, get over it," I said, tugging on her harness at the end of the leash and leading her toward the pier. A string of costumed adults climbed into a pair of heavily decorated canoes, balloons and streamers trailing in the water, the wobbling of the two craft as the excited crews laughed and piled in without the kind of care they likely should have taken making me wince and hope for the best. Robert stood to one side, and to my utter shock, he wasn't alone. Rose, her narrow face attempting a coquettish smile, hung off his arm.

Oh. My. God. I suppressed a stomach heave at the adoration she beamed up at him. When? What? Why? Gag. The fact Daisy's stepsister was into my disgusting cousin just plummeted her in my estimation. Regardless of how she treated my bestie, having any kind of romantic feelings for Robert ruined her for me forever.

Just yucksky. And hang on a second. Daisy's reaction this morning to her criticism of Robert… had she known Rose and my cousin were dating? Why wouldn't she tell me? Whatever her reason,

Daisy didn't owe me an explanation, I guess. But it certainly went a long way to turn Rose over from frenemy to just plain nope. Not trusting her was pretty much exactly par for this particularly hideous course, thanks. Girl had zero personality, lacked in ambition, and, obviously, had no idea what taste actually was.

"Looks like they're ready, sheriff." Rose's voice carried from the dock below, the floating decking wobbling under her feet as the last of the passengers boarded the two canoes without dumping themselves or their craft into the water. Her narrow gaze met mine, her giggle grating over my nerves about as much as that title did. We'd just see how much she liked her Robert-snookums when Crew came back.

I was about to loudly and firmly correct her on her use of the term—was I the only one in town willing to defend our actual sheriff's honor or what?—and likely embarrass myself and start a fight I knew better than to set off when stomping footfalls caught my attention and turned me around. Just in time to avoid being shoved out of the way, though from the grim expression on the woman's plain and angry face I wasn't her target, just in her path and she wasn't letting anything get between her and her goal. I followed her trajectory with my gaze and understood about ten seconds before she reached our mayor that it was Olivia Walker who was about to bear the brunt of the furious woman's temper.

Shame on me. I didn't defend Olivia, did I? Where was my loyalty now? Well, considering the mayor was here to defend herself… sure, Fee. Sure.

I was so transparent I could see through myself.

"This is outrageous!" The woman came to an abrupt halt, one hand swinging upward, finger shaking in Olivia's face. "You're having a party. A party! All of Reading is celebrating your stupid plans, aren't they? Meanwhile, those of us suffering from your lack of care about our town's wellbeing are kicked to the curb, right, Olivia?"

CHAPTER SEVEN

I eased a few steps closer, nearing the stairs to the lower deck where even normally clueless Robert turned his head to look up at the woman's attack on our mayor, a frown on his face. I paused to listen, Petunia firmly at my side, panting as she sat on my foot and waited my curiosity out, like always.

"This is neither the time nor the place for a discussion of this nature, Wanda," Olivia said, her best politician's tone doing nothing to shut the woman down.

"I warned you," her confronter snarled. "I said there'd be casualties in your little agenda. My fishing business is one of them. But do you or the council or this pathetic excuse for a yacht club care one scrap about a small business you're supposed to be helping?" She spun, her wide shoulders and barrel chest more masculine than feminine inside her khaki shirt and baggy pants, lined face and dark blonde hair laced with gray in a tight ponytail down her back. Everything about her screamed no-nonsense, including the precisely stitched "Beaman's Fishing" that spanned over her shoulders. "No, you don't. You're celebrating while I'm losing business thanks to the yahoos in this club who dump their waste and their fuel into our lake and kill my fish!"

That wasn't good. If the status quo old boys' club that ran the marina weren't toeing the line that had the rest of us run off our feet...? While I was all for everyone benefiting from Reading's boom in tourism, if some of our residents were knowingly damaging our natural beauty, something had to be done. After all, what else really was Reading's claim to fame without the gorgeous views, the lake and our mountains?

Robert was striding past me before I could stop him, though I don't know if I would have, given the choice. In fact, instead of getting into the fray, I got out of the way while my idiot cousin tried to throw his nonexistent weight around, descending the steps to the lower deck, Petunia huffing beside me.

To my disappointment, Rose closed the gap between us and, with her hands on her chest and her breath—I kid you not—bated in anticipation, we stood together and watched Robert try to do what would have taken Crew five seconds, hands down.

"Threatening our mayor will get you arrested," he

said, taking exactly the wrong tact against the aggressive and clearly furious woman. I glanced back and forth between Robert—scrawny but for his potbelly and clearly out of shape compared to Wanda who looked like she could lift the front end of a pickup truck with one hand—and anticipated him flying over my head and into the water. The quiet that had fallen over the two canoes told me everyone was watching, waiting to see what would happen.

Was it wrong I hoped she'd land him on his ass and maybe break something he valued in the process?

"Back off, poser boy," Wanda snarled at him, barely glancing his way. "This is between me and Olivia."

The mayor looked briefly concerned but quickly covered, her fake smile pulling at her lips, her eyes flickering to me with a kind of hopeful question that made me freeze in place and swallow hard. Why was she looking at me like that?

"Let's go inside, shall we?" Olivia gestured toward the yacht club entry while the gathered crowd's tension did nothing to make me feel better.

"I'm not going anywhere," Wanda snapped. "You're not brushing this under the rug. I want my problem solved, Olivia, and I won't take garbage talk for an answer ever again."

If anything, I knew a blowup was pending. Mom looked startled, even stunned, and would be no help. And Doreen just stood there, one hand over her mouth. As for Robert, he had a hand on his gun, started to reach out to grab Wanda by the arm. Seriously? Did he have a death wish? I grunted to myself and, to my shock, heard myself speak up.

"I'd like to hear what she has to say." And, just like that, I was the center of attention. Yay, me.

My interruption did the trick, though. Wanda spun toward me, brown eyes meeting mine, and as if for the first time, she seemed to realize there was a huge crowd staring at her waiting to see what she'd do. Olivia's quick frown at me disappeared as fast as it came while I shrugged at her and waited for Wanda to speak.

It seemed my willingness to hear her out was all Wanda needed for validation and to shut her down. Instead of launching into a tirade publically, she grunted at Olivia and headed for the yacht club door, the mayor trailing after her, Geoffrey following with a sly grin on his face. I let them go, raising my eyebrows at Olivia on her way by. She could be pissed at me if she wanted, but I got the job done without my ridiculous cousin shooting anyone, or himself, so it was a win, right?

Right?

"You know," Rose said, startling me, speaking up reminding me she was there at all, something I'd forgotten in the heat of the moment, "you really need to learn to mind your own business, Fiona Fleming." And then she sniffed at me.

Sniffed. At. Me.

I pushed her. Watched her topple into the water, laughed with my hands on my hips as she spluttered and screamed for Robert-snookums to pull her out—

The vision that flashed in my head was so real I had to blink to snap myself free of it, about half a heartbeat from actually shoving the arrogant little snot as my furious brain told me I already had. Robert saved her, huffing his way down the steps and joining us, confronting me with his mustache bristling, hand still on his gun, the doofus.

"Mind telling me what that was?" He sounded pathetic so I didn't answer, tugging my pug, looking for a way around him and Rose to the steps so I could just get out of there before I did something I'd regret. Like push both of them. Yup.

"Excuse me." It rankled to even have to ask with that measure of not really politeness.

Neither of them moved, Robert leaning forward and getting in my face, Petunia softly growling at my side, something she never did. But she must have sensed his animosity because I could feel the rumble of her discontent through our contact, where her warm, furry butt perched on my foot. Well, we were of the same mind there, weren't we?

"No one asked you, Fanny," he snarled, poking me in the chest with one index finger. Oh my god, he actually touched me. The pit of my stomach tightened in a rush of rage that he seemed really good at triggering despite my resolve otherwise. "You might get away with butting in when Crew is sheriff, but this is my town. My rules." He jabbed me again. "And you keep your mouth shut, you hear?"

I have no idea what I would have done next.

Likely something that would have gotten me arrested. I know I was furious enough, in a red-hot rage so deep I don't think I would have regretted a single moment, not even when they took me away and put me in prison for murdering him. Nope, would have laughed. Out loud.

Instead of being arrested, though, instead of having the chance to do something my extended family, at least, would regret, I was stopped by an unexpected interruption. That of my normally mild-mannered and contented pug, she of the quiet happiness and eager tummy, who loved everyone and never, ever took sides where the chance for food of any kind was involved—and, as far as she was concerned, food was always a possibility.

But whatever triggered her unhappiness in that moment, she took it and ran with it, literally. With a deep growl and the kind of yipping bark that she reserved for squirrels who tortured her from behind windows, she stood up, fur bristling and challenged Robert to say that to me again.

Shocked by her defense of my person, I looked down at her, hand slack on the leash, just as Robert grunted and his foot lashed out, impacting her firmly in the chest. Sending my pug, her narrowed eyes now gaping wide, her comical face shocked if possible for a dog in transit, over the edge of the decking and into the water.

Where, thanks to her dense and ungraceful nature, she promptly sank like a stone.

CHAPTER EIGHT

There was no thought, no inhale, nothing but panic and instinct. I dove into the water after Petunia, hands grasping desperately for the disappearing leash end that trailed away from me far too quickly. The water wasn't that deep, but it was deep enough and dark, the inkiness of it engulfing me as I propelled myself beneath the cold surface of the lake after my pug's plummeting form.

Time stood still, my chest aching from the lack of breath I'd failed to take, my eyes stinging from something tainting the water, heart pounding doing nothing to help me conserve the little oxygen I had in my lungs, in my system, to sustain me for the dive.

She hit the bottom before I ran out of air, a puff of dirt rising under her butt, the impact pushing her up toward me again and just within reach. I grasped for her harness, caught it and the end of her corkscrew tail, jerking firmly on both and hauling her up toward the light and the surface there. My eyes skimmed over something, a large rock embedded next to the dock, a strange dark symbol etched in the surface trying to distract me. But Petunia twitched in my arms, drawing my desperate panic back to her, the whites of her eyes glistening as she sagged against me.

And then I was on the surface, coughing, gagging on lake water, hands reaching out for me, many more than I expected, pulling me onto the decking and relieving me of Petunia. One of the costumed canoers laid her out, hands pressing firmly on her ribs, steady and kind as he massaged her torso with the kind of reassuring confidence that told me he knew what he was doing. Though he might look ridiculous in his clown attire and fuzzy red nose and wig, it was pretty clear he'd handled a drowning victim—maybe even a drowning dog—before.

She coughed softly, choking up water, yipping a little before righting herself and shaking firmly, moisture spraying everywhere. The cheer from the watching crowd made me sob once in relief, Petunia hobbling to me and landing in my lap, panting as she laid her heavy head on my leg and groaned.

"Robert Andrew Carlisle." I knew Mom's voice anywhere. Looked up, dazed and recovering from the adrenaline rush to find her shaking her fist at my cousin. He actually looked contrite while everyone glared like they knew just what he'd done. "What is the matter with you? How dare you do such a horrible thing?"

"It was an accident." Yeah, like anyone was going to buy that.

"I saw it happen," Rose spoke up instantly. "It was. The dog got in his way. He didn't mean it."

That was it. Daisy's stepsister or not, she was dead to me.

The clown who'd performed CPR on Petunia pulled his nose free and bobbed me a nod. "She should be okay, Fee." I finally recognized him past the white makeup and the wig. Dr. Fred Miller hadn't been our local vet for long, but I was definitely grateful he was there. "But bring her in Monday morning just in case and I'll give her a checkup, okay?"

I nodded in gratitude, squeezing his hand and letting him go before trying to stand up. Meanwhile, the crowd was dispersing, though Mom wasn't done with Robert by a long shot.

"You just wait until I talk to your mother," she said. Robert winced. I wasn't a huge fan of Aunt Doris thanks to her favoritism of her wretched son. And it wasn't like his mom really cared about me at all. "When she finds out you did such a despicable thing to her mother's dog, she'll have your liver on a plate." Oh, right. Grandmother Iris. Petunia had been hers. Well then. Maybe I was Aunt Doris's fan after all.

Robert and Rose hurried off then before I could

recover enough to say anything or confront him. Honestly, I wasn't in the mood. I just wanted to get my dog home and pamper her and stuff her full of her favorite foods until she couldn't eat another scrap. She seemed listless but eager to keep up as always, so I let Robert go and focused on her.

I'd find a way to deal with him later.

Mom hugged me, Doreen joining me, while Robert and Rose got back to starting the canoe race. I carried Petunia up the steps to the main dock and set her down, feeling her wriggle in response, knowing she was going to be okay but hugging her an extra moment anyway. Tears burned behind my eyes, my heart pounding. I could have lost her. She could have drowned, and it would be my fault for not keeping my mouth shut.

From the way Mom glared at me she knew what I was thinking and when she spoke, I discovered I was right.

"Don't you dare," she said. "He's an ass and he'll pay for that." She hugged me, trembling just slightly, enough I knew she was as worried as she was angry. When she let me go, Mom bent and stroked Petunia's head. The pug let out a happy groan and leaned into her hand when my mother scratched her ear.

"I need to get her home." I looked down at my soggy clothes, just grateful I'd left my wallet and phone in the car. Sucked I'd have to soak my seats on the drive, but there wasn't much I could do about it. I wasn't driving home in my underwear.

Doreen joined us, looking horrified, tsking over the state of my clothes. "I have a t-shirt and shorts you can wear, Fee," she said.

That was a huge relief. I smiled my gratitude at her but waved her off when she moved to lead me inside. "Just tell me where," I said, handing Petunia's leash to Mom.

"Same linen closet as the tablecloths," Doreen said. "You can change in the locker room at the end of the hall."

I headed inside before I could change my mind and go back for my pug. The urge to hug her and never let her go ever again was as powerful a feeling as anything I'd ever dealt with, and I suddenly wished Crew was there. Weird. I didn't need a man to protect me or keep me safe or anything. I was perfectly fine, thank you. But now that the adrenaline was wearing off, I could have used a little tall, dark and handsome to lean on just for a moment so I could cry my eyes out in a safe place.

But he wasn't here, and I was on my own. Okay then. Big girl panties, Fee. Or yacht club t-shirt and baggy shorts. I entered the back hall, turning the corner and getting the third shock of the day, almost enough to send me to the floor as the last bit of adrenaline I possessed surged up and smacked me in the face.

But instead of a threat, I came face-to-face with Heather Parborough. The attractive brunette gasped at the sight of me, hastily closing Lester's office door behind her, looking guilty enough I knew she wasn't supposed to be there. Yes, she was a rep for one of the boat companies who hung around the club offering deals on new products all summer, but the likelihood Lester allowed her into his office on her own seemed slim.

"Hey, Heather," I said. She was a regular at Petunia's, staying with me right now, in fact, and I felt comfortable enough to address her with the familiarity of a sort-of friend.

"Fee!" Her guilt turned to surprise at the state of me. "Swimming? In the harbor?" Her nose wrinkled, faint smile lifting her lips. Was that a sheen of sweat on her brow? What was she up to? I liked Heather, had coffee with her a few times over the course of the last two summers. She was quiet but knowledgeable about the boats she sold, kept to herself, seemed competent and nice enough. I hated to think she was up to no good.

I winced at my wet clothes, pretended I didn't wonder what she'd been up to because it really wasn't any of my business. "Petunia took a tumble," I said. "Just need to change."

She shook her head, looking distressed. "I hope she's okay?"

I nodded, noted Heather's clenched hands at her sides, the way she didn't quite keep eye contact, glancing over my shoulder and out toward the front entrance of the club. "She'll be fine," I said. Waited. If Dad taught me anything, it was that silence had a power to it that the guilty couldn't bear.

But rather than blurt out what she'd been doing

in Lester's office, Heather just forced a smile. "Good to hear. See you, Fee." She turned and strode off in the opposite direction, toward the back of the building and the rear exit. I let her go, dripping on the carpet while my overactive mind begged me to investigate.

Silly brain. Investigate what? I shook my head like rattling my mind inside my skull might shut it up for once and moved on. Honestly, I wasn't in much of a mood for curiosity and nosiness be damned. Instead, I headed for the closet, clothes and the chance to go home and forget Petunia's near-death ever happened.

Sounded like the perfect ending to this particular brush with disaster.

CHAPTER NINE

So, my guestimate as to the attractiveness of the offered attire was about as accurate as I could have imagined. Feeling out of sorts and uncomfortable despite the dry clothes thanks to the massive t-shirt hanging almost to my knees and the awkward way I had to bundle up the waistband of the men's basketball shorts that could have passed for old-fashioned culottes, I did my best not to let my fashion fiasco get me down. Hadn't I rescued my pug from certain death and garnered enough sympathy for her as well as animosity toward Robert—who didn't love a sweet-faced animal over that mug of a worthless human being?—that I should have felt far better about the whole thing than I actually did.

I returned to Mom who handed off Petunia's

leash with a sad smile and concern on her face. The pug, on the other hand, seemed totally fine, cinnamon bun tail twitching spasmodically from side to side under the wrinkle of the skin over her butt, her big eyes staring at me with the same adoration she always showed, long, pink tongue hanging sideways out of her wide, smiling mouth like she thought this whole thing was actually fun or something. Or maybe she was laughing at my outfit. Either way, I was ready to take her home, give her a good looking over and change into my own clothes. Anything to forget this regrettable event ever happened

And make no mistake, if she even coughed, I'd be going to the vet lickety-split with the bill landing on the sheriff's desk about half a second later.

The pug perched on the passenger's seat, her harness buckled securely into the seatbelt, airbag safely turned off. She preferred to perch in my lap, but I wasn't taking any chances with her today, not after such a near miss. I had myself so worked up with what-ifs and could have beens, tears threatening all over again, that by the time I got back to the B&B I had to take a moment to hug her tight, something she didn't exactly protest but wasn't on her menu of expected responses to riding in the car. She finally whined softly, wriggling enough I let her go and wiped at the wetness on my cheeks.

"Sorry, Madame Petunia," I forced a smile at her, stroking her soft face, the wrinkles moving comically under my fingers, taking her from perplexed joy to scrunchy good humor and back again with that simple manipulation. "I'll stop being a weirdo."

She huffed at me, grinning before snorting so forcefully I had to wipe droplets from my cheeks. Awesome.

I should have realized the cat—or pug, as it were—wouldn't stay in the bag for long. Especially with someone like Daisy ferreting out news like a natural-born journalist. Speaking of which, maybe she should have been writing the column for Pamela and not me. Whatever the case (or excuse not to follow through, see it for what it is, Fee), I was instantly engulfed in a massive hug the second I walked through the front door of Petunia's. Off-balance from the force of Daisy's embrace, I teetered as she released me in a rush to bend and give yet another big squeeze to Petunia, my best friend's face twisted in fear and concern.

"Oh, Fee," she said, heaving the dog into her arms and standing up to snuggle Petunia against her cheek, her gray eyes next to the pug's brown ones, the two of them staring at me though with disparate expressions about as far off each other as possible. "I heard what happened. Is Petunia okay?"

Um, she was holding her, right? Kind of a silly question. I felt myself sag in response to the query, though, while my best friend cooed and rocked the happy pug. "She's fine," I said. "Dr. Miller was there." I felt panic wake in my chest yet again and shoved it firmly down. Later, I'd curl up on the couch with Petunia and smother that terror in chocolate and cheese puffs. For now, I was done crying over what could have been. "He said she should be fine, but I'll take her for a checkup Monday anyway." Yup, the Reading Sheriff's Department was going to foot that bill, hopefull,y Robert personally, but I'd take the revenge I could get.

Huh. Wasn't expecting to feel so pissed at Crew for not being here. I shoved that down, too, and watched Daisy set Petunia on her four little feet, the pug seemingly disappointed at her loss of height and status.

"I can't believe Robert would do such a horrible thing." I knew she meant the opposite. Neither of us were fans, after all. "He's such an ass. Poor baby." Daisy made a sad face at the pug who panted happily back.

"He is," I said. "He tried to say it was an accident." I considered mentioning I now knew Rose was dating said ass but waited to see what Daisy would say. And wondered again why she hadn't brought it up before.

She snorted, though with far more delicacy and attractiveness than the pug ever managed. "I bet. I hear your mother gave him what for." Sparkle returned to her eyes.

"Yeah," I said. "Might have gone better if your stepsister hadn't stood up for him." Okay, I didn't mean to come across so bitter in my reveal of the truth, but seriously. I wanted Rose out of my place. But she was Daisy's family, and my bestie had a say, right?

Daisy flinched, looked down, face settling into a kind of tight mask that told me she wasn't going to back me on this one. "I'm sure she was just trying to diffuse the situation."

Grunt. Not. And proof my best friend had known about Rose and Robert. But before I could call her on her attitude, Daisy took the leash from my hands and led Petunia toward the kitchen, her heels tapping on the wood floors, the pug happily trotting along beside her. Because didn't the swinging door at the end of the foyer always mean food?

I followed them, determined to mind my own business and keep my mouth shut. That lasted about a minute while Daisy fetched a bag of frozen strawberries from the freezer and proceeded to cut them up. I'd taken to freezing the treats in an effort to slow Petunia down, to make her chew, at least, before swallowing. Daisy handed the drooling dog bits of red with an indulgence that made my jaw clench. Not because I minded how much Daisy loved Petunia, but because I loved Daisy and it was clear she wasn't willing to face the monstrosity who was her (former, come on, Day, snap out of it) stepsister.

Thus, the utter lack of staying quiet that meant my lips parted and words came out before I could stop myself.

"How long is Rose staying?" Yes, I was grumpy. I sat my butt on a stool at the island, glaring when Daisy refused to meet my eyes.

"I don't know," she said, fingers and knife dark crimson with strawberry juice. Made me think of murdering someone. Well, two someones. Robert and Rose. Right? Or was Crew on my death wish list too? Why did I feel like he'd abandoned me all of a sudden? Silly, and shook me out of the deep resentment funk that plunked me down to face off with Daisy in the first place.

But I'd already pitched the question, and it was out there, waiting to be answered. Funny thing, I almost spoke up, the silence between us making me feel bad. This wasn't Daisy's fault and family was family, whether still in that category officially or not. Apparently, though, I'd been silent long enough it pushed her own discomfort into the realm of guilty answering.

"I'm sorry if she's not fitting in," Daisy blurted, finally looking up, huge eyes so innocent and full of hurt I sighed, leaning my elbows on the counter. "She just doesn't have much of a life right now and she really needed someone."

I didn't know Rose played the victim card to get Daisy to agree to let her come to Petunia's. "I'm sorry to hear that," I said, grudgingly, yes. But it seemed to placate Daisy who beamed a smile at me.

"Dad's being a jerk to her mother," she said. "They got back together after all these years. Did you know that?" I hadn't. Why did Daisy seem hurt by that? Well, her father wasn't a saint, or much of a parent, for all that. "You know what he's like." Daisy's father had been pretty absent her whole life, my dad more of a role model to her than hers ever was. So honestly, I had very little idea what her male parent's skills looked like. But I nodded anyway, let her ramble. "Rose just wanted out of the whole mess. They've been dragging her into the middle of their fighting and she's tired of it." More like the sniping little whiner was either a) the cause of the fighting or b) feeding off their angst. Still, she was here, wasn't she? So maybe I had to give her the benefit of the doubt after all.

Sure, I did. Right after I got over the fact she was hanging off Robert. Shudder.

"You're very patient," I said, implying, of course, I wasn't. "You do know she's dating Robert of all people?" Yup, tossing chum in the water.

Daisy's wince told me what I already knew, that she'd known and had kept that juicy bit of gag-worthy gossip to herself. Not like her at all. "She'll come to her senses."

Grunt. We'd see about that.

Daisy shrugged, smile fading, sorrow returning as she scooped the last of the berries into one palm and deposited them into Petunia's bowl, going to the sink to rinse her hands and the blade of the knife. Light from the sun caught the edge, flashing into my eyes while she spoke.

"She's my little sister," she said, soft and gentle. "I wasn't there for her, Fee, all those years. If I can be now, I want to be."

Huh. Okay then. If she said so. Despite the technicality of their lack of blood ties, it was Daisy's way. Still, this morning's subtle jibes at my bestie sat about as well as this stupid t-shirt across my shoulders, and it certainly wasn't the first time since Rose arrived that I'd witnessed the younger handing passive-aggressive crap to the gorgeous woman in front of me. But she wasn't my problem, was she? Unless she interfered with our business, or how Daisy handled her end of things.

Then? Yeah, then Rose and I would have words. But did I dare to let this relationship go that far? I had a bed and breakfast and annex and restaurant and event center to run...

Daisy's gray eyes flickered to mine. "I'm sorry she defended Robert."

Not for her to apologize for. "And I'm sorry she makes you feel like you're not good enough." Yikes, I had to say that out loud, didn't I? Honestly, I had no proof it was Rose who'd been undermining Daisy's confidence all these years, but from what I'd witnessed since she'd arrived? I had a great circumstantial case. Maybe it wasn't just Rose. Maybe Daisy's former—wait, was she current again?—step-mom and her own father were part of the problem. Likely. But Rose certainly wasn't innocent.

I knew I'd gone too far, though. Daisy's usually open expression shut down in a flash, a mask of hurt falling, smothered in brusque tightness that wasn't like her at all. "I'm going to run to the annex and check on messages," she said, hurrying off before I could apologize. I heaved a sigh into the quiet kitchen, the pug now at my feet, licking her chops like the strawberries Daisy gave her only whetted her appetite.

I stared down at the happy creature and found myself grinding my teeth. You know what? Daisy might not like it, but she was my best friend and more family to me than Rose would ever be to her. I loved her and honored her for who she was. And I refused to stand by and allow anyone to treat her like she wasn't good enough. No one hurt my Daisy, especially when she'd done so much to increase her confidence and joy in her work. Maybe Rose was just jealous. Didn't matter her motives. Next time I heard her say anything to my bestie that didn't fit the woman she was becoming I'd be shutting that down.

Knowing I'd likely just decided to put a massive strain on my relationship with Daisy but the redhead in me not caring very much, I headed downstairs to my apartment to change, sizzling with determination, frustration and the uncomfortable need to call Crew and blame him for everything despite the fact he had nothing to do with it.

Yikes.

CHAPTER TEN

It wasn't until I went looking for my phone and wallet a few hours later I realized I'd done the unthinkable. My money and credit cards were safe, thankfully, still in the dash of my car. But my phone? My most precious of lifelines to the outside world? Missing.

For a moment I felt a flash of panic not unlike that I'd experienced when I'd seen Petunia go over the edge of the dock. Please, please let me have left the phone somewhere and not at the bottom of the harbor where it must have died a tragic early death. I'd just upgraded, too, damn it.

I checked my clothes again, damp in the hamper, coming up empty, mind turning over and over as I tried to remember where I'd left it. After a long, desperate think through, I exhaled in relief. Hadn't I set it in the box of food on my way from the car? Yes, yes, I had. Right, so that meant Mom probably still had it. Awesome. My day was looking up again.

But when I called my mother, she was already home, naturally. It was near dark, the party at the dock long over, dinner served and cleaned up, her part done for the day. "Sorry, sweetie," she said when I asked after my phone. "I left the boxes and the leftover food at the yacht club. Doreen was going to put everything in the fridge."

I was already searching the internet to find out if refrigerating a cell phone would damage it (short term was probably okay but I had condensation to worry about, apparently) while thanking Mom and hanging up. A quick call to the yacht club ended in a message and I was forced to leave one of my own, annoyed with myself for the slip of memory. I quickly called Mom back.

"I'll call Doreen myself," Mom said, queen of efficiency that she was. "I'll have her meet you there. Okay?"

"Thanks, Mom." Phew, saved by the mother. I turned as I hung up, finding Daisy exiting the kitchen. "I need to run out for ten minutes," I said. "Are you good?"

She hesitated before shrugging, still a bit stiff with me. She had been for hours, so not like her at all but I guess to be expected when family was involved. Even my amazing Daisy wasn't immune to hurt, and she was emotional enough and honest enough she struggled to hide it when she was upset. I'd have to deal with the mess I made of our friendship after I got my phone back.

I nodded thanks, ignoring the plaintive look on Petunia's face as I headed for the door. She'd had enough excitement for one day and taking her with me would add another ten minutes to my trip, including putting on her harness while she danced around like she didn't want it on, hustling her into the car, settling her long enough to put on her seatbelt and the reverse since she'd insist on getting out of the car with me once we arrived. Instead, I chose expediency, grabbing my keys and wallet and heading for the driveway, wincing at the sight of a car with New Hampshire license plates parked in front of Petunia's.

Just what I needed. But instead of turning back to ask Daisy to deal with it, I felt my chest tighten in rebellion and annoyance. You know what? Let Robert try to ticket my guests. I'd be in Olivia's office so fast he'd get seasick from the motion.

The yacht club building was dark when I arrived, though a few of the boats were out on the water rather than moored at the long, narrow pier. The majority of them sat quiet and I wondered about the appeal of owning what amounted to a floating cottage. Who needed two homes, anyway? Yeah, okay, so I had Petunia's and the annex, but that was my business. Thinking about the waste of owning something that cost more than my renos on the new place just sitting there and doing nothing gave me hives.

I peeked in the windows of the club, but except for some emergency lighting the place was dark and locked up tight. I paced in front of my car, wondering at the wisdom of coming down here without a phone and no confirmation from Mom she'd even reached Doreen in the first place. I needed my cell to check so that Catch-22 wasn't lost on me or anything.

I finally dug a quarter out of the folds of carpet in the driver's side of my car and headed for the payphone at the end of the dock. The thing had seen better days, handle faded from deep black to near gray, the silver buttons worn so the numbers barely showed. But it worked, the blank dial tone answering me as I lifted the handle and slipped the quarter into the slot.

Now, what was Mom's number again? Ack. I had it on my cell. And I knew her old one, of course, I did, the one from when I was a kid. But with the rezoning and changes Olivia had made, the phone company updated certain streets with new numbers about two years ago. I hadn't taken the time to learn Mom's new one. Or the number for Petunia's, either.

Well, wasn't that a heaping pile of steaming frustration.

I didn't slam the receiver down. Didn't swear that the stupid antiquated thing didn't give me my money back, either. Didn't kick the post the box sat on or throw a hissy fit as I spun back toward my car. Nope. Didn't. Proud of me? I know I was. Though, to be fair, the reason I didn't? Wasn't my firm and complete hold over my temper. Surprised? Instead, it was the sound of water splashing behind me.

Now, I was standing on a dock, so splashing wasn't exactly a foreign sound or anything. But this wasn't the gentle lapping of waves. This sounded like floundering, like someone struggled in the water and not swimming, either. I frowned into the darkness, aware at that moment the big light over the dock was out, the boats at the far end smothered in night. Any normal person would have retreated, right? Gone back to her car and drove home, worried about her phone tomorrow and kept her nose out of something that was likely nothing.

Me? I did the horror movie heroine thing, like always, and followed the sounds of splashing. They died out pretty quickly, mind you, so by the time I reached the end of the dock and the last boat moored there I wasn't following anything but my nosiness. It took a moment for my eyes to adjust to the dark, the stillness of the water black and unfathomably deep, though I had just been in it so I knew it wasn't as bottomless as all that. I was about to turn and go back to my car after all when I spotted something pale floating in the water and paused.

It looked like a sail or a bag of some kind and bobbed peacefully, the soft waves carrying it closer. A tall, wicked-looking boat hook hung from a spike driven into the last light post, offering my curiosity a chance at answers and I took it. Just some flotsam from today's festivities, likely. I was doing my part to keep the harbor clean, right?

Sure, I was. I poked at the rolling debris, the end of the hook's barb nabbing the fabric. It floated easily toward me, though as I tugged the weight behind it became apparent, even more so as it rolled over, bumping the dock and dislodging the hook, flipping upright in the dim light of the stars.

Lester Patterson looked more peaceful than I'd ever seen him, at least, though that was a small consolation considering he was dead.

CHAPTER ELEVEN

While I was used to filling in town sheriffs on the details of discovering dead bodies, this particular stand-in wasn't my first choice, not by a long shot. But the fact that Robert was all I had to talk to, with Crew and Jill both out of town, left me with no choices and little hope anything I said was going to be taken seriously outside of the actual discovery.

The way his beady eyes narrowed while I walked him through why I was at the yacht club in the first place and the jumpy twitching of his mustache told me I was far more likely to get invited to the Oscars by some handsome A list star than to be asked for help in this particular investigation. Which meant, knowing Robert's terrible track record when it came to police work, there was an excellent chance this murder—okay, I was guessing, jumping ahead to foul play, but my previous encounters with death all led to horrible people dying at the hands of those who thought they deserved it—would go unsolved without Crew here to handle things.

I blinked into the glaring lights Robert ordered set up around the dock, Dr. Aberstock already arrived, two paramedics pulling the body from the water so he could have a closer look. Never mind my cousin's inflated ego and the way he glared at the local medical examiner, muttering about disturbing his crime scene or the fact Dr. Aberstock had seen more death than Robert ever had. I guess procedure was procedure, but still, Crew never said boo when the doc arrived first or questioned the fact the older man knew what he was doing.

Doreen hovered nearby, hugging herself, her pale yellow sweater tight around her round torso, shivering though the evening was warm. She'd arrived about a minute after I'd found Lester, huffing her way toward me and the sound of my quick scream. Okay, yes, I screamed. Despite seeing multiple dead bodies in the last few years, I still had that crawling sensation up the back of my spine when I came face-to-face with unexpected death. At least I wasn't hanging next to him or pinned under him like had been the previous experiences that marred my psyche for life. Still, turning over what I thought was an innocent bit of litter only to have his bulging eyes stare up at me from the cold, black water? Yeah, scream-worthy, if I do say so myself.

At least I hadn't been alone when Robert showed up. Doreen handed me my phone—she'd found it in the box before putting the food away, thank goodness—leaving me to call the sheriff's department. While I was grateful for the presence of another person when Robert pulled up, scowling at me like I'd interrupted something important (please, no visuals of him and Rose in a compromising position, I'd throw up) with his uniform shirt rumpled and his expression decidedly grumpy.

"So, you're telling me this is all a coincidence," he said as I rambled to a halt. "That you just happened to be at the yacht club, and you just happened to hear splashing and you just happened to find the body. Is that it?"

Holy guacamole, did he hear a word I just said? "Um, yes." Sigh.

"Right." He wasn't even taking notes, hands on his hips, glaring like I was the one who kicked his dog into the water to drown. "Just like always, Fanny. In the middle of a murder you claim you stumbled on." Oh, he was not going there. Was he, really? "See, I'm not Crew Turner. I don't assume you're not guilty." Considering Crew had me as his prime suspect in the death of Pete Wilkins when that real estate swindler did his best to steal Petunia's from me? Yeah, Robert could choke on his attitude. "In fact, I'm starting to wonder about you, Fanny." Argh. Could I please just smack him and get it over with? "Everyone around town thinks you're so smart and so clever, that you're some kind of super sleuth detective or something." Huh, I didn't know that. "But there comes a time when the girl who cries wolf is in the wrong place at the right time one time too often."

I spluttered a second before eye-rolling. "You can't be serious." And besides, his little metaphor attempt made zero sense. "I'm not crying wolf, you idiot. The guy is dead. The fact I'm here is a fluke. As for the death toll in our town, maybe you should worry more about finding out what happened to this guy instead of giving the person who found him a hard time."

I was so tired of going down this road. I barely tolerated it with Crew, let alone my jerk cousin Robert. While the handsome sheriff might have gotten away with his veiled accusations (and sometimes not so veiled), I'd known and despised Robert since I was a child. So, he could piss off.

"You really need to respect the sheriff." Oh my god. If Rose opened her mouth and spoke one more time I was absolutely going to go to prison for murder, but it wasn't going to be over Lester. I ignored her, just like I'd been ignoring her since she climbed out of the passenger's seat of Robert's cruiser—at least he didn't have the guts to claim Crew's truck for the duration of his temporary position—and high nosed her way around the crime scene, acting like she was some kind of police presence herself.

Thankfully, I was saved by the huffing, frustrated form of the primly suited and shining bobbed Olivia who appeared shortly after Robert had, whispering into her cell phone and acting about as agitated as I'd ever seen her. As I inhaled to tell Robert where he could shove his little girlfriend's attitude the mayor stepped between me and the acting sheriff, her back to me as she confronted him.

"Stop being a moron," she snapped, voice low and harsh, "and go look for clues or something. I need to talk to Fiona."

Robert's initial startled reaction flickered into the kind of dark and dangerous rage I'd only read about in books that dealt with over-the-top villains. He smothered it quickly, jerking himself around without protest, but by the stiffness of his shoulders and the way he walked off, like a rod of iron had been shoved down the back of his shirt to the soles of his feet, I actually felt a surge of fear of him. Not that I really believed he'd ever hurt me. But this was the first time I realized real hate lived in my cousin, the kind that could set fire to a man who I'd always discounted as a pain in the butt nobody.

Before I could think on it further, Olivia grasped my arm and pulled me aside, the bright light of the spots making the fine hairs on her cheeks stand out, the pale powder she wore obvious in the glaring illumination. "I've called Crew and Jill back," she hissed at me. "They should be here in the morning." Thank goodness for that. No way could Robert handle this without bungling.

I hadn't noticed Geoffrey's arrival, probably thanks to the fact I'd spent the last ten frustrating minutes answering ridiculous questions my cousin really didn't have to ask. But, when the councilman sidled into our conversation, I was acutely aware of his presence, thanks to his proximity—ew—and the scent of his cologne—yuck.

"That's a mistake, Olivia," he said, voice as low as hers. Eavesdropping was a horrible pastime. Yeah, like I didn't have a history of it myself...? "Robert can handle things."

"I have no idea what actual planet you come from," I snapped at him, though I kept my tone as low as theirs, "but the incompetent excuse for an acting sheriff couldn't find a clue if it goosed him in the rear end." I hadn't meant to be so harsh, and I certainly hadn't had the opportunity to snark back at Geoffrey in the past. He didn't seem surprised by my words, though, and instead of looking angry he just seemed amused. Whatever. I turned back to Olivia. "Don't let Robert screw this up in the meantime," I said. Realizing even as I did, I really didn't get a say in the matter. Sure, my father was the former sheriff before Crew, and I might have played a pivotal role in uncovering the perpetrators of past murders, but honestly, I was just a local business owner.

Didn't faze Olivia one bit. If anything, my confidence seemed to boost hers. "I'll make sure Dr. Aberstock doesn't release anything until Crew gets back." She seemed a bit relieved. "Is your dad in town?"

I shook my head. "Still gone on a case, but I know he'll come back if you need him." Shouldn't, though, not if Crew was on his way.

Olivia chewed her bottom lip a moment. "Any ideas what happened?" She hesitated before rushing on. "Is it murder, Fee?"

Right, because I could pull clues and answers out of thin air. "Sorry," I said. "Not my department." I groaned at the sight of Robert arguing with Dr. Aberstock, the volume rising as the two faced off. "You might want to go handle that?"

Olivia huffed off, a woman on a mission, Geoffrey lingering a moment like he wanted to talk to me. But I was already turning my back, scanning my phone. Noted a missed message from earlier, Crew's number. Well, I'd get it later or he could tell me in person. Likely just a good night since I hadn't been home to take our usual evening call. I pulled up Crew's number and dialed.

After three rings, his voice answered, but not the fresh, friendly and present one I was hoping for. "You've reached Sheriff Crew Turner. Leave a message."

The long beep made my stomach ache. "Hey," I said. "Olivia said she called. Yeah, I found the body." Wince. "No surprise there, right?" Nice attempt at a joke, Fee. "Anyway, could use you back here ASAP. Robert's being a total dick." I watched him fight with both Olivia and Dr. Aberstock, their voices loud enough I caught the gist but not the details. "Call me and I'll fill you in, okay?" I hesitated before hanging up, wanting to add more, to tell him I missed him, that I wished we had more time together lately, that

I'd done more to advance our relationship past the few dates and private moments we'd managed to wrangle. Instead, I chose to go for professional, because maybe murder, right?

Coward. I hated feeling like I'd chickened out. I took a moment to check his message, hoping to savor the sound of his voice saying a sultry good night. Instead, goosebumps rose on my arms when I took in the tense, quiet tone he used.

"Something came up. I have to take care of it. I'll be in touch." A woman's voice said his name from somewhere behind him just as he hung up.

And that was it. I checked the time of the message, found it was from this afternoon, shortly after Petunia went into the water. Who was the woman? It didn't sound like Jill. Had Olivia spoken to him directly? I almost turned to ask her, but her argument wasn't over and I needed to hear things from the man himself. I dialed him again. This time, though, while I held my breath and hoped he'd answer, the other end clicked and a voice said, "Hello?"

Thing was? That voice wasn't the deep, graveled tone I was expecting. Nor was it male at all. Instead, some strange woman was answering Crew's phone and the instant I heard her voice my chest knotted, stomach fluttering while I clutched the cell to my ear and tried to catch my breath.

"I need to speak to Crew Turner." Wow. I sounded rational and put together, not at all like I'd just heard a strange woman answer his phone. Wait, had I dialed the wrong number? Nope, speed dial told me otherwise.

"He's unavailable." She sounded brusque, annoyed. "Please stop calling. He'll be in touch when he's free." And then, just like that, she hung up.

I gaped at my phone for a long moment, heart pounding suddenly, though I instantly shut down any jealousy that surged into place of shock. Crew and I had a thing, didn't we? He told me so. Told me I was the woman he wanted to be with. So why then was some other female presence answering his phone when he was supposed to be at a conference?

I didn't even know I was scrolling my numbers until my thumb chose Jill and I dialed. She answered almost immediately, second ring echoing in my ears, the huffing sound of her voice telling me she was on the move.

"Fee." A car door slammed, and an engine turned over. "I'm on my way."

"Jill." I almost choked on her name. "Where's Crew?" I'd just spoken to him this morning. He hadn't said anything about any trouble or another woman. Choke.

Her hesitation told me a lot. Like I needed to be worried. "I should be back tonight, late. You found the body?" She didn't sound surprised, but it was pretty obvious to me she was deflecting.

Fine, whatever. I told her what I knew, oddly comforted by the cool and professional way she talked me down from my hysteria just by being Jill. "It's going to be okay," she said. "I'll see you soon."

When she hung up without telling me anything about Crew, I let it go, though her calming influence wasn't lasting now that she no longer talked to me from the other end of the line.

That's how I found myself dialing one more time, this person, I realized without surprise, my go-to when the chips were down, and I needed someone to talk to. Dad answered like he already knew why I was calling.

"Fee," he said in his rumbling Dad voice. "Tell me what happened."

That was all I needed to launch into a breathless, rambling blurty rant about everything. Dad listened with his usual patience, only occasionally grunting or muttering some supportive sound that kept me going. When I stumbled to a halt, he sighed into the phone, but as he spoke, I felt his strength behind his words like I always did. Jill might have brought me comfort, but Dad took my fears away.

"I'm already home, honey," he said. "I'll meet Dr. Aberstock at the hospital and Robert be damned. As for Crew, I have no idea what he's up to, but I'll help you find out, okay? I'm sure it's nothing." Right, he was right. Nothing. Crew would call and clear things up and it would be fine. He'd be back, he'd solve this case, murder or not, and life would go back to normal. I'd make a huge effort to forward our relationship and I'd have my happily ever after. Thanks, Dad. "Tell Olivia I'll be in her office in the morning. She has to make it official, but I can flub the paperwork if she wants to hire me in the interim."

"Done." I turned to find Geoffrey standing far too close to me, watching me with his careful eyes. I stiffened and when I spoke again it was as much to my father as to the Patterson council member. "I'll see you in the morning, Dad."

I hung up, tucking my phone into my pocket, while Geoffrey closed the last of the distance between us and spoke quietly, his words making it through the distant shouting that still went on over the body of Lester Patterson. "I'm sorry you had to yet again be the bearer of deadly news, Fiona," he said, in a tone that told me he was trying to be sympathetic but just gave me the willies. "And that you had to tolerate Robert's accusations. Of course, no one believes you're a murderer. In fact, you've proven an invaluable resource in multiple crimes over the years. He needs to learn to be grateful and accept help when it's offered."

Playing both sides, Geoffrey? Why? I didn't get a chance to find out. Doreen suddenly burst into tears not too far from me and I found myself hurrying to her side to hug her while she cried, watching Geoffrey exit to his car and drive away even as I made a mental note to call Mom and have her check in on Doreen. The poor thing was a wreck.

I knew how she felt.

CHAPTER TWELVE

Tired and completely over today, I skirted the side of Petunia's after I parked in the driveway—noting the car that had been outside was long gone, thankfully, though that didn't mean I'd miss out on a ticket—and headed up the sidewalk. We'd converted the lawn between the two houses into a parking lot to circumvent the increasingly irritating town rules about cars on the street, making for a bit of an unsightly curb appeal but keeping me from being cited regularly for illegal use of curbside space.

I bypassed the front entry altogether, just wanting to sneak inside, check on things and slip downstairs to a hot shower and bed. And maybe a snack of some kind involving too much sugar and salty goodness. Yeah, it had been that kind of miserable day, the kind that either needed strong arms as support or a bowl of heavily processed snack foods. Since the arms I longed for weren't here (wasn't thinking where those arms might be or what they might be doing or who they might be holding right now), I'd have to make do with chocolate and chips.

Naturally, instead of my plans for peace, quiet and a bit of feeling sorry for myself, I stumbled into the kitchen to find Daisy and Rose deep in conversation. I guess I was quiet enough on my entry and their focus so tight they didn't hear me enter because neither looked up when I stepped inside and softly closed the door behind me.

Just in time to hear Rose, who had beaten me home thanks to my lingering to support Doreen while Daisy's stepsister and my cousin drove off in his cruiser, delivering one of her passive-aggressive, lip curling and vastly irritating suggestions.

"Oh, Daisy," she was saying, one hand on my bestie's arm and the other pressed to her chest with that fake care etched into her plain face, bulging brown eyes locked on and not letting go, "are you sure you can handle everything yourself like this?" Everything like what? I held still and listened instead of speaking up like I wanted to. Just to hear what the nasty piece of work had to say this time, without my interference. It was, after all, the first time I got to hear how Rose talked to Daisy without anyone else around. "You take on so much and you know you're just not great at juggling too many things. You're so forgetful." I felt my stomach clench as Daisy sagged and Rose went on. Was that a faint smirk on her face? I'd smack it out of her right before I kicked her butt to the street and let Robert write me a ticket for his smarmy little girlfriend parked on the side of the road where she belonged. "You know you always mess things up if you have too much to do. It's not your fault." Daisy didn't even try to protest, rubbing at her arm with one hand, head drooping. "You're just so much like your mother, you know. Your father says so all the time."

Daisy nodded, dismal expression pulling her full mouth down. "I know," she whispered.

Rose patted her arm, smiling for real now, too much satisfaction in her expression for her continuing health and safety if I got my hands around her neck. Any second now. "There, there, Daisy," she said. "Admitting you're not up to the task is always the best, isn't it? Do you feel better?" I was feeling rather murderous, personally, while Daisy bobbed a nod. "I'm happy to take the weight off your shoulders," Rose went on while alarm bells sounded in my head and my chest tightened so far, I was positive I wouldn't be able to take my next breath. "It'll be okay. You'll see. We'll just tell Fiona in the morning."

"Tell Fiona what?" Yeah, that came out as a rough growl akin to the pending attack of a vengeful she-wolf about to pounce on her prey. Snarl.

Daisy almost leaped from her skin, spinning with a shocked expression to face me, Rose looking about as surprised and barely hiding a flash of worry that crossed her face. Probably because I more than likely looked ready to take her head off and toss it in the koi pond for Fat Benny to nibble.

No, forget it. I wouldn't poison my fish with her tainted flesh. Maybe a shallow, cold grave where the coyotes would find her.

"Fee!" Daisy wavered, looked like she wanted to come to me, eyes huge, but Rose's hand never left her arm and now I could see it wasn't just a touch but a grasp, an iron grip. On just her bicep or on her soul? Since she didn't pull away and come to me, I could only guess both while my heart plummeted to my shoes. "Are you okay? Rose told me about Lester."

And yet, no rushing to my side to hug me, her gray eyes hollow and her own heart not in her sympathy, I could tell. I grunted my disgust and glared at Rose before returning my gaze to Daisy who looked beaten while I wondered what the hell just happened to the vibrant, amazing woman I adored.

"I'm fine," I said, crisp, angry, crossing the kitchen and purposely getting between them. Rose took a hasty couple of steps back, her foot catching Petunia's toes. I hadn't seen my pug lurking, though of course, she had been, her favorite when anyone was in the kitchen. Though Rose looked quickly contrite and offered the dog an awkward pat on the head like she'd rather do anything else, considering her boyfriend had almost killed Petunia earlier today her attempt at an apology wasn't buying her any kind of leeway with me. I turned to Daisy, cutting Rose out of the conversation completely, treating her like a plant or a piece of furniture while I faced down my slightly trembling best friend with the kind of expression I normally reserved for Crew when I was pissed at him.

Too much? Maybe, but again, the day I'd had? Yeah.

"Tell Fee what?" I repeated the question, softly, without anger at least but with enough intensity Daisy blinked, glancing over my shoulder at Rose who inhaled to speak. I waved her off with an upraised hand, sitting in the silence a moment, still staring at Daisy before my best friend finally met my eyes again. Only for an instant before dropping her gray gaze to the floor as she spoke.

"I was going to ask you if it would be okay to make Rose a more permanent part of Petunia's and the annex," she said, voice soft, wavering. "To help me with the event planning and the staff."

I should have been surprised. Wasn't. Though the need to choke her and shake her and ask her what the hell was wrong with her devoured me to the point I had no choice but to inhale. Exhale. And force the kind of response that might do more damage than good.

"No." End of conversation. "Now, I'm going to bed."

Rose spluttered, Daisy holding her back, while my pug followed me out through the swinging door, the only witness to me swearing softly under my breath all the way down to my apartment where I took a few minutes to privately scream into a pillow instead of going upstairs again to commit murder.

One death in town at a time was enough for today.

CHAPTER THIRTEEN

Morning broke, my alarm blaring at me at the usual 6AM wakeup, though I wasn't exactly in the mood to rise and shine. Considering I'd spent the majority of the night tossing and turning and arguing with multiple people who only existed in my head—hello, straight jacket, padded room and three shots a day—it was a wonder I wasn't a walking zombie by the time I emerged, grumpy and blinking into the bright Sunday summer morning, into the foyer of Petunia's. My pug was equally quiet, though her reserved behavior shifted the moment we entered the kitchen and found Mom stirring something that smelled delicious enough to break me out of my funk. The pug waddled and wiggled her way to Mom's feet where my darling mother and partner promptly handed over a small plate with a serving of fruit and freshly cooked hamburger for the hungry pug.

"Spoiled," I muttered, helping myself to coffee.

Mom took one look at me, her spoon raised over the pot of simmering oatmeal that almost smelled like Christmas thanks to the cinnamon wafting my way, her green eyes tight. "You really need to stop finding dead bodies," she said. "They're bad for your complexion."

I rolled my eyes and went in for a hug which she offered instantly, cooing soothing sounds while she kissed my cheek before letting me go.

"I'm sorry I didn't rush over last night," she said. "I shouldn't have listened to your father." She set down her spoon and cupped my cheeks in her hands, looking me over with more care, her attempt at humor gone with her usual Momness washing over me and making me feel better. "He said you were fine, that he was taking care of talking to Dr. Aberstock for Crew."

I nodded, leaning against the counter, sighing. "Mom, do you think I'm cursed?"

She laughed, soft and kind, patting my cheeks before letting me go. "Silly," she said, "it's just bad luck, sweetie. I do wish it would stop happening to you. But this is a small town and you're a big part of it. So, it's not so surprising to me you stumble on these things." She returned to her spoon. "You and your father, both with that nose for crime. Makes you a magnet, Fee, not a victim of a curse."

I guess she was right. Funny how finding the body was taking second seat to my anxiety over Daisy, though. Priorities, yeah? I quickly and quietly filled her in on what I'd witnessed the night before, Daisy's shift back into her old lack of confidence, worse than ever, actually. Mom's jaw tightened, her head bobbing an almost endless nod until I finished. After which she set down her spoon again so roughly the small plastic drip catcher rattled with the force of her motion.

"I haven't said anything to her directly," Mom said, "but I've been witnessing the same thing, Fee, on far too regular a basis. And I don't like it one bit. Yes, Rose is family, but honestly." She huffed a breath, her redhead temper firing up just as mine had, though Mom was usually better at hiding hers. Good to know I had her on my side in this mess. "We really need to corner Daisy and have a solid heart-to-heart."

Awesome. "Exactly," I said. "Let's do that, okay? Sooner rather than later?"

"This morning." Mom nodded sharply then beamed a smile at me like making that decision actually fixed the matter before it was even addressed. Well, if she was so confident, I'd do my best to be as well if only to present a really solid united front when we talked Daisy down from the ledge of Rose she was standing so precariously on.

And no way—NO WAY—would I ever let someone like Rose take any kind of responsibility. With Mom on my side, two partners against one?

Relief gave me the lift I needed, and I found myself finally relaxing long enough to yawn through the realization I was tired from my lack of sleep and had a huge day ahead anyway.

Great. Still. Progress.

When I told Mom about Doreen, though, she immediately flinched, her face tightening into worry for her friend as thoughts of Daisy and Rose left my caring mother. "I'll head over to see her right after breakfast," she said, fretting herself while I hugged her around her shoulders, leaning my cheek into her hair, remembering the distance there had been between us only a short time ago, a distance created by my mother's own walk down the path of self-recrimination and doubt. If anyone could convince Daisy to come back to us it would be Mom.

"You're awesome," I whispered, surprised to find I was choking up.

She paused, squeezed my arm with one hand, leaning into me, too. "I love you, Fee. Now," her brusque professionalism returned, flashing smile all Lucy Fleming, "I have a horde to feed in the next little while and a ton of food to prepare. Shoo!"

I hustled, mood lifted despite my weariness, Petunia staying with Mom while I made my rounds. With all rooms full it was a busy morning of finishing laundry the staff started yesterday, restocking closets with linens, checking and cleaning communal areas, and, finally, paperwork. Daisy arrived shortly after 7AM, though she avoided me, hurrying past the front desk with a small smile in my direction, head down as she rushed to join Mom. Rose wasn't with her, so I let Daisy go. We'd be talking to her shortly, and I wasn't in a hurry to confront my bestie alone anyway.

I took my usual morning break and paced my apartment for twenty minutes, knowing Crew wouldn't be calling like he'd failed to call last night despite his usual contact. His short, unhelpful message weighed on me and left me frustrated. When I emerged from downstairs I was about as agitated as possible, though I did my best to hide it as I exited through the kitchen door on my way across the property.

With Petunia's handled, I headed outside to the now expansive garden, crossing the bridge on my way to the annex. The carriage house would have to wait until the guests were out for the day for restock. I'd leave that to the staff when they did their cleaning rounds after 9AM. The morning sun washed over the pond beneath me, the chubby, bright bodies of the koi within swimming lazy paths beneath the pretty wooden structure. Jared's last project had turned out perfectly, the dark wood smooth and heavy, the boards of the bridge solid under my feet. I loved the curved feel of the railing, the way the sun heated and made it feel almost alive under my hands. Though it only took three or four strides to cross, the bridge felt bigger, metaphorically, anyway. Like crossing from my old life to my new every time I set foot on it.

Making that crossing finished the job Mom started, my heart light and my thoughts on the day rather than my worries. I was almost to the back door of the annex when I heard someone calling my name, a familiar voice that turned me around with a smile and open arms. Dad caught up with me, hugging me tight, rocking me a little, the strong, firm embrace so familiar and comforting I exhaled in a final release of tension before looking up at him with a grin.

"Guess I have a thing for dead bodies," I said.

Dad winked down at me, blue eyes sparkling. "Did you scream?"

"Like a little girl," I laughed.

"Get a good look?" Just like the former sheriff to ask.

"Close enough," I said, shuddering.

"Anything stand out?" That was Dad, all right.

I thought about it a moment then shrugged. "It was pretty dark. All the lights down the dock were out." Broken or dead? I hadn't thought to check. "Did you talk to Dr. Aberstock?"

Dad grunted something then shrugged, hands in his pockets. "Tried," he said. "Robert was there, being an ass." My father's whole body tensed, jaw clenching. "Guess he's not so happy about the trouble I've been making for him since I left office."

Crew had mentioned Dad was giving my cousin a hard time. "Like he doesn't deserve it." Shoddy police work should have been grounds for firing him. Why he was still even in uniform, let alone acting sheriff...

Dad didn't comment, didn't have to. "Whatever

his reasons, it put the brakes on my questions last night. But I'm going to pop over to Doc's office today and buy him a coffee."

Worked for me. And saved me asking the doctor myself. Yes, I was going to investigate this case, thank you very much. At least until Crew managed to get his butt back here and take over. Or someone told me definitively it wasn't murder. No way was I letting Robert mess things up.

Which raised an interesting question I posed to Dad on impulse. "What's with Geoffrey, anyway?" My father's bushy eyebrows raised in response. "It's like he's playing both sides or something." I told him what happened, about his support of Robert in public before he came to me privately. Dad's gaze narrowed, a flash of anger showing, and I wondered just what he knew he wasn't telling me. He was like that, still protective enough he hid things from me despite the fact I was a grown-ass woman who could take care of herself. Sheesh.

This time, though, instead of stonewalling like he usually did, Dad spoke up. "He's been up to something since he took his seat." My father's deep voice had dropped to a low rumble. "I've been trying to figure out what, but so far, he's keeping his plans to himself. Whatever it is, it's not good for you, Fee." Dad's worry translated into his big hand touching my cheek before returning to his pocket, almost as if he was holding himself back from hugging me again, this time out of protective instinct. "Just do your best to stay out of his way. I'm doing what I can to keep

Olivia afloat, meanwhile, and the Patterson interests from screwing up our town."

I wanted to ask him point-blank what he was talking about, but Dad cleared his throat and straightened his broad shoulders, lips twisting into a little grin full of mischief. Which meant he had his own plan in mind. And wanted me in on it. I already had yes on my lips when he asked. "Speaking of our mayor," he said, "I have an appointment to talk to her about the sheriff situation. Want to come with me?"

Um, double yup with a shot of are you freaking kidding, of course. Because I *was* a Fleming, after all.

CHAPTER FOURTEEN

I guess I shouldn't have been surprised to find Jill, dressed in her deputy's uniform, entering town hall ahead of us. Even without her gun belt around her narrow hips and the telltale khaki shirt over jeans she favored, I would have recognized that blonde ponytail bobbing against her back anywhere. When I called out to her, she jerked around, looking startled and then, oddly, guilty as Dad and I crossed the small parking lot beside the building to join her.

Was it just me or did she have a deer caught in the headlights of an oncoming freight train look that made me nervous? She smiled at Dad, then at me, not really meeting my eyes as we came to a halt next to her. Jill's knuckles were white where she clasped the handle of the entry door, the set of her broader than most women's shoulders telling me she wasn't comfortable with this meeting. All of which boiled down to something I didn't want to know but really, really had to ask.

"Jill," I said without preamble or niceties usually involved in saying hello to someone who's been gone a few days, "where's Crew?"

Dad cleared his throat and interrupted before the flush on her face could turn any brighter than it already had. "Conference okay?"

Jill seemed grateful for the deflect while I glared at Dad for interfering. What did he know that I didn't? If he had info on Crew's whereabouts—and the strange woman on the other end of his phone—I wanted to know about it. Didn't I? On the other hand, shame on me for jumping to inappropriate conclusions. Mind you, I had precedence in my past, enough to make me anxious about the possibilities. My ex and his cheating, for example. Yeah, big example. Still, Crew had never given me reason to doubt his sincerity or the fact he wanted to be with me and me alone. For all I knew, there was a perfectly logical and non-other woman explanation for the sheriff's absence and silence.

Trying not to play the crazy jilted woman card when I had no idea if that was the case or not, I held my tongue and my temper while Jill responded.

"You know, John," she said, false brightness in her voice. "Too much talking for my liking."

He grinned, nodded, gestured at the door which she pulled open with extra enthusiasm, gesturing for both of us to go ahead of her. I entered the cool dimness of the stone and dark wood-paneled lobby, still under firm control and unsure how long that would last.

"I hear you," Dad said, voice carrying in a faint echo in the quiet of the front entry to town hall. "Great place to make connections, though."

Jill spluttered a moment while I turned to face her, eyebrow raised. Was that what happened? Did Crew "make a connection" and Jill didn't want to tell me about it?

She averted her eyes from mine before we could really connect. "I guess," she said. "Shouldn't keep the mayor waiting, right?"

"You were invited to this meeting?" Dad didn't sound surprised, now following the tall blonde deputy to the right and up the wooden stairs to the second-floor offices. I ignored the pair of young women giving a tour to a small group of tourists, keeping my arms tight at my sides, wanting to shake Jill for not giving me the answer I was looking for right now, damn it.

Jill glanced back over her shoulder, speaking directly to Dad, sounding worried, now. "I'm sorry I wasn't here," she said. "Though from the sounds of things it wouldn't have mattered anyway."

As in, she wouldn't have been offered the acting sheriff position. I wasn't surprised there, though as far as I was concerned Robert's tenuous connection to Dad and the fact our town, for some dumb reason, preferred to have even a nephew of their former sheriff in the primary law enforcement role was about as bad a choice as anyone in this crazy place had ever made. Jill was a million times the cop my cousin pretended to be.

We turned left at the top of the steps, approaching the large double glass doors that led to the mayor's office, the grand entry rather ostentatious as far as I was concerned for a small-town officiant's place of work. Not that I got a say or anything. Dad didn't knock, opening the first door and letting himself into the reception area, the perky young man at the desk looking a bit harried as he nodded to us. I nodded back, not really feeling it but attempting to at least pretend to be a well-adjusted member of society while my constricting heart beat a bit too heavily in my chest. Hugh Farcourt's black, horn-rimmed glasses caught the light as he placed one slim hand over the receiver of the phone he cradled between his clean-shaven cheek and narrow suited shoulder, gesturing for us to go inside with a mouthed, "She's waiting," looking like a warning.

Kudos to him, as far as I was concerned. He'd tolerated working as Olivia's assistant since I'd moved home and seemed to be holding his own. But was that some premature gray in his dark hair? A bit early for someone in his mid-twenties, right? I'd be shocked fully white or in prison if I had to work for her, so I forced a wave as an added gesture of humanity on my way by while he grimaced at me like he understood completely.

See? I could be a good girl. Uh-huh.

I followed Jill and Dad through the door, keeping back as they greeted Olivia. She stood from behind her desk, looking a bit harried herself, but clearly happy to see both of them. I accepted her firm handshake before sinking into a chair in the corner of her big office, the breeze through the tall windows behind her cooling my temper as my father and the deputy took their own places in the heavy leather seats flanking the front of Olivia's workspace.

"You have to replace Robert as acting sheriff," Dad said. Looked like I came by my demanding with barely a howdy-do honestly.

Olivia sank into her seat, grim and quiet. "I'd love to do just that," she said, pointing an index finger at Jill, the nude polish fresh enough it still shone. "Trust me, Deputy Wagner is my first choice in this whole mess. No," she slapped the desk in front of her, making her green felt blotter shift. "I want my sheriff back." Her glare matched mine. "Where is Crew Turner?"

"Unavailable," Dad and Jill said together, which made my whole being twitch in irritation. So, my father did have information. Which I'd wring from him without mercy in short order. If Olivia didn't do the job for me.

Didn't she go and let me down? Instead of pushing, she sighed, leaning back into her leather chair, the shoulder pads in her cream suit scrunching as she shrugged. "I'm up against a wall," she said, sounding tired, but what else was new? I'd watched our mayor carefully since I arrived home and she always seemed to be in a balanced state of outward forward motion and verve and inner spiral into imminent collapse. Whatever worked for her. "The council is on Geoffrey's side in this issue, not to mention the fact Robert has the Fleming name behind him."

"I thought I took care of that." Dad's gruff response narrowed my eyes and finally shook me out of the concern I felt about Crew. Was that why my father had been calling out Robert on his bad police work? To distance him purposely from the Fleming name?

Apparently. But Olivia's second shrug told me Dad's plan wasn't working out.

"Maybe if Geoffrey wasn't behind Carlisle's support," she said. Her eyes found me and locked on. "Or if there was another Fleming willing to step up in times of crisis." My heart thudded once while Dad's shoulders shuddered faintly, about the same moment Olivia glared at him. "Either Fleming," she said.

Um, huh?

"We've had this conversation," Dad growled. "Get over it, Olivia."

She steepled her hands in front of her, elbows on the arms of her chair, dark eyes narrow and lips pursed. "I'm on the razor's edge here, John," she said. "And you know it." She sagged then, slight and subtle but there despite her continuing scrutiny of him and, oddly, me. "We both know this reprieve I've been handed the last few months won't last.

103

Next election there will be a new mayor in this chair and everything I've built will crumble to dust."

"How dramatic," Dad said, sounding amused. Olivia's anger flashed, and insight woke. Dad was manipulating her, pushing her. I watched her reject his humor and stiffen, chin rising, resolve returning. Respect for my father renewed, I firmly shoved aside my personal crap and paid closer attention.

"I can't risk rocking the boat," she said. Winced. "No pun intended." Olivia stood then, paced to the window behind her, hands clasped at her lower back while she spoke in a low, soft voice, in a tone I'd never heard from her before. Was this the real woman speaking? "There are rumors of a special election being called. That November isn't soon enough. I have to be prepared and doing that means giving in to certain things that keep the council happy."

"Even if that means a botched murder investigation," I spoke up before Dad could.

Olivia spun around to meet my eyes, though there was no anger in her. "Maybe that's a good thing," she said. "If Geoffrey's first choice for acting sheriff—for sheriff once I'm out of my seat if you want the bald truth of it—is discredited, it might work out in my favor."

So, my suppositions and fears about Crew's job weren't fantasy. "You're hoping Robert screws up," I said. "And that Crew or Dad or someone you support will then sweep in and fix everything and make him look like the idiot he is." Politics. I hated them. But I understood them. At least, once things were spread out in front of me.

"This is a wait-and-see proposition," Olivia said. "Though, I'm not telling anyone in this room not to poke their nose in if something happens to fall in their lap." Was that aimed at me or Dad or both?

Jill exhaled, shaking her head while her ponytail danced in echoing protest. "I can't condone that," she said, sounding weary herself. Met Dad's eyes with a weak smile. "Not officially."

"Since the mayor's office asked for Fleming Investigations to look into the possibility Lester Patterson's death was murder," Dad said, "you're off the hook here, Jill." Dad hadn't called it murder outright. Had he spoken to Dr. Aberstock yet? If so, was there no solid information either way of foul play? No one protested, so I could only assume, but I'd be asking later, anyway.

She nodded, turned at last to look at me. "I assume you officially work for said investigations agency?"

I said "No" the same moment Dad laughed and said, "Yes." Huh. Well now, there was a world of possibilities opened up with a single word I wasn't expecting.

Olivia waved off the conversation, looking pained but also a bit hopeful. "I don't want to know the details," she said. "But if Fleming Investigations uncovers any evidence in the course of a perfectly legal support process, the town of Reading and the sheriff's department," she nodded to Jill, "will be very grateful."

That was our cue to leave, apparently. I stood as Dad and the deputy did, exiting after them, turning to meet Olivia's eyes when I did, the doorknob in my hand. Neither of us spoke, though there was a level of discomfort in her scrutiny that made me close the door a bit more firmly than I'd planned, the glass rattling its unhappiness at my attention.

Dad and Jill were already on their way out into the hall, and I had to hurry to catch the deputy as she hustled toward the steps. But when I grabbed her arm and turned her around, she exhaled like she was expecting a fight.

"I can't tell you anything," she said, with conviction that shut me down. "He's okay. I promise. It's got nothing to do with Reading or you or any of us. No, I have no idea how long he'll be gone. No, I don't have details, okay? All I know is, he told me he had to go and that it was important. If he hasn't contacted you, there has to be a good reason." She softened a little, then whispered her next words into my ear. "All he did all week was talk about you," she said.

My heart fluttered a happy pitter-pat—yeah, I was pathetic and gooey and needed that, I guess—as she pulled back and shrugged.

"Okay," I said, now worried for different reasons. "Thanks, Jill." I really did feel better.

She left with a salute for Dad, her heavy boots tromping on the steps as she hurried off. I held back, mind spinning before I turned on my father with a scowl.

"You're going to tell me everything you know," I said.

His slow, wicked grin informed me otherwise. "Aren't you more curious to know when I was going to tell you you're a full partner in Fleming Investigations?"

CHAPTER FIFTEEN

He said *what* now? I was left speechless for the time being, forced to stumble after my father who exited town hall with the kind of pep in his long stride that told me he was enjoying himself far more than was good for either of us.

I crossed the street with him, heading for his office, conveniently located just down the block while I wondered if he made a habit of using the lot at the hall for his truck just to tweak Robert's enforcement of parking violations. The acting sheriff wouldn't have the nerve to call Dad on leaving his vehicle there, I was positive of it.

Not that I was really thinking about Robert as I joined Dad, catching up to him with my heart now pounding and possibilities raging, a million questions on my mind. Only to run right into him, oofing out a breath as my nose impacted his back, my hands catching his biceps to keep me from falling backward. Dad didn't even seem to notice we'd collided, and it wasn't until I peeked around him, catching sight of the faintly mocking smile on the face of the silver-haired Irishman leaning so casually against Dad's door I realized why.

"A bright and happy morning to you both," Malcolm Murray, the alleged mobster owner of The Orange pub said, white teeth flashing at Dad while his green eyes settled on me.

Dad's good humor had faded, everything about him tense and ready though his tone of voice was all soft, soothing former sheriff.

"Malcolm," he said. "I trust you're moving along, now?"

"Not just yet," Malcolm said, wiggling his fingers at me. Weird to actually witness an interaction between these two. Typically, their face-to-face confrontations lasted about half a second when I was around. And there was no sight of the pub owner's bully boys, either, though I had little doubt the casually clad, jeans and button-up wearing sixtyish Irishman was perfectly capable of taking care of himself. "How lovely to see you, Fiona, darlin'," he said, heavy on the accent today. "Have you had the opportunity to reach out to dear Siobhan yet? She'll be delighted to hear from you, I imagine."

My mind flashed to the white business card tucked away in my music box, safe with the treasure clues my grandmother left me. I hadn't the courage as of yet to call the woman, though her name and number were etched into my memory thanks to the countless times I'd stared at the same card, the one Malcolm handed me in the back of his car, the only clue I had as to what my father was hiding. And it was obvious he was hiding something.

Dad growled under his breath, his body dodging to the left to keep me from circling him, leaning back as if to protect me from some threat. "I told you to back off my daughter," he said, voice so deep and graveled I was a little afraid.

But Malcolm didn't show a hint of nervousness, just shrugged, hands in his pockets, the flash of a diamond on a heavy gold ring he wore catching the sunlight before it disappeared behind denim. "She's going to find out sooner than later, Johnny me boy," he said. "And when she does, I'll be here to answer her questions." He met my eyes, his now slits as his false humor faded. "I'm tired of waiting, lass. I'll force my hand if need be. Call her or I'll have her call you."

"Get out of here," Dad snarled, and I barely caught him before he lunged for Malcolm, feeling his tall, strong body vibrate under my grasp while the Irishman faced him down, almost a foot between their heights but not a scrap of fear in Malcolm's lean form.

"A reckoning is coming, Johnny," the Irishman said. "You have a nice day now, the two of you." With that, he strolled off, whistling a catchy tune that sounded like some kind of jig meant to be played on a fiddle.

Dad stood there a long moment before spinning on me, his broad jaw tight, eyes so fierce I almost took a step back. "He's trouble, you hear me? And so is digging into the past, Fee." My father had refused to tell me a thing about his interactions with Malcolm. Maybe I should have just taken his reticence about the mystery at face value instead of letting it eat at me the way it did, but I couldn't let it go. And yet, I'd done everything in my power to step away from it despite the name on the white business card burning a hole in my mind and heart. What was Dad hiding?

And what did Malcolm intend to do about the reveal if I didn't act?

"Dad," I said, "I'm a big girl. Whatever it is, you can tell me." Fear my father might have cheated on my mother with this Siobhan Doyle had never left me. Why was that always my go-to? Ah, right. I owed my ex so much for being a cheating bastard and tainting every relationship with men from the day I found out about his infidelity forward.

Dad shook his head, glaring after Malcolm. "He'll be out of town soon enough," he said, "and no longer a problem."

"Oh?" I followed him into his office as he jabbed the key into the lock and opened the glass door, stomping his way inside. "Why's that?" I'd always assumed he and Malcolm had some kind of agreement, considering the kind of sheriff Dad was, the dog with a bone type who didn't let anything go. Always struck me as odd he didn't chase the Irishman off before now. I just hoped Dad's assertion didn't mean he was going to risk putting himself in harm's way—either physically or his reputation if it came out, he'd been colluding or giving Malcolm special treatment for some reason as yet unrevealed. Wow, I was great at doubting the people I cared about most in the world, right?

Dad seemed mollified by my question, flipping on the lights and bypassing the desk at the entry—he had a receptionist? Since when?—heading into the back of the long, narrow space he'd rented and taking a heavy seat in his chair before shoving a file across the desk at me. With a key glistening on the surface, a new ring with a rectangle and "Fleming Investigations" written across it. A key to his office? Our office? Wait, this was moving far too fast for me to keep up with all the questions in my head. But Dad wasn't slowing down. In an effort to make me forget Malcolm?

If that was his goal, it worked. Because what he said next caught all of my focus. "There's been a rash of thefts at the yacht club and the cottages along the lake," he said. Then he went and brought Malcolm back into it, didn't he? "I'm investigating, but it would be just like Murray to have his boys out liberating some easy pickings from tourists if he thought he could get away with it." The scowl on Dad's face told me this might have been a pattern he already knew about.

"Dad," I said, glancing at the file, the stack of reports he'd collected and duly filled out with details and thefts, enough I wondered why this was the first I'd heard of it. Swallowed my nervousness and the faint taste of bile that my anxiety forced up to the back of my throat. "Did you and this Siobhan have a history you don't want to tell me about?" I met his eyes, kept all judgment out of my voice, at least as best I could. "Something you and Mom might not want me to know?" Okay there, I said it about as politely as I could but clearly, I hoped, so he'd get the idea and where my heart was hoping this wasn't going.

Dad's gaze widened and his mouth popped open as he sat upright, his shock at my suggestion so real I almost cried in relief. "Fee," he whispered, choked up. Cleared his throat, big hands clenching then settling flat on the surface of the desk in front of him. "How could you ever think that of me?"

And I was the worst daughter on the planet, in the history of daughters who had the most amazing father ever. "I'm sorry," I said, eyes burning with tears that really, really wanted to fall. "I just don't understand what you're keeping from me or why."

Dad sat back, nodding slowly, but when he spoke it wasn't with the information I wanted. "I love your mother," he said, sounding sad enough I did finally feel two tears escape and slide down my cheeks. "Fee, I would never." He coughed softly, face darkening, frown deep and troubled. "He's caused our family enough hurt," he said, obviously referring to Malcolm. "I'll take care of it, okay? Just promise me you'll let this go. There's nothing to be done, Fee. Nothing. I've spent my whole adult life trying to put it right and there's nothing to be done."

Okay, that didn't help matters, that brief whiff of a suggestion of information. If anything, it fired me up more, though I nodded just to ease the tension between us, rising to go to him, hugging him and whispering an apology while he hugged me back, awkward from his seated position.

I wanted to beg him to forget what I'd suggested, but I didn't get the chance to find out if he'd forgiven my assumption or not. The door to the office swung open and we were interrupted, forcing me to drop the issue, to wipe at the tears on my face, and I found myself standing at Dad's side, one hand on his shoulder, as Chris Noltz strode in, nodding first to my father then to me as if he was unsurprised to find me there. Which led me back to Dad's initial reveal, that he'd made me a full partner in his little enterprise without telling me first. Who else knew when I hadn't a clue?

CHAPTER SIXTEEN

Chris didn't wait to begin complaining, his mouth open and his brain running through it even before he settled in the chair I'd just vacated.

"This is all Olivia's fault," he groused, smacking the top of Dad's desk with an open hand. "Three of our local owners are listing because their water quality has been compromised by fuel spills near the marina." Yikes, that wasn't good to hear. "Wanda found evidence someone's been dumping garbage illegally just down from the harbor. And another visiting cottager at one of my rentals just reported valuables missing. This has to stop, John. Our town is being ruined by all this new activity."

Dad's expression had leveled out, no sign of our previous conversation showing either on his face or in the sound of his voice as he responded.

"I'm happy to help, Chris," he said, "you know that. I've been working to uncover the culprits. But I'll remind you, just a week ago you were telling me how business is booming and you're thinking about building three new units for next summer." The irony of the statement wasn't lost on me, nor was the fact I'd done just the same thing in creating the annex. Did that mean I didn't have the right to complain if something went wrong involving Olivia's plans for our town?

Chris spluttered a moment, one beefy hand rising to slide over his slicked brown hair, receding hairline pink from too much time outside unprotected. "Maybe if Lester and his ridiculous yacht club would upgrade security," he said, "or would monitor who's dumping waste, this might not be an issue." Dude liked to pass the buck, did he? "That acting idiot sheriff tells me it's not his department and the park rangers won't help, either. Do we have to police the lake ourselves?"

I could understand his frustration, even if Dad wasn't willing to go there.

"I'm looking into it," Dad said, hand on the file he'd retrieved. "As promised. You'll be receiving my first bill shortly." Nice reminder my father's particular skills didn't come for free.

Chris waved that off as if unimportant. "Damned sheriff's office is useless, John. That nephew of yours can't find his own car keys let alone catch thieves stealing from my cottagers and vandals ruining our lake."

"I understand your frustration, Chris," Dad said, reaching into his desk for papers he slid over the surface to the cottage association president. "If you'd like to fill out the information of the new cases, I'll add them to the list. But in thc mcantimc, I really need you to step back and let me do my job."

"We both know you were making Lester's complaints the priority." That seemed to fire up Chris's attitude all over again. Wait, hadn't I heard him arguing with Lester during the yacht club party? "I'm the one who hired you, John, not that weasel of a Patterson."

"Well, now that Lester is dead, you don't have to worry so much about him, do you?" I hadn't meant to speak up, but his attitude was getting to me. Feeling a little guilty about thinking badly about good old Dad, Fee? Enough defending my father wasn't beyond my scope of please forgive me for being a horrible child.

Chris spluttered at me then blanched, his slightly bulging pale brown gaze falling to Dad. My father's faint smile but otherwise calm, empty expression with his big hands folded in front of him, utter silence as intimidating as ever, did nothing to ease the cottager's sudden worries.

"Surely you don't think I had anything to do with Lester's death?" Chris looked back and forth between us.

"I hear you and he had a bit of a falling out the other day," I said, as casually as possible. "A fight about boat owners making cottager lives miserable?" I hadn't told Dad what I overheard because, quite frankly, I had no idea it was even an issue. Besides, I hadn't put anything together yet, too busy with Daisy and Crew and Olivia and now this thing with Siobhan and my father to really even think about who might have wanted to kill Lester Patterson. Way to focus on the crime at hand, Fee. That was if Lester was even murdered. Right? Argh, what had Dr. Aberstock uncovered?

Gun jumping was my favorite.

Chris jumped to his feet, big hands rattling the chair as he shoved back and stood, backpedaling his way toward the exit. "Just find out who's stealing from my renters and ruining our lake," he said before stomping out into the sunlight.

I wanted to talk to Dad more about the hurt I'd delivered, doubting his faithfulness to Mom, but he was all business, staring after Chris like he wanted to go after him and ask more questions.

"Tell me about the argument you mentioned," he said.

I sat again, told him everything, which wasn't much. Dad nodded his thanks before exhaling, sitting forward with his pen in his hand. "Did Dr. Aberstock say if Lester was murdered?"

"Not conclusively," Dad said, "but he said he'd have more for me shortly." That non-answer wasn't very satisfying. "I'm going to make some calls," he went on. "We'll talk tonight, okay, honey?" His soft, steady expression did help me feel a bit better, but I wished I hadn't said a word, now. The very idea Dad could be unfaithful to Mom seemed utterly ridiculous.

"Dad, did Crew know about the thefts?" Not like him to drop the ball on something like this.

My father shrugged, reaching for the phone. "I don't know, kid," he said. "The incidents seem pretty recent, maybe a week since Chris came to me. And since the sheriff left about that long ago, maybe he didn't. You can ask Jill."

That was a dismissal if ever I heard one. But I wasn't done. Dad paused, eyebrows raised, finger poised over the keypad but waiting for me to speak again as I leaned forward.

"You know where he is," I said. "Crew. What he's doing."

Dad hesitated before looking down at his notepad. When he met my gaze again, his was shadowed and walled off. "I don't know anything for sure," he said. "But if I get confirmation of where I think the young fool went, I'll let you know. I promise, okay?"

That didn't sound good, but if Dad was working on it, I'd let it be. Yeah, sure I would.

"We'll have a nice, long talk tonight," I said, standing up, like I was choosing to go. My father nodded. "About everything, Dad. Including this partnership thing you think is a good idea."

He grinned suddenly, everything forgiven. "You bet." Joy sparkled in his gaze. "Now git. I'm busy catching bad guys."

It wasn't until I hit the sidewalk, I realized I had to walk back to Petunia's. Not that it mattered. The gorgeous sunny morning paired with the short jaunt of a few blocks wasn't exactly a chore. Besides, it meant passing Sammy's Coffee, and that meant my favorite latte was in my near future.

But instead of stopping, I kept moving, feeling the nervous energy in my body stirring, the pressure of the last day or so building up so much by the time I reached the front door of Petunia's I knew I wouldn't be able to settle without burning off some energy. I ran up the front steps and through the door into the foyer where, with a faint squeak of shock, I almost collided with Daisy.

She grasped me with a breathless laugh, her old happiness back for a moment. Then, inevitably, the shadows she'd been carrying around lately returned, her gray eyes hooded, full mouth pulling faintly down as she let me go and backed away. The sunny foyer was empty and usually felt welcoming, warm. Instead, in that moment, the air turned cold, dank and I caught a shiver before it raised goosebumps on my arms.

"Day." I whispered her name into the sun-filled but chilled air. "Please, we really need to talk."

She shook her head, looked away. "I have to run to the annex," she said. "Your mother is in the kitchen." Daisy spun and ran off as if she hadn't just been heading out the front door. So, an excuse, then? Where had she been going?

I let her leave, nodding to the young woman at

the sidebar counter who bobbed a nod with a quick smile of her own. Young but perky enough. I really had to learn their names. And while maybe it was a bad idea to take off in the middle of the morning, I just couldn't get my mind to come to heel without wearing out my body first.

I slipped downstairs and changed quickly into shorts, t-shirt and sneakers, poking my head into the kitchen a moment to check in with Mom. She waved me off when I told her I was going for a run, deep in conversation with two of the servers. Petunia glanced my way but Mom's conversation involved a tray full of some kind of confection, so the pug didn't even bother to come say hello. I grabbed my keys and headed for the lake, already feeling lighter and eager for the miles ahead.

Crew and I had started running together, an activity I found I immensely enjoyed, though often the route we took along the lake passed in silence as both of us fell deep into thought, occasionally sharing our worries, where our minds were at as we ran the edge of the lake in the kind of companionable silence that felt like we'd been together forever. Hitting the path alone bothered me more than it should have, and the first person I pondered as I tucked in my earbuds and let my feet move on their own while my mind took over was tall, dark and delicious himself.

It didn't take me long to circle around my fear of infidelity and back to worry he'd gotten himself into something he couldn't handle. Dad seemed to suggest that might be the case. Who was the mystery woman on the other end of the phone? And was I really feeling that lost without the handsome sheriff that I couldn't bear to be without him for a week?

Yeah. Actually.

I worked out my concerns with a burst of speed before sighing through my parted lips and inhaling a giant gulp of air despite knowing it might trigger a stitch. Crew was a big boy, I was a grown woman and he'd be fine long enough for me to kick his butt for not telling me what was going on himself. There. Stress solved. Uh-huh. At least lying to myself hadn't gotten old.

Not hard to segue into Dad and Malcolm and that whole mess, though I was only just dipping into that particular spiral into frustrated unknowing when the sight of a familiar face up ahead on the trail slowed my pace.

CHAPTER SEVENTEEN

Wanda Beaman didn't seem happy or unhappy to see me, though her expectant expression told me she figured I'd stop for a chat despite my present activity. I did just that, curious enough to find her standing on the side of the path, not walking as most people did, but staring into the lake with a sour expression on her flat, plain face.

"Miss Fleming," she said, nodding to me. "Shame about you finding Lester Patterson's body like that. You okay?"

I wasn't expecting sympathy from the hard-faced and rather blunt businesswoman, so her attitude startled me enough I felt a pang of connection I wasn't planning on. "I'm kind of used to it by now," I said, not as much of a joke as I'd originally meant.

After all, I'd been stumbling over death since I got home, hadn't I?

Wanda grunted a faint sound that was apparently her laugh, at least if the slight lift to the corners of her mouth was any indication. "Been a hell of a few years," she said without a hint she blamed me for bringing murder to Reading, unlike other locals I knew. Which endeared her further to me, again totally unexpected. I hated misjudging people and actually focused on her, rather than on what she could give me, observing the lines of age on her tanned face, the way she carried herself carefully, her square body rather hunched and misery showing when I actually looked for it.

"I'm sorry things haven't been going well for you," I said. "I feel pretty lucky aside from all the dead bodies." Again, an attempt at a joke that didn't hit the mark.

She didn't seem to mind. "It's not anyone's fault, really," she said. "Mine more so for being a stubborn old fool. Should have moved on from the business long ago when things started to slide. But it was my granddad's, don't you see, and I just couldn't abandon it without a fight." She shrugged, crossing her arms over her chest, glaring at the water. "Stubborn runs in my family."

She wasn't the only one. "Is there anything I can do to help?"

That perked her a bit. "I'd be obliged if you'd keep some of my brochures in your foyer," she said, hesitant before tossing her hands, her long, thick braid bouncing with the motion. "Who am I kidding? My fishing business is on the way out. I need to move on, not throw more logs on the fire."

My heart ached for her, this straightforward and strong woman I'd never had the chance to get to know. Funny how people can touch you when you least expect it. "I'm happy to hand out brochures," I said. "We're all in this together, Wanda. Or we're supposed to be." Had I lost sight of that myself? I didn't want to think so. But I'd gotten so busy I hadn't even had a chance to visit the equestrian center—not that they needed my help—or have dinner at the new restaurant on the edge of town. What was it called again? Didn't matter, not while Wanda shrugged and smiled faintly again, turning away from the lake.

"I've been tracking pollution in this water for the last five years or so," she said, changing the subject as if realizing there wasn't much either of us could do to help her at the moment. "The fish are dying, Miss Fleming. In fact, there was an odd rash of dead trout in the water just yesterday morning, washed up on this bank." She pointed to the side of the path where the water lapped against the shore. "If the tracking I've done counts for anything, those fish died right around the time you found Lester Patterson."

Interesting. "Any idea what killed them?" Maybe it would help Dr. Aberstock figure out what happened to Lester? Or I was, quite literally, fishing.

She rubbed at her chin, eyes narrowing as she stared into the water again. "Not sure," she said, "but whatever it was took out a dozen or so of my favorite breed, so I'm worried."

Well, if it was murder, she wouldn't have anything to worry about further, but if not? Poison was an option. But who would be poisoning the fish—or the water for that matter? The fuel spill Chris mentioned was troubling and could have done the deed, perhaps.

Wanda sighed, hands stuffed in her pockets as she turned back to me. "Sorry to keep you from your run," she said. "Thanks for listening to an old woman. I'll drop the brochures off if your offer was good?" Was that hopeful concern? A trace of doubt? Did anyone in this town actually support her at all?

I hugged her on impulse, feeling her stiffen before she tentatively hugged me back. "Come to Petunia's for dinner on me," I said, wondering why I was suddenly choked up. "We'll get to know each other a little better, okay?"

Wanda seemed floored by my offer before nodding. "Thanks for that," she said, gruff and brief. Hesitated before grimacing. "You'll be wanting to know Lester and I had a history, I suppose. Ever so long ago, so long it doesn't count for much." Romantic? Well, everyone was young once. Wow, that was insulting, Fee, like people her age just stopped wanting to be loved. "I'm on the list of suspects for those wanting the old bastard dead. But I didn't have anything to do with his death."

If he was even murdered. "All the more reason for you to come for dinner so I can grill you for clues." I winked, pretty sure she was innocent but finally finding my funny bone.

She barked a laugh. "He broke a lot of hearts," she said, "before girls our age figured out he wasn't worth bagging as any kind of catch." Hmmm. Very interesting. "As for me, I had mine broken enough times I learned my lesson." That was just sad. "Any news if it was an accident or not?" I shook my head and she sighed. "Would be easier for everyone if the old bastard just keeled over." Tell me about it. Without another word, she walked on, heading back the way I'd come, waving as she did. I ran on, earbuds in place, mind spinning as I thought things through.

Without murder confirmed, it was rather silly to dig into motives, but I couldn't help myself. So far there were enough suspects to keep me from narrowing anything down, as far as I was concerned. Wouldn't hurt to keep my thought process open, right? And Dad's attitude was enough for me, so I made the decision to trust my instincts until I knew better.

Without any kind of hard evidence to ponder, though, I was left wondering rather than deducing. When the official trail ended, circling back toward the parking area, I ignored it and ran on, keeping close to the edge of the bank now rising up from the water's edge to avoid too much overgrowth of grass that caught at the toes of my sneakers. I loved this part of the run, though it wasn't groomed or cared for like the one the town maintained. The wilder feel left me more in tune with the world. I usually ran this with Crew, though, not alone, and after a few minutes and a sharp turn around a corner into a large stand of trees had me feeling a bit uncomfortable.

Silly, but true. Which fired up my stubbornness and forced me onward. The road was close, after all. I could hear the hum of cars passing just a quarter mile or so inland from the edge of the lake. Not like I could get lost or anything. But there were bears and other predators out here and running alone wasn't exactly the smartest choice.

Since when did anyone accuse me of doing the smart thing, anyway?

I finally gave myself a mental kick for being an idiot when the brush grew so thick, I was forced to the very edge of the bank, dangerously close to slipping down toward the water. When I felt something tug on my sneaker, I looked down in time to stop myself from tripping over my loose shoelace. Ready to turn around at last, I crouched to tie it, and, as I did, caught faint light from the corner of my eye.

If I'd been upright, I would have missed what came next, I'm positive of it. The shine of metal only showed up when I dropped to my knee, sunlight catching whatever it was reflecting into my eyes. I squinted down the side of the bank, this area elevated, access to the lake impossible thanks to plant growth and a marshy stretch that dominated. But from this vantage point, I could make out at last what looked like some kind of ghillie net covering what had to be the hull of a small boat.

Huh. Someone was hiding a boat here—were they fishing illegally? Or maybe they just didn't want anyone messing with their property. Made sense. Then again, my suspicious nature made me wonder why anyone would hide a boat all the way out here off the beaten path instead of keeping it in an area more easily accessed.

Then again, who was I to judge someone for where they moored their boat?

Before I could slip down the bank and investigate my phone rang. I recognized my mother's number and answered accordingly. "What's up, Mom?"

"Daisy's out and we have three new check-ins coming." My mother didn't sound harried, exactly, but I knew a cry for help when I heard it.

"On my way." I hung up as I turned around, dialing Dad, but got his voicemail. Rather than leave a message, I made a mental note to mention the boat to him in person and headed for home, mind shifting from murder to what I really should have been focusing on—Petunia's.

CHAPTER EIGHTEEN

I was in time to grab a fast shower, though the three new sets of guests had to deal with my damp hair in a messy bun. Not that they seemed to mind, or even notice. I left the last couple, a lovely pair of middle-aged women from Connecticut, to settle into their third-floor suite and hustled back down to the foyer to finish their paperwork.

Mom was right, no sign of Daisy, not even when I called over to the annex to see if she was there. Weird for her to disappear like this. I texted her briefly, but when I didn't get an answer, I shrugged it off. We all had our moments and our issues. I was just out for a run at probably a terrible time, wasn't I? Daisy had the right to vanish now and then just like I did. Still, she loved being here to greet new guests.

That and party planning were her favorite parts of being at Petunia's. I hated to think she was off somewhere with Rose and that the creepy stepsister of hers was filling my bestie's head with more crap about her not being good enough.

Not much I could do about family, though. At least, not until Mom and I managed to corner Daisy and smack some sense into her.

I took two seconds to dial Dr. Aberstock, though when he answered he sounded reluctant enough I suspected my long stretch of good luck with him might be coming to an end. The kindly older doctor who always resembled Santa Claus and of whom I carried many happy childhood memories had treated me almost like I was supposed to be investigating murders since I stumbled on the body of Pete Wilkins in my koi pond. Obviously, someone got to him, though, because he sighed over the phone, sounding tired.

"I was wondering if I was going to hear from you," he said, the rattle of something metallic in the background ending in a faint crash. "Be more careful, please, Mr. Jones. Sorry, new intern."

"I can have Dad call if you'd rather," I said. "I really don't want to put you in a bad position, Dr. Aberstock."

When he grunted faintly, I wasn't sure if it was at me or his clumsy helper. Until he spoke again, anger in his normally level voice. "I've been informed I've been speaking out of turn," he said, "and that my position as county medical examiner might be at risk if I share information again."

I figured as much. "Got it," I said. "And that makes sense. Thanks anyway."

"I'm not done, young lady." Wow, he was pissed. I pictured his round cheeks pinked with irritation, though it was hard to imagine the normally jovial doctor as anything but his typical cheerful self. "If for one second I thought you or John Fleming weren't helpful in every case you've gone and solved, I'd have kept my observations to myself. As things stand, if that young idiot who calls himself acting sheriff comes into my office one more time, I'm going to be the one you're investigating because he'll be meeting an untimely end."

Robert was making friends again, was he? "Did you find anything?"

Dr. Aberstock paused a moment, taking a deep breath. "You're working the case with your father?" He asked in a rush, as if making a decision he would never let himself regret. I assured him I was. Seemed to be good enough for him. "I'm telling you to pass on to him."

"Since Olivia hired him to investigate," I said, "and I'm a partner in Fleming Investigations, you're within your rights to tell me what I need to know." So there, Robert.

Dr. Aberstock fell silent before breaking into a belly laugh that made me grin. "Something Acting Sheriff Carlisle clearly doesn't know, is that right?"

I guess he didn't. But at least it absolved Dr. Aberstock from wrongdoing, so I was happy about that. "Time and cause of death, Doc?"

"About 9PM," he said.

"Drowning?" I'd assumed as much, but it would be nice to have confirmation.

"Actually," Dr. Aberstock cleared his throat then, exhaled. "No. There was water in his trachea and lungs, and I supposed technically he died from inhaling water."

Odd. "So, what caused his death?"

"There was no sign of a source," he said, "but I've seen cases like this before, where underwater lines are broken, and victims succumb to the effects the closer they get to the source."

Source of what?

"Electrocution," he said then, brusque and all business again. "Lester Patterson's heart stopped before he could drown."

Grunt. "So, no proof it was murder." Damn it.

More hesitation. "He doesn't have any definitive marks on him, no defensive wounds, no head trauma. There are faint bruises on the backs of his thighs as if he hit the rail before going over." Dr. Aberstock didn't sound like he was convinced it was accidental, though. "And more bruising with what looks like a friction burn on his wrist, but not from ligature. More like whatever was around his wrist pulled free when he fell. He might have simply slipped overboard and whatever electrocuted him shorted out or was shut off."

"Could he have been electrocuted on land and fallen in the water?" That might have been accidental, too.

"No," he said. "His heart was still beating when he entered the water. He took a final breath. If he'd been dead before he went in his lungs would be empty."

"So, he fell in, was electrocuted and drowned while his heart stopped." Still sounded like maybe a terrible twist of fate and not intentional death. Well, for once it might be nice if it wasn't murder and someone actually died due to bad luck. If anything was nice about death, I mean.

"Another boat in the harbor could have had an electrical issue and, after Lester fell in, they left, taking the danger with them."

I thought about the dead fish, Wanda's trout, and nodded to myself. "Thanks for the help," I said. "I'll pass this information along legal channels to the head of Fleming Investigations." I couldn't help grinning at the receiver as I heard Dr. Aberstock chuckle in response.

"Have a great day, Fee," he said, cheerful as always. "Say hello to your mom for me." And, with that, he hung up. I might not have had the answers I was looking for, but I had at least thwarted Robert's attempt to bully someone I liked and trusted. Score for the Fleming team.

I was still grinning, just hanging up, when the front door opened, and Pamela and Aundrea stepped through. The happily married newlyweds waved and smiled in return, though the narrow-eyed look Pamela gave me told me she knew I wasn't just happy to see them. She leaned over the short counter that served as a desk and winked.

"Murder in the air again, Fee?"

I shrugged. "Not sure," I said. "Might want to ask Acting Sheriff Carlisle about that."

She rolled her eyes at me, Aundrea making a soft sound of amusement she hid behind one hand, eyes sparkling. "Don't mention him to my darling Pam," she said, her formerly pretentious tone long gone in the wake of the happiness she and her long-lost love rekindled. I found I liked her more and more as I got to know her, though she was still a Patterson at heart. I really had to sit down with Aundrea at some point and ask her pointed questions about her family. And if she knew anything about the mysterious Blackstone Corporation that troubled us not so long ago. "He's been nothing but a thorn in her side since he took Crew Turner's desk."

"Temporarily," I said, about as firmly as I could manage without being cranky.

Pamela's eyes didn't leave me, her gaze as watchful and careful as ever though her lips twisted into a grin. I couldn't forget she wasn't a small-town newspaperwoman at all, though she filled that role since I moved home. She'd been an award-winning investigative journalist at the *Boston Globe* for years and her sense of curiosity was even stronger than mine. "Hopefully," she said. "Regardless, I know I can count on you to fill me in, right?" She flashed her teeth in a feral smile. "One busybody to another?"

"We're here for dinner," Aundrea said, hooking

her arm through her wife's, pulling Pamela away. "Not work."

I nodded, though I felt it was proper to at least offer condolences, remembering in the last second who Lester was to her. "I'm so sorry about your loss, Aundrea." Yes, he'd been her first cousin, but still.

She didn't look all that broken up about his death, though, waving off my offer of commiseration. "I'm surprised the reprobate didn't keel over years ago," she said, sniffing like he offended her just by existing. There was the Patterson in her showing through. "And you won't find one person in the family sorry to see him go, either." She patted Pamela's hand where it rested on her elbow. "Pretentious old windbag."

Okay then. "I take it no one in the family had motive?"

Aundrea looked startled. "You mean he was murdered?" She met her wife's gaze before turning back to me, free hand now pressed to her heart. "I'd heard he'd had a heart attack and fell into the water."

Interesting. "Still not sure what happened," I said. "But no love lost?"

Aundrea looked distant, suddenly, musing as she tapped her long, manicured fingertips against her collarbone. "He lorded over everyone," she said, "and was only ever home summers, like most of the cousins." That sounded like she judged them for not living full-time in Reading. "And that son of his, Luke, is it?" She turned to Pamela who nodded like it was her job to keep track of Aundrea's family, not hers. "Troublemaker from the start." The family seemed to breed them. I thought about Mason Patterson and wondered if that was the road the young man I met was heading down, though Luke hadn't seemed as arrogant as Mason the night the young Patterson heir died in his chocolate cake.

"I hear he's been kicked out of a number of private schools," Pamela said, casually, like she had to tread carefully with her wife when it came to family. But Aundrea seemed enthusiastic enough as she nodded in answer, voice dropping to a gossiping whisper.

"Born late, to that third wife Lester married. The one who left him to live with her bodyguard in California." So not a suspect unless she figured out how to murder Lester from the other coast. "Left to run wild, from what I hear."

But would he have motive to kill his own father? I remembered then Kiera begging me not to tell her dad, that David Campbell and Lester weren't exactly friends to begin with. Which made me wonder what David had against the deceased that kept the two young lovers apart. Another motive, perhaps? For a death I still didn't have confirmation was murder in the first place.

I waved Pamela and Aundrea on to dinner, finishing up my paperwork for the day and doing a quick run around both locations to make sure everything was running on schedule and without hiccups. I caught distant sight of Daisy in the dining room at the annex, though she avoided me, hustling back across the bridge to Petunia's when I tried to corner her. Fine, whatever. I let her have her space, spending the remainder of the evening answering emails until I shut my laptop at 8PM, my mind prodding me instantly, unwilling to let go of the conversation I'd had with Aundrea.

Impulse control never one of my strong suits, I left Petunia's, my pug staying behind once more—no way I was letting her near the docks again—as I took a quick spin out to the club to look for Luke, to ask him about his father's conflict with David, to feel him out for possible conflict with his own dad. Yes, I was chasing my tail and clutching straws and all those terrible clichés that nosy girls like me used as taglines. And I'd tried not to let my mind get away with me. I'd lasted a whole five minutes on the couch, staring at nothing and my brain buzzing. But when my thoughts spun sideways and crashed into Crew Turner's missing in action act, evening phone call once again a victim of his disappearance, I found myself behind the wheel and driving to the lake, if only to keep from making myself crazy.

CHAPTER NINETEEN

I shouldn't have been surprised, I guess, to catch the handsome young Patterson sneaking over the side of David Campbell's boat, considering the embrace I'd caught Luke and Keira in the day of the yacht club party. Though the audacity of the kid to be stealing time with his girlfriend under her father's nose like that? Yeah, either he was a thrill-seeker with a death wish or just had a cast-iron pair born of being a Patterson who got away with everything. Not that I cared, though I couldn't stop the grin that crossed my face as the erstwhile young Romeo landed softly on the dock only to turn, shock registering, to find me standing there watching his exit.

"Nice night," I said. "How's Keira?"

Luke stammered something, cheeks pink, the

recently refreshed lighting of the dock doing nothing to hide his embarrassment at getting caught. Even more daring of him to risk slipping on and off board without the cover of darkness to keep him safe. And now I was just judging him as a dumb kid with a terrible sense of entitlement or the sense Mother Nature gave him not to put his own life in danger.

And when the cabin door of the boat beside us banged open, a large and angry man emerging, I choked on my amusement while David stormed out into the open, roaring the kid's name.

I hooked Luke's t-shirt with one hand, though he didn't seem ready to run just yet, sullen scowl settling over his face while he glared at the boat owner. Keira emerged behind her father, grabbing his arm, weeping. She at least didn't seem averse to begging him to back off, her words barely comprehensible beyond, "Dad, don't!" and "Please!" while Luke just stood there beside me, like he'd resigned himself to whatever was coming.

"How dare you, you little punk?" David roared over the side but made no effort to come down to the dock, heavy forehead pinched, broad shoulders looming. Keira looked like a scrap of fluff compared to her tall, broad father, more than a match for the lean young man who stood at my side. If I was Luke I'd be hoofing as fast as I could, not lingering with what could barely be called the hold I had on him by the hem of the thin cotton of his shirt. I released him and still the young Patterson made no move to leave while Keira burst into fresh tears.

"Leave him alone, Daddy!" She wailed, hanging off his forearm. "I love him!"

I almost sighed. Almost eye rolled. Almost. Ah, young love. Barf.

"Stay away from my daughter," David snarled while Luke gave him an extremely rude gesture in return involving the middle fingers of both his hands. The big man roared something I can't repeat while the young Patterson smirked at me before spinning and finally running off, his sneakers thudding on the dock as he disappeared into the evening. I found myself turning back just as David leaped down to follow and, to my own shock at my bravery, stepped in front of the juggernaut of angry father. Maybe I surprised him as much as myself because he stopped, staring down at me from the foot or so he had on me, though he seemed to relent instead of his anger increasing which helped ease my tension and the fear I might have gotten between a charging bull and his target.

"Fiona Fleming," David grunted at me. "Sorry to hear about you finding Lester like that. Hell of a way to go, heart attack and all. At least he went quick." For once, it seemed like the people I encountered actually felt badly for me uncovering a dead body. Maybe because everyone was assuming his death was an accident or even natural causes. Did that mean I was wasting my time?

"I understand there was conflict between you and the deceased." If he was going to play the sympathy card, I was happy to ask questions.

David shrugged, brow darkening, thick eyebrows pulling together. He had the kind of heavy dark beard and mustache that made him look like maybe there was a bear or two in his lineage. Never mind the beefiness of his big hands or the way his barrel chest expanded as he inhaled like he wasn't above intimidation if necessary.

"Not sure why that's your business," he said.

I could have thrown the Fleming Investigations thing at him, but I went instead for innocent bystander just worried about a fellow business owner. "I hope he wasn't making trouble for your hardware store." Campbell's was a staple in town, had been around as long as Petunia's.

David appeared to soften somewhat. "Listen, Lester and I were friends." Why did it sound like that friendship wasn't valid any longer? "We had a falling out, that's all." Now he seemed uncomfortable.

"That's never easy," I said. "Do you know of anyone who would want to hurt him?"

David flinched. "You think he was murdered?" He glanced back over his shoulder at the boat behind him. But why? What was he thinking? When he turned back to face me, his expression was dark, troubled. "You might want to talk to a few people," he said, voice low. "Like maybe the woman I bought the *Keira Sky* from."

I remembered seeing her yesterday in Lester's office, sneaking out, looking guilty. What was her tie to the dead man? "Heather Parborough?"

David shrugged his big shoulders. "Lester had

issues with her." He seemed hesitant to say anything but sighed at last, anger leaving him. "And she had issues with him."

"No idea what those issues might be?" What else was he hiding?

David growled, voice even deeper than Dad's or Crew's, enough gravel in it he might as well have been crunching rocks right then and there. "I told you, you should talk to her." He glared at me like it was my fault Lester was dead. "What's it to you, anyway?"

I didn't have an answer for him, no proof Lester was murdered. "Just wondering," I said.

"I heard you were as nosy as your dad," he grumbled, turning to go back on board his boat. He shot one last angry look back the way Luke had retreated before finishing his thought. "Maybe you'd like to mind your own business." The cabin door slammed shut behind him while I turned slowly on my heel and followed the young man he'd let get away.

I was getting really tired of people telling me that.

But when I entered the club, instead of finding Luke, I instead stumbled into Doreen and, with a soft inhale of worry, hugged her immediately. She looked terrible, dark circles under her eyes, her normally prim hair disheveled. I led her through the entry into the empty bar, seating her beside me on a stool and holding her hand. She hiccupped, fishing tissues out of her pocket and dabbing at her nose and eyes, distress so obvious I wondered why she was here at all and not at home.

Before I could ask that question, though, she waved at my clear concern with that handful of dampness and forced a small smile. "I can't stop thinking about poor Lester," she said, catch in her voice. "Sitting around makes it worse." Well, I was just as guilty of needing something to do to take my mind off things so I couldn't really argue her reasoning, nodding instead. "I came to get some work done. To distract me from everything. And I still have a job to do, whether Lester is here or not." She blinked behind her glasses. "It's so quiet here at night, you know. Peaceful, with no one else around."

Yikes, poor old dear. I had to call Mom. "Doreen, why did Lester and David Campbell fall out?" I patted her hands, knowing my empathy for her would take second seat to my curiosity even before I opened my mouth.

She seemed grateful for the distraction, frowning down into her tissues, shaking her head finally. "I don't know," she said. "He never actually came out and told me. But he seemed to think it was funny. Talked about David owing him from now on. That a lot of people did, whatever that meant." She exhaled heavily, her lips pursing, regret flashing as she spoke ill of the dead. "He wasn't a very nice person sometimes."

Yeah, I had gotten that picture loud and clear, even when he was alive. But what could David Campbell possibly owe Lester? "How long was he president?"

She wriggled in her seat, face calming, whole demeanor settling down as she was forced to focus on my questions, so I didn't feel so badly grilling her when she was down. We were both getting something out of it, right? "Oh, ages," she said. "No one else wanted the job. At least as long as I've been treasurer, and that has to be ten years now." She blew out a soft sound of regret before her face tightened and she leaned closer, drawing me to her with her hand grasping mine tightly. "They used to be thick as thieves, those two," she said.

"David and Lester?" David said they were old friends.

"Something happened between them," Doreen said, eyes flickering to the entry and back to me like she expected to be called out for speaking about it. "Right around the time David bought his boat. The funny part was no one can pinpoint why they fell out—no big blowup or anything. Just a quiet and sudden break and then they were enemies."

Huh. "No guesses?"

She hesitated, wiping her nose with her wad of tissues. "Money," she finally said. "It has to have been over money. But I don't know why or what happened."

I'd take it. Money was a good motive to kill someone.

If only I knew either way if this was murder.

CHAPTER TWENTY

Doreen returned to her office, claiming she had work to do though I knew from the haunted look on her face she was just keeping busy. Fair enough. As I turned to exit the building, still on the lookout for Luke though I was fairly sure he'd already left the area, I caught sight of a deputy's car pulling into the parking lot. It didn't take much encouragement for me to pounce on Jill as she emerged from the driver's side, and the grimace on her face told me she wasn't happy to find me there. I tried not to take her attitude personally, knowing it was her reticence to talk about where Crew went that had to be feeding our newfound distance.

"Hey, Fee." Jill sighed, shook her head. "I don't know anything, I swear."

Okay, fresh tactic to maybe soften her up and get info another way. "How's Matt?" She and the handsome park ranger had really hit it off since he'd stopped being a blind idiot and realized she was into him. Sure, he'd come onto me at probably the least opportune time ever—during a murder investigation while Crew and I were finally making headway into our relationship—but Jill didn't seem to mind the ranger had to be guided in her direction by yours truly. If anything, she'd been pretty grateful, though all I did was kick his butt that he'd been missing out on her awesomeness.

It wasn't that she (cough) owed me (cough) or anything. Right?

Jill softened slightly, grinned. "He's great," she said, that dreamy look in her eyes telling me they were still in the enraptured honeymoon phase. "Missed me." It was bright enough with the renewed lighting I caught her cheeks flush before she cleared her throat and gave me a guilty grimace. "I see what you're doing." I didn't say anything. If Dad taught me a skill it was to stay quiet in the face of someone who had something to tell you even if it was their intent not to spill. Silence and guilt typically led to confessions. I just waited, faint, friendly smile firmly in place and let her babble her way to what I wanted to know. "You're trying to make me talk. Fee, there's nothing to say." She looked away, shrugged, sighed. "Look, fine, be like that. I thought we were friends." Jill needed to buck up on her own interrogation techniques if this was working. Either that or she felt really guilty. "Okay, you win, here's all I know. Some woman showed up yesterday morning. Wearing a suit, looking like she meant business." I ignored the tightening in my stomach and let her go on. That was me trusting him. "I was leaving for breakfast when she came knocking, so I didn't get a good look at her. I was still eating when he texted me he had an emergency. That's it." She huffed at me, eyes sorrowful. "You happy now?"

I hugged her before stepping back. "Thanks, Jill." Not much to go on. But growing suspicion was leading me away from another woman in his romantic life and toward something far more worrisome and likely dangerous. "As it turns out, I have something for you, too." I filled her in on what I'd seen, about Luke and Keira and David's conflict with Lester. Jill listened carefully, nodding at the right places before hitching her belt.

"Thanks," she said. "I'll go in and chat with Doreen, see if I can't convince her to head on home and get some rest. Think I should call the doc?" That was Jill, caring enough to worry about the woman's state of mind. I felt a bit guilty I hadn't gone there myself.

"I'll leave that up to you," I said, heading for my car, waving goodbye as she disappeared into the club. I slipped into the driver's seat and called my dad, getting him on the second ring. When I told him about David and the kids, he just grunted his usual quiet acceptance of the details.

But when I broached the topic of Crew, Dad cut

me off. "I promise I'll tell you when I'm sure of my source," he said. He sounded grim enough I let it go because now I was pretty sure I knew exactly what Crew Turner was up to and I really didn't want to worry about whether he was coming home or not.

Instead, I drove back to Petunia's, cranking the radio of my car and forcing myself to sing along so I didn't drive myself nuts with the need to call Crew over and over again until either he picked up or the woman did. Because that would get me nowhere fast except on a crazy train I refused to board just now.

I'm not sure if it was a good thing or a bad thing that distraction found me the moment I walked through the door of Petunia's, though perhaps I should have been grateful for the chance to stop thinking about Crew and focus on something I could take action on. Though, dealing with the smug expression on Rose's face and the source of that personal victory—real or imagined—was likely going to give me heartburn and an excuse to kick her out onto the street.

Still, here was my chance to dress down the woman doing damage to the self-esteem of my darling Daisy. Not to mention the fact she stood behind my counter, fiddling with my computer in my foyer when her "job" entailed helping Daisy. I hadn't given Rose permission to access my files, had I? Awesome. The yelling would commence in three, two, one...

"Fiona." Rose stepped back from the keyboard, faintly guilty, enough I pounced on the fact she knew she wasn't supposed to be doing whatever it was she was up to. "I booked in a new guest for you, since no one was here to answer the phone." She sniffed like she'd done me a favor. Like I'd dropped the ball.

"The next time," I said, keeping my voice low and cold, "don't." Was it possible I was overreacting? That my redheaded temper was getting the better of me and I was seeing things that weren't actually there out of jealousy Daisy's stepsister seemed to have more influence on her these days than I did? Maybe. Snarl.

Rose's face tightened, her snotty little nose rising as if she was queen of the bed and breakfast and not a temporary pain in my backside. "You're welcome," she snapped.

"Didn't ask for help," I cracked back. "As a matter of fact, just for future reference, I don't appreciate you interfering with my business or treating my best friend like she's not good enough." I should have kept things professional, left Daisy out of it. I had ground to stand on, after all, when it came to Petunia's. But Daisy was her sister. I realized I had clouded the issue even as the words left my mouth. Too late.

Rose shrugged, crossing her arms over her chest, lips pinched as she tilted her head to one side, self-righteousness almost getting her a punch in the face. I'd do it, too, precedence had been set when it came to Daisy. Though Vivian French and I had been young enough I had an excuse for breaking her nose.

"I have no idea how you stay in business," she

said. "You're never here, always gallivanting around Reading being nosy about things that don't concern you."

Back to Robert, were we? That didn't help my temper and neither did the crack about my busybody nature. I was well aware of my failings, thanks, and the guilt I felt over slipping away was mine to deal with, not hers to shove in my face.

I was about to deliver a blistering and likely untakebackable rant that would have devolved into me shouting and her hitting the pavement with the kind of force that broke bones when Daisy appeared through the swinging kitchen door, her face closed off, gray eyes unreadable. She came to stand next to Rose while I finished my tirade inhale, stopping with the sort of hurt, pinched expression that was probably the only thing that could diffuse me in that moment.

So, instead of blowing off steam and telling Rose what I thought of her and where she could take her opinions, I instead found myself deflating somewhat unhappily, dissatisfaction burning a hole inside me but unable to push myself past the knowledge that yelling at Rose would mean hurting my best friend.

Well, crap.

Rose, meanwhile, turned to Daisy with disdain, pinching her side with her index finger and thumb. "There you are," she said. "Fee's been mean to me, Day." Her pout was near enough to ridiculous I almost ignored my instincts and chose in favor of yelling all over again.

Daisy sighed, barely perceptible, before gesturing for the front door. "I'll meet you in the car." At least Rose wasn't staying here, small blessings. I could only imagine constant contact with her stepsister wasn't doing my bestie any favors. Maybe I should have invited Daisy to stay with me for a while, to let Rose have the run of the apartment. Instead, I watched Rose stomp her way across the foyer and out the front door, positive at the last second she'd turn and stick her tongue out at me or something equally childish. Instead, she flounced out, her skirt—wait, that was Daisy's new dress she had on, wasn't it?— flaring around her thighs as she went.

I waited until the door thudded shut behind her before inhaling once again, but Daisy beat me to the conversation. From the low vibration in her quiet voice, she'd been holding back, too.

"I asked her to help," Daisy said. "Okay?"

I shook my head. "Not okay," I said. "This is a partnership, Day. You, me, Mom. All three of us have to agree or no go." Mom would side with me. I was sure of it.

Daisy twitched, stared at the door. "Then maybe this was a bad idea." She left without another word, my mouth hanging open as she softly closed the door behind her. Wait, what? How had our friendship and partnership and everything turned around so fast? Where was the Daisy I loved and adored? Gone without a fight, with a whimper. Was I not even going to get a chance to fight for her?

No way, not acceptable. I spun and stomped into

the kitchen, finding Mom there with Petunia at her feet, my mother frowning into a giant pot of something that seemed to have offended her somehow.

When she looked up and met my eyes, hers were angry. "Did you talk to Daisy?"

I stumbled to a halt, stared at her. Wait, had the conversation I'd just had with my best friend begun here? "Mom, what happened?"

My mother's shoulders twitched, her green eyes snapping. "That fool of a girl seems to think she's a liability to the business," she said. "She actually asked me just now if I would consider buying her out."

So, the parting shot wasn't something she pulled out of the air. "Mom." I choked on the word, sagging against the counter. "This has to be Rose."

My mother nodded, her long spoon stirring far more aggressively than was necessary. "Agreed."

I wanted to scream, to go after Daisy, something, anything, but every scenario I considered ended in disaster. And from Mom's sullen silence and the way she abused what smelled like stew in the pot she was spiraling down the same road.

Thankfully, our mutual black mood wasn't meant to last. Dad appeared at the kitchen door, took one look at both of us, and came in for a group hug. Mom resisted far more than I did—what did Daisy say to her exactly? Had to be a lot more than what my mother gave up for her to be so upset—but we both caved at last, my dad's shirt smooshed against my nose, Mom's green eyes glaring at me while we let him have his way.

When he released us both, I actually felt lighter, like maybe the world as I knew it wasn't coming to an end. Mom exhaled sharply, crossing her arms over her chest while Dad kissed the top of her head. Instead of asking us what was wrong, he turned to me, grimaced a bit, then touched the tip of my nose with his right index finger.

"Hate to add to the mood," he said, "but I found out where Crew went. And you're not going to like it."

I sighed. "With a woman," I said. "Likely FBI." Because that was the only logical explanation, right?

Dad grinned but without humor. "Should have known you'd suss it out," he said. "None other than Crew's old partner, Special Agent Elizabeth Michaud."

I swallowed hard, remembering her from a few months ago. She'd seemed happy to see Crew, the pair with obvious history. And while I knew nothing romantic happened between them, it was the call of the FBI that worried me more than feminine wiles. He'd left to become sheriff of Reading. But what if getting a taste of the Bureau again changed his mind?

"What's he doing running off with and FBI agent?" Mom sounded cross enough I almost hugged her.

Dad shrugged. "Not sure, though from what I could find out it's tied to an old case, one he worked when he was still with the Bureau."

If it was an old case and he felt responsible... it

would be like Crew to want to help.

I left Mom to Dad, to the sound of him cajoling her into leaving, retreating to my apartment where I could call Crew in private. And, despite my previous agreement with myself not to bother, I called three times in a row, finally leaving him messages to get back to me. Followed by an email. Two texts. Pissed off texts, because seriously.

Knowing I was playing the crazy almost girlfriend but unwilling to let him jerk me around like this—there was a supposed murder to solve for goodness's sake (sure, that's why I was mad)—I stomped my way back upstairs, looking for an outlet for my irritation and fully intending to comb through the front desk computer for evidence Rose screwed up just to make myself feel better. At least I could distract myself from one worry with another.

Instead of diving in, though, I was startled to stumble across one of my guests slipping quietly through the foyer, one who created an even better distraction than more worry.

CHAPTER TWENTY-ONE

Heather Parborough nodded to me, clearly nervous. "Hi, Fee. Sorry to be coming in so late." It really wasn't that late, only about 10PM. Her anxiety reminded me I'd caught her sneaking out of Lester's office, hadn't I?

"No problem, Heather," I said. "Can I offer you anything?" We'd had coffee enough times in the past surely it didn't sound like too fishing of a question.

She hesitated, like she wanted to take me up on my offer but shook her head. "Thanks. It's been a long day. Just going to get some sleep."

I spoke up quickly before she could head for the stairs. "A shame about Lester," I said. "They still don't know what happened to him." Wow, was that a flinch of guilt? Sure, looked like it. "I know you two worked closely together to build interest in the marina." Okay, I was guessing, but she nodded so my guessing paid off. "I hope his loss won't mean trouble for you and your business."

She swallowed hard, gaze flickering to the stairs and retreat before she shrugged. Something was obviously weighing on her. Was it his death? Or whatever she'd been up to in his private office the day he died? "It definitely complicates things," she said. "Paperwork, that sort of business. You know." Like her vague answer should offer the kind of information I was looking for.

"I get it," I said, trying for an easy grin and rewarded when she seemed to relax somewhat. "Can't be easy, your job. Selling those big, expensive boats. Especially in such a small marina."

She paled, so ghostly white I actually took a step toward her, one hand extended in concern before I could stop myself. She recovered quickly, but not nearly fast enough.

"You work for a small boat company, don't you?" Idle chitchat to fill the moment between her horrified response to my seemingly innocuous comment and her next inhale. At least, I hoped she thought that was all I was asking. Otherwise, she'd be clamming up before I got another thing out of her.

Her faint grimace at the question made me pause. It was a straight-forward enough inquiry and shouldn't have elicited such a response. Unless, of course, she had something to hide about her employment.

"Yes, that's right," Heather said, slightly breathless now, not meeting my eyes any longer, a faint flush hitting her high cheekbones. "Buckley's Marine out of Boston."

"I guess your bosses will be worried about the rest of the season's sales." Come to think of it, it was August. Why was she still here? She'd been hanging around for over a month, hadn't she? I wasn't an expert or anything, but wouldn't selling boats be more an early summer kind of thing? And surely this was a tiny market for her to be putting in so much attention. A sneaking feeling of more to the story that had nothing to do with her guilty reaction made me pause and wonder just what kind of relationship she might have with the deceased yacht club president. The fact he was wrapping up on his fourth young and pretty wife wasn't lost on me, nor the fact Heather herself was about as young and pretty as they came.

Not to judge her choice in men, but yuck.

"They trust me," she said, sounding like that was about as far from the truth as anything she'd ever said in her entire life and raising my hackles so far, I had to fight off the need to pounce and demand she tell me everything.

Was she in trouble at work, something to do with Lester? Would that explain maybe her being in his office? Had they been dallying there? Or was she looking for something that had nothing to do with my suspicions about how close the two of them might be, something instead hinging on her job?

Only one way to prod this pony, especially when her clear desire to run away from me had come back in a visible rush of nervous anxiety. "Heather, what were you looking for the day Lester died? In his office?"

Heather's dark eyes met mine and for a moment she seemed totally taken aback by my question. Like I'd struck her instead of asking a (far from) innocent question. I couldn't help my own eyes widening at her response and found I was at a loss for words when her expression shut down and she looked away again.

"I don't know that's your business, Fiona," she said, curt and sharp, finding her backbone past her anxious guilt. "Now, if you don't mind, I'm going to bed."

I could have pushed her further, I guess, but it just didn't seem worth it and besides, I was kind of out of steam when it came to poking my nose into other people's business. I just had too much of my own worry on multiple fronts to drive myself nuts over the death of Lester Patterson. A death that, until proven otherwise, might very well have been natural causes.

A few minutes later, Heather ensconced in her room with her door firmly locked behind her, I stood quietly in the foyer of Petunia's, prepping for my final evening check, sighing as the pug at my feet sank to her haunches and yawned.

When the front door opened one last time, Dad stomping through, I was startled enough by his return I stayed silent, at least until I realized he wasn't alone. And that the mustached acting sheriff on his heels was going to be a pain in my butt whether I liked it or not.

"I'm talking to you, John." Robert had the audacity to grab Dad's arm and tug him around. Okay, so he tried to turn my father. Instead, all he got was two very angry Flemings—I wasn't about to let my cousin manhandle my dad and get away with it—leaping on him in tandem.

"That's Uncle John, boy," Dad snarled.

"Don't make me call Olivia," I snapped at the same moment.

Robert backpedaled, but just barely, his face darkening to deep red a moment, that same dangerous look I noticed returning. I really had to take him more seriously, though from the way Dad's eyebrows shot up, he caught the expression too. Which meant I wasn't the only one to underestimate my cousin.

"I'm tired of you two Flemings interfering with official police business." I hadn't listened to Crew on that matter, what made Robert think I'd pay attention to his attempt to keep me out of things? Not to mention Dad.

"The town of Reading has employed us," nice of my father to include me, "to investigate alongside your department, Robert." Dad wasn't backing down. "You know that. I was there when Olivia told you as much. So don't tell me you're holding a grudge when we're doing the job we're being paid for."

"Just stay out of my way," my cousin snarled, though he seemed fully aware he had no grounds to demand such a thing. "And out of my cases. Or I'll have you both arrested and let Olivia deal with the consequences."

I opened my mouth to interfere because that was how I rolled. But Dad cut me off, stepping between me and his nephew, towering, looming like he did when he wanted to shut someone down. "You listen to me, Robert Carlisle," he said, voice low, deep, more graveled than ever. "There have been times I've let your incompetence slide out of respect for your mother, and times I've covered for you because you're family. But I'll be damned if I'll let you threaten me or Fiona. You do the work the town's paying you to do and we'll do what Olivia's asked of us and we won't have a problem." Dad closed the distance, Robert standing his ground just barely, mustache quivering. "You decide you want to come after me and mine, boy? Let's just see how far you get."

I loved my dad so freaking much. And yet, as I watched Robert finally back down, that horrible, nasty expression returning long enough to make me worry, I wondered just how far he'd go if pushed.

Not that we'd be finding out tonight. Robert muttered something I didn't catch before spinning and striding out of the foyer, slamming the door behind him. I winced and scowled, knowing I'd be handling a noise complaint from a few of the guests thanks to his rude exit but not really caring much.

When Dad turned to face me, he looked worried enough I figured the complaints were the least of my concerns.

"That boy is on the edge," he said, soft, thoughtful. "Wonder what it'll take to make him break?"

Did we want to know? "He wouldn't have the nerve to come after you, Dad," I said.

My father shrugged, sighed, one big hand rubbing over his face. "Let him try," he said. "But I've let a lot ride over the years, Fee. Maybe I should have a chat with your Aunt Doris."

Mom joined us, startling me as she slipped up beside me, her face creased in a frown. I didn't realize she was still here, but Dad's reason for returning was now obvious. He was here to pick her up. How much of his interaction with Robert did she witness? Enough, I guess, my mother went right to him and hugged him before meeting my eyes.

"Doreen called," she said. "She needs us to pick up the things we left behind on the weekend. Dishes and whatnot."

Right. "I'll take care of it, Mom," I said. Watched my parents leave, Mom whispering to my father while I contemplated what I'd witnessed.

I'd already been out to the club tonight once already, so the pickup would have to wait until morning. Though, when I finally made it to the parking lot the next day, I wished I'd just gotten it over with. The fast run to Dr. Miller's office with Petunia went well, no adverse effects from her dip in the marina apparent. She was just as happy for the drive in the car as much as the freeze-dried liver treats the vet and his cheerful staff seemed to think the pug earned for being a terrible swimmer. Nice of Dr. Miller not to charge us for the checkup, though I did tell him if anything came up on later tests to make sure to bill the sheriff's department.

But that trip meant two jaunts out into the world when I needed to be at the B&B. And no, I wasn't yet prepared to bring the pug with me to the yacht club. So, after running her home and delivering her into Mom's care, I sighed over yet another drive that felt like a waste of precious time. Doreen was nowhere in sight when I slipped inside the club, finding the pile of boxes with my belongings at the entry. Either nice of her to prep everything for a fast getaway or she was evicting me without wanting to see me. Whatever. I wasn't going to take this as an insult.

I stumbled over the curb on the way to the car, fumbling one of the boxes which landed against the garbage, dumping three of my favorite plastic containers into the trash. Awesome. Fishing out my property meant leaning over the edge of the dumpster, forcing me to not only touch the side of the disgusting bin but to inhale the unhealthy aroma emanating from within. The polite thing to do would have been to close the stupid lid, something whoever used it last failed to do. Had they, I wouldn't have found myself sighing as I stepped up on the lip of the dumpster and leaning far over to grab the plastic container while wondering to myself if this really was necessary.

I slipped. Of course, I did, almost falling face-first into the vile sludge at the bottom of the trash. One hand leaped out, caught the slimy side of the container, my legs swinging under me on the outer wall, sneakered toes scrambling for purchase, even as my gaze caught sight of something tucked into a corner, sparkling in the morning sun.

Containers forgotten, I twisted sideways and lunged for the bright object, fingers closing on a black wire, tugging loose the long string of lights, a few of the decorative bulbs broken. I pushed off, balance restored, landing on my feet, frowning at the string of lights.

And the burned-out plug at the business end.

CHAPTER TWENTY-TWO

Of course, my mind told me this was the murder weapon. Had to be. And though yes it could still have been an accident, the fact that someone hid this juicy piece of evidence was all the proof I needed that Lester Patterson's death was, at best, manslaughter and, at worst, first degree hate his guts and purposely electrocute him then bury the proof.

Okay, so this was far beyond my sleuthing skills. I needed help, and though I could have called Dad—planned to, yes—I knew it would go over much better with Olivia and the rest of the town if I instead called Jill. No, not Robert. Jill. And it wasn't going to hurt when Crew got back when he found out I cooperated and went to his favorite deputy, either.

I winced that I'd touched the string with my bare

hands as I dialed my friend and waited for her to answer. Oh well, nothing to be done about it now, and seeing all the bits of yuck clinging to it made me shrug and deduce finding my DNA was going to be the least of the deposits the forensics folks uncovered. I set it carefully on the top of my trunk, placing the boxes of goods I'd retrieved inside first and closing it firmly before looking up and around as the phone rang. Surely there'd be some kind of security camera placement nearby that might give me—Jill, Fee, not me—a good view of the person or persons who'd deposited said evidence into the dumpster? Lo and behold, there were two, one high on top a pole near the front door, around the corner from the waste bin and another pointed at the side of the building, though without a clear view of where I stood. It looked like whoever aimed the cameras did so with the safety of the boat owners in mind. Fair enough. Who would have considered aiming one at a garbage bin? Still, it would have been nice to have a clearer shot at the dumpster. Yet, I was fairly confident that whoever did the dumping would have been caught on camera at one point or another. So, finding the perpetrator would be as simple as reviewing the footage the night of Lester's death and pinpointing the individual closest to this side of the building as possible.

Easy peasey, lemons and all that.

Jill finally answered as I scanned the area for more cameras, the softly pained anxiety in her voice an uncomfortable but expected response. If Robert was trying to push Dad around, I could only imagine what he'd been saying to Jill. But when I told her what I found, her worry turned instantly to excitement.

"I'll be right there," she said. "Don't move a muscle."

Since she didn't tell me not to call Dad, I did that next. He heard me out, though I could tell from the sound of a chair squeaking suddenly and the slamming of a door he was on the move even before I finished filling him in on the discovery. Not surprisingly, he showed up first, his pickup truck spitting gravel as he came to an abrupt halt, parking askew next to me, though Jill was a close second, her cruiser traveling at a somewhat more sedate and careful pace.

Jill didn't protest when Dad did a quick examination of the light string, though she only gave him a moment with a disposable glove she surreptitiously handed to him to do his look-see before she liberated him of the cord and hefted it at me with a grin.

"Thanks, Fee," she said. "You heard from Dr. Aberstock?"

At least she wasn't beating around the bush. I didn't have to be evasive with Jill. "He mentioned electrocution," I said. "And Wanda Beaman said some fish died, washed up down the lake. I'm guessing they were in the wrong place at the wrong time."

"Makes sense," Dad said. "The fish would have

been in the harbor looking for food from the party and got caught in the jolt. They must have been right beside Lester's boat when he went in." Dad paused a moment, nodded. "The doc said he found some odd bruising around Lester's right wrist like something restrained him briefly and rubbed off some skin. It could be the cord of this string wrapped around him and he pulled it into the water when he fell."

"Meaning an accident," I said.

Dad shrugged. "I'm still thinking manslaughter. Doc said there's no evidence of Lester's heart giving out on its own. The electrical shock was what killed him. And hiding this kind of evidence leads me further down the road to murder. Or, at least, someone who's very happy he's dead whether they arranged his end or not."

Agreed. Jill seemed on our page, too, so I was going to call it murder from now on, thanks.

"Now we need to find out who tried to hide evidence," Jill said.

I pointed upward at the cameras, not saying anything and not needing to. Grim now, Jill nodded.

"I already checked the footage from that night," she said. "Or I tried." Dad frowned at her while she shrugged, looking uncomfortable. "Turns out neither of the cameras were functioning properly. The video is spotty, at best." She flinched slightly, met my eyes, then Dad's before exhaling heavily. "At least, according to Robert." Jill was really having a hard time with silence and guilt lately. She tossed her hands at both of us, frustration so clear I felt horrible for her suddenly she had to bear the brunt of what had to be a crappy time to be a deputy in Reading. "Fine, he won't let me review it," she said. "I'm telling you both, if Crew doesn't come back soon, I might not last until he does." Hands shaking, she looked down at her feet, clenching her fists at her sides though it did nothing to stop the hot points of red on the tips of her cheekbones. "I've barely been back a day and he's driving me mad."

No need to say who "he" was. "Hang in there, Jill," I said with an awkward pat to her shoulder. It might have felt that way to me but the quick, grateful smile she flashed me, her big eyes wide with concern, told me I'd made a better impact than I expected.

"He won't last much longer." Dad sounded so sure of himself I wondered if he had a plan he wasn't telling me. Like that wasn't his usual way of doing business. I didn't ask, personally didn't care. I just wanted Crew to come back.

Pathetic, really. I didn't need a damned hero.

Jill left with the evidence, promising Dad she'd let him know on the sly when she heard back from the lab. "No matter what Olivia says," the deputy told us both, halfway into her car as she paused, "or who's paying you to investigate, Robert's on a warpath over you two. Watch your backs." She drove off without another word while I hugged myself, scowling after her, though obviously not aimed at her.

Nope, aimed full speed at my annoying and suddenly kind of scary cousin.

Dad grasped my arm and steered me toward the

front door of the club as soon as Jill's car was out of sight. I looked up at him with surprise, pulling free while we strode together through the front door. "I want a look at that footage," he said.

"Jill said Robert has it." I wasn't trying to be a wet blanket or anything but surely, he'd heard her, too.

Dad shook his head, pointing at Doreen's office door. I joined him as he entered, finding the small, older woman huddled in her seat, staring at the wall, tears streaming down her face. My eyes followed her gaze, settled on a photo framed in an old-fashioned wooden rectangle, the image of four smiling women staring back at her. I recognized her as one of them, and, to my surprise, realized the one next to her was a young and vibrant version of my Grandmother Iris. But who were the other two? The one on the far left seemed very familiar for some reason. I just couldn't put my finger on why.

I didn't get to ask about it. When Doreen looked up at the sight of Dad she sobbed once and stood up. My father engulfed her in a hug, nodding to me with a slight widening of his eyes, glancing sideways at the far wall where a cabinet door stood open.

Revealing a bulky security setup complete with two monitors. But before I could sneak my way over and have a peek, Dad came right out and asked.

"Reenie," he said, "we need to see the tapes from the night Lester died."

She hiccupped, shook her head. "That wretched Robert Carlisle took them."

Dad grunted, let her go. "You're sure there are no copies? You know Lester liked to keep backups of everything. For safety's sake." Sounded like Dad knew more about the habits of the disliked Patterson than he'd let on.

Doreen just shrugged. "If there are copies, I don't know where they are." She shivered, dabbing at her nose with her ever-present wad of tissues. "It's just horrible, John. Horrible."

He nodded, patted her shoulder. "Can I have the key for his office?" Just like that, point-blank. I half expected her to hand it over, considering the way she leaned on him. But Doreen shook her head, sitting down again, faint frown on her face.

"I can't do that, John," she said. "You'll have to have the sheriff come down and ask."

Dad sighed, shrugged. "Worth a try," he said. "I'll have Lucy come by and sit with you a bit tonight, Reenie."

She swatted at him with her tissues, face settling into a forced state of serenity. "I'm fine," she said. "Just a struggle, not knowing what happened. Get on with you both." She met my eyes. "You got your things, Fiona?"

I nodded, not sure what to say. And followed Dad out when he left.

He paused at the front door, scowling up at the two cameras. "I need to see what's on those tapes."

Tell me about it. But before I could ask him what he was planning, Dad strode off, climbing into his truck and driving away. At least he took a second to wave goodbye, though the whole "partner in investigation" thing seemed not to extend past his need to tweak the noses of those he deemed troublesome—like Robert.

Fine, then. Let Dad play his games. I was done for today. Petunia's called and I had a real job to do. Now, if only I could get the stench of the dumpster off my hands, that would be just peachy.

CHAPTER TWENTY-THREE

The rest of my day passed without incident, though I seemed to spend more time looking for Daisy who continued to avoid me than I did actually getting work done. And while I tried to corner Heather a time or two, she did a great disappearing act herself, vanishing either into her room or out the front door before I could pretend to find a reason to pin her down.

Without word from Crew, the smirking face of Rose lingering seemingly in every room I ventured into as she, on the other hand, followed me around as if looking for a reason to piss me off, and with Mom still upset over whatever Daisy said to her, I found myself wrapping up my day with knots across my shoulders and the kind of bubbling in my stomach that told me I should have a snack before bed or I'd be up with heartburn halfway through the night.

Morning broke, clear and lovely, my usual 6AM wakeup a whole hour early as my body, wound tight by continuing anxiety, drove me out of bed and into my sneakers. Ten minutes later I was running down the lakeside path, the first of the morning staff covering for me, Mom not yet arrived but due at any moment. I just couldn't stand one more minute inside.

This was the time I really missed Crew, I realized, more so than I expected and I found myself fighting off tears that I dashed aside with annoyance and impatience. No, I would not cry over him. Not this girl, not ever. He might have thought running off to do whatever heroic or idiotic thing he was doing was the right choice, that failing to even send a text update was acceptable, but I disagreed wholeheartedly. It wasn't so much the fact he disappeared, not really. I was a grown woman and, I at least told myself in no uncertain terms if Crew Turner wanted to live his life this way that was up to him. But have the freaking courtesy to tell someone, anyone, where he was going. While not abandoning the people who came to care about him and the job he left behind for some kind of covert whatever this was he'd gotten himself into.

So there.

I was so far gone into my pep talk of screw you, Crew that I failed to realize I'd passed the end of the trail again until I was almost as far as I'd gotten two days ago, the long grasses lashing at my legs, my sneakers slipping on the edge of the high bank. I paused, bending with my hands on my knees, realizing I was panting at full force, my chest heaving. That I'd pushed far harder than I usually did and was only noticing now.

Yeah, not worked up about this or anything. I took a second to crouch, to bow my head and catch my breath, to hug my knees and inhale, exhale while the morning sun washed over me, the soft breeze from the lake cooling the sweat beading my skin. I was almost back to normal, shaking my head at my own foolishness, red hair sticking to my cheeks that I pushed away with hands now tight from excessive blood flow when I caught my breath for a different reason, freezing in place.

I wasn't alone. Damn it, I had to come out this far again, didn't I? Knowing there were bears in the area? Seriously, Fee, what the hell was wrong with me? But before I could freak out and run off or utterly freeze in place while trying to figure out what a bear might want to snack on that wasn't Fleming related when I realized it wasn't a giant, hulking furred creature of the forest that crept past where I crouched, not twenty feet from me, but two dark figures in hoodies.

"I'm telling you," one of them whispered, his voice carrying but too low for me to identify who he was past gender, "they're going to find out."

"Just shut up and move it." The second, bigger

figure's gruff response was just as quiet, his identity as lost to me as the first. Damn it, I needed a closer peek, but the way the pair moved, how they slunk toward the hidden vessel, told me I'd stumbled on something that would likely get me in more trouble than I could handle alone if I confronted them.

"But what if they find out we were on his boat that night?" The first sounded anxious enough and guilty enough I had to wonder who I was allowing to escape.

"So what if they do," his partner said, the splash of water the only other sound, followed by the swish of what had to be the ghillie net being pulled free. I risked a glance, but the high weeds blocked my view. "They can't prove anything. Now, get in the damned boat already. We need to ditch this stuff before anyone finds us. Tonight's our last run. Let's make it count."

I held my place, holding the air in my aching lungs, waiting for the chance to take a safe look in the hope of identifying who they were. I stretched out on my stomach, creeping to the edge of the dirt, looking down the bank, watching the smaller of the two jump in next to the bigger and push off. The pair crouched low in the boat while it coasted away, a small engine coming to coughing life a moment later. The low hum of the motor echoed back toward me as the two in the small craft puttered down the lake in the direction of the cottages dotting the other side of the bank.

Now, I wasn't exactly suspicious by nature—ha!

Just had to get that out of the way—and while there was likely a perfectly good explanation for two people to sneak around shortly after dawn, taking a well-hidden boat out for a spin, I couldn't think of any. Didn't help their little conversation brought to mind Lester's death. They had to have been talking about the yacht club president, right? "His" boat? That put them right at the top of the suspect pool. But it was the recent reports of thefts from the cottages that got my hackles up enough I made note of my exact location, and, when the boat was out of sight, I crossed to retrace the path of the two the way they'd come, though there was no sign of a vehicle or a means of arrival when I reached the road, nor any tire tracks to follow.

Time to head for home and hand this particular mystery over to Jill. If these two were connected to the thefts, not to mention the death of Lester Patterson, it would give her a solid win and might grant her the leverage she needed to oust Robert. I swallowed hard as I ran back toward the main path, wondering when I stopped believing Crew was coming home.

CHAPTER TWENTY-FOUR

I found Dad sitting at the counter in the kitchen when I returned to Petunia's, enjoying a plate of breakfast while Mom worked on feeding our guests. He looked up when I entered, bushy eyebrows raised, and didn't move or eat another mouthful while I filled him in on what I'd seen.

To my surprise, he didn't comment right away, and it wasn't until I heard a familiarly irritating voice pipe up, I realized we weren't alone.

"You did inform Robert, I take it?" Rose sneered at me as she sashayed her nosy way into my private conversation with my father. Mom glared at her, the rigid way she clutched her spatula making me wonder if my normally reserved mother was planning something violent. Likely. "Or are you too busy poking your nose into other people's business?"

Snarl. "If I wanted your opinion," I snapped back, "I'd ask for it." Yup, had it up to here. Time to take out the trash. "Don't you think it's time you headed home to Montpelier, Rose? And didn't come back?" And there it was out in the open. Get lost in the nicest way possible. Okay, not so nice, but it was the best she was getting and all I had in me.

Leave it to Daisy to walk in on that little statement and miss the rest, naturally. My bestie's big, gray eyes stared at me like I'd run over her puppy instead of telling her irritating stepsister to get the hell out.

"How dare you," Rose said, turning to stomp to Daisy's side, hooking her arm through my best friend's like she owned her. "Are you going to let Fee talk to me like that, Day?"

Mom grunted, an uncommon sound from her, far more familiar from Dad. But she didn't comment, glaring while her spatula still hovered, dripping oatmeal all over the floor, a fact that made Petunia infinitely happy. The pug snuffle-snorted her way around the tile at Mom's feet while Daisy looked back and forth between Rose and me before saying a word.

"Fee, Rose is welcome to stay for as long as she wants." She sounded like she was trying to convince herself. "This is my business too." Standing up for herself finally? I wished she'd done so against Rose, not for her, but at least her backbone was returning.

"Our business," I said, nodding to Mom who

stayed quiet. "The three of us. You seem to think because you want her to work with you, we agreed to such an arrangement. We didn't." And we hadn't. I'd kind of taken Daisy's quiet request at face value initially, but the more I got to know her nasty ass little piece of trash stepsister, the less I wanted anything to do with her. Or to have her in my house, thanks. "We need to discuss this in a meeting, Daisy. Not out in the open." There, I was being a proper businesswoman, all professional and whatnot.

"Right so you can talk about me behind my back." Rose's hands clutched at Daisy's arm. "You know they're going to turn you against me." Her wheedling, whining tone made my best friend— former? Still? Hard to tell at the moment—flinch.

"We can talk about it right now," Daisy said, firm and flat.

I kept expecting Mom to speak up, but my mother held her tongue, though it was apparent she wanted to say something. Was she worried she'd fly off the handle? What, did she think I was about to do much better? Great, leave it to me, then.

"Fine," I said. "Two against one, Daisy. Rose is out. Now."

Daisy glanced at Mom who just nodded. That seemed to set her off like my rejection hadn't, her normally lovely face settling into something I didn't recognize, something much closer to Rose's pinched and judging expression, far too close for comfort.

"If you're going to ask Rose to leave," Daisy said—where exactly did she get "asking" out of "get the hell out"?—"then I'm going with her."

The two spun and left as a unit while I stared after them, not sure what to do or say from here. This changeover in the woman I'd come to adore all over again was so abrupt, so painfully uncomfortable and shocking I could barely breathe. Mom sagged into the counter, dropping her threatening utensil at last while Dad sighed and shook his head.

"That girl needs a serious reality check." Whether he referred to Daisy or Rose I wasn't sure, but he was right. And maybe I did, too. Was Daisy not the woman I'd thought? Was I underestimating everyone in my life these days, from Crew running off without notice to Robert's deeply hidden rage now coming to the surface and even my own father's willingness to use me as a tool to get what he wanted when it came to our town's officials? I didn't like where my thoughts were going, nor the tight, angry expression on Mom's face as she finally met my eyes.

"You have to do something, Fee," she said. Like I had any kind of recourse.

"Thanks, Mom," I shot back at her. "For all the support and everything."

"Would you rather I turned her over my knee and spanked her? Because that's the direction that child is heading." Mom's sharp tone made Petunia whine softly. And kind of shocked me, since I knew for a fact Mom had never in her life even threatened to strike anyone. She didn't believe in it.

Rather than argue with my mother, because we were heading for a fight, that much was clear, I stormed out of the kitchen and to my apartment to clean myself up for the day. Ten minutes later, a fast shower and quick change under my belt and a list of things to do a mile long to distract me in my grasp and I was climbing the steps to the third floor and my day's work.

I was passing the far door when I heard someone crying, pulling me to a halt and tugging me out of the lingering anger that seemed to hover over me these days whenever I thought about Daisy and Rose. I paused at Heather's door and listened, looking for a distraction if nothing else and getting exactly what I was hoping for.

"Please, you have to listen." She was obviously on the phone because she paused to no audible response. "I just need a few days. I know I can make this right. Please, give me a chance to get the money."

Hmmm. Money, was it? A great motive for many things. Including murder? My mind went to the string of burned-out lights, the night of Lester's death. Was Heather linked to the dead Patterson somehow through financial problems? Who did she owe money to and why? And was she somehow connected to the two men I'd encountered this morning? If they were the thieves Dad was hunting, could they be tied to Heather's money troubles?

So many questions, so little information. My favorite. Sigh.

As I stood there, listening to her beg and cry, I missed the fact the sound of her voice was closer to the door and, as she promised whoever it was she spoke to she was close to an answer, I found myself face-to-face with her as she tried to storm out of her room.

She squeaked as she confronted me, her face wet with tears, eyes huge, anger flashing over her expression when she realized I'd been listening in.

"Did you kill Lester Patterson?" Yeah, that was subtle. "Over money?"

She pushed past me, scowling back over her shoulder, stuffing her phone into her purse and wiping at her cheeks with her free hand. "So much for your pretense at friendship," she snapped. Why did that make me think of Daisy and the fight we'd had? Guilt smacked me harder than it should have, considering none of this was my fault. But it kept me from trying to stop Heather as she pushed past me. "I'll be out of your establishment before nightfall," she said. "And I'll never be back. Just be grateful I don't call the sheriff's department and report you for eavesdropping." Pretty sure listening in to private conversations wasn't illegal, but whatever, Heather.

I let her go, my own mood sour and grumpier than ever. Absolutely the worst time to call Crew and leave him a choice message about just how I felt about his absence and why it was I hoped he survived whatever it was he was up to so I could kill him myself.

Grand day. Just grand.

Another lovely one spent snarling at the staff, fighting off a mix of crankiness and a vague despair that everything that was supposed to be going right was actually going wrong while the world spun on around me.

For a brief instant of worry I caught myself frozen at the top of the steps just as the dinner rush started, the thought that Daisy was intimately tied into the pirate treasure mystery and, now that Rose had her ear, likely told her stepsister everything. Not that I really believed in the Reading hoard, but the hurt that my former best friend—yes, I was thinking of her in those terms, shame on me—might have spilled our secret to that hideous creature gave me a long instant of wanting to sit on the step and cry my eyes out.

Wow, talk about an emotional train wreck. I had to shake this funk somehow, move on from it. Yes, Crew was MIA. Yes, Daisy was acting like a psychopath. Okay, so Robert was a scary freak and I had too many mysteries floating around for my own comfort. So what? Not like life hadn't handed me lemons in the past.

Big girl panties firmly in place, Mom handling the meal for the evening with her staff in full force and Daisy—to my shock—hustling to help, I slipped away from Petunia's and out of their way, heading instead for my other place of business, even if it wasn't by choice.

I arrived at Dad's office with a million questions tucked neatly away for the expected interrogation, only to find his door locked. But despite his absence, it appeared I wasn't the only one looking for him.

When I stopped outside his door, it was to the watchful, angry double gaze of Wanda Beaman and Chris Noltz, both of whom seemed more than willing to turn their irritation on me as a surrogate.

Except, as I inhaled to protest I wasn't Dad, Wanda's hand came up, a small something in her grasp held out to me like an offering. And, as she spoke, qualifying her gift, I realized it was a thumb drive in the shape of a trout.

"We have something you need to see."

CHAPTER TWENTY-FIVE

The key Dad gave me worked, at least. I let the pair into his office (ours, I guess) and down to the end of the long, narrow space, inviting them to sit while I carefully perched on the edge of my father's chair feeling like a little girl invading a grownup's private lair but not sure what else to do. A call to him ended in voicemail, so I left him a quick message while the impatient Wanda and Chris watched me with narrowed eyes and the kind of insistence that told me I wasn't necessarily their second choice.

Okay, breathe, Fee. If they had no problem bringing me their evidence, I shouldn't feel guilty looking at it without Dad present.

"What we have to tell you, well, it's not exactly legal." She glanced at Chris who looked angrier than before. So, was that the source of their unhappiness? They were working on something together and fighting over how to deal with the consequences? I waited for her to go on and, when Chris finally nodded and looked away, arms crossed over his chest, Wanda met my eyes again. "We set up our own cameras," she said. "At the yacht club and at different points on the lake." On their own property? Perfectly legal. On someone else's? Yeah, I didn't need to go to the police academy to know that was illegal surveillance and couldn't be used in any kind of court. But it might give valuable information, right? And since I hadn't gathered it, I was all eyes and ears. "I've been missing a few things along the way, small things. I didn't really put two and two together until Chris came to me a week ago and mentioned the thefts at the cottages." She handed over the thumb drive which I plugged into Dad's laptop and booted up to have a peek. Wouldn't you know his computer was password protected? Only took one try—Mom's birthday—to get in, though.

Really, Dad. Sloppy security.

"Lester didn't seem to care about the thefts," Chris said, his anger from our first encounter not any less than when he'd confronted Dad. "We had to do something." Illegal or not? Well, I hardly blamed him. "Not to mention the dumping." Wanda nodded like that was worse than the disappearing property. "We need to know who's destroying our lake so we can put a stop to it."

"We couldn't take this to the acting sheriff,"

Wanda said, voice low and angry. "You were the only one I trusted, Fiona."

I'd earned her trust, had I? The fact she and Chris were handing the footage over to me helped, quite frankly. I had them on the original suspect list for Lester's murder, though Wanda's involvement seemed farfetched. If she was going to kill anyone it would have been Olivia. But Chris's falling out with Lester wasn't lost on me.

Wanda seemed much calmer than he did now that the evidence was coming to life on the screen. I noted the poor quality of the video footage, disappointed to discover they hadn't made the dumpster area a priority either. Well, I could hardly blame them for that.

"Sheriff Turner knew about the thefts," Wanda said, sounding grumpy about the whole thing, "though, in his defense, it was pretty minor before he left. And I know he told Acting Sheriff Carlisle to look into it while he was gone. But that was a week ago and the losses have ramped up."

"I overheard Geoffrey talking to Carlisle," Chris said, leaning across the desk toward me, heavy brow furrowed, double chin accentuated as he shook his head. "That we weren't a priority. Imagine that. Olivia's really losing touch with her council if elected officials in her ranks are openly telling law enforcement not to care about what happens to us in this tourist climate."

Agreed. I knew if it was my establishment losing out, I'd be furious. Come to think of it, did I have anything to worry about? I needed to talk to Daisy about doing an inventory to make sure nothing was going missing.

My mind went to the boat this morning, to the two figures in hoodies heading out on the lake, and I pondered their secret surveillance as Chris went on.

"I wish Wanda and I had talked sooner," he said.

The fisherwoman nodded. "Me too," she said. "Look, I know I had a grudge against Lester and that Olivia and I don't see eye to eye on the tourism thing. But I'm willing to put all that aside." She glanced at Chris next to her, shrugged. "At least the cottagers are consistent clients. If they start jumping ship because of these thefts, I'll lose the last of my revenue." When she met my eyes again, hers narrowed. "We have enough evidence on the footage to prove Lester and his boating friends were dumping garbage into the lake." I scrolled through a few scraps of footage, watching in fast forward as the laughing Patterson's boat passed the camera and tossed a bag of trash over the side like it was hilarious to him. "I don't have proof, but I wouldn't put it past Lester to be involved in the thefts as well as the dumping." She shifted Dad's computer around, scanning for a particular timecode in one of the files. I watched as two hooded figures—the same two from the boat? Certainly, it looked that way, enough to renew my thrill of nerves over the encounter that morning—talked in the shadows with someone else, a someone that walked away from them with a nasty grin on his face. Lester Patterson crossed the light in front of the clubhouse door long enough to identify him, though his two companions disappeared into the shadows.

"Rumor has it Lester's been having money problems," Chris said. "That he was in deep debt and that the family had cut him off."

Interesting. I didn't really believe, it, but interesting.

"This is the part I want you to see." Chris took control of the computer this time, scanning the final file before letting the footage run. I watched two hoody-clad figures climb out of a small boat—it had to be the same one I'd spotted on the lake—and slide onto Lester's. The timecode told me they visited a half-hour before his estimated time of death.

Hadn't the first one said there'd be evidence they were on "his" boat? Here it was, plain as day (well, night). But, when the two reappeared moments later and slunk off, it was the last visitor who made my breath catch, her face clear as she turned with what looked like guilt, slipping off the dock and into the cabin just as the footage went black.

"The drive space ran out," Wanda said, sounding frustrated by the equipment failure. "But I'm positive the last person on board Lester's boat the night he died was Heather Parborough."

CHAPTER TWENTY-SIX

Chris and Wanda left a short time later after I saved copies of the footage they took. I sat at Dad's desk and perused the video files, disappointed that the pair hadn't caught the killer on tape. Heather's appearance was damning, I'd give them that, though, and her apparent distress with Lester and whoever it was she'd been talking to this morning at Petunia's made her seem pretty guilty to me.

If she had accidentally caused the yacht club president's death, why was she lingering in Reading? Right, something to do with recovering lost money. But where did it go and how did she lose it?

I was about to call Dad again when the phone rang. I recognized his number and answered, knew from the sounds in the background he was on the move, the hum of his truck's motor discernable as was the faint country song his radio played.

"I had to leave town for the rest of the day," he said. "Unrelated case."

I filled him in on what Wanda and Chris told me while Dad listened with his usual silence.

"Any idea who the two you saw might have been?" Dad sounded worried.

"Not sure," I said. "I'm going to head back out to the lake and check out the site. See if I can find anything that identifies them. But Dad, it's got to be the thieves. And from the sound of things, they are getting ready to wrap up their operation." And we'd lose the chance to catch them and question them about their involvement with Lester Patterson. They were nervous enough about being on board his ship they might have killed him and run, leaving him for Heather to find, right? Rather than jump to the conclusion that Heather was the killer, I wanted to give her the benefit of the doubt.

"Fee." The vibration in Dad's voice told me he thought that was a terrible idea before he even said so. "Stay out of it until I get back. I'll be home tomorrow morning. We'll go out together, okay?"

It would be too late by then, I just told him that. "I'll be fine, Dad," I said. "I'm not going to go anywhere near them personally, I promise. But if it is the thieves, if I don't do something they'll vanish and with them our chance to catch them."

"Just wait for me," he said. "Please, Fee."

I grumbled and I growled but I agreed at last,

hanging up with a promise I wouldn't go looking for the thieves alone. The door to Dad's office locked behind me as I pondered calling Jill. If I took her, I wouldn't be breaking my promise, would I?

But she just reiterated what Dad said, sounding angry. "Fiona Fleming," she snapped, voice very low like she was trying to keep our conversation a secret. "If you do anything to put yourself in harm's way, I'll kill you myself. Because Crew will strip my hide if even a hair on your head gets harmed." She paused a long moment before exhaling. "Just tell me where you saw the boat and I'll do my best, okay?"

"Never mind," I said in a rush. "Dad's back." Yup, just lied to her. "He'll call you." And I hung up, feeling guilty and frustrated and more than a little rebellious. Crew might not be here, but his smothering protectiveness was in full evidence.

As I turned, considering doing as the deputy told me to (snort), a black sedan cruised past, familiar enough without the bulky sunglassed bully in the driver's seat I knew exactly who sat in the rear passenger side.

I should have gone home to Petunia's. But I'd long given up on not following my nose when the chance came up. Instead, I crossed the street and headed for the edge of town, approaching the front entrance of The Orange with growing trepidation. Dad mentioned he thought Malcolm might be behind the thefts, but I had other ideas. No way someone as smart as the Irishman would make a mess where he lived. More likely he either had no idea or was monitoring the situation himself.

Time to find out which.

The bully at the door towered over me but didn't try to stop me as I slipped past him, wishing Malcolm would hire guys with necks for once. His suit just made him look bigger, too, intimidating, though I was used to big men thanks to growing up with my uniformed Dad. Honestly? I found men like Malcolm far more frightening. Slim, contained, with faint deprecating humor hiding who knew what behind eyes vaguely reminiscent of a shark watching prey, the handsome silver-haired Irishman didn't comment as I approached and sat at the bar he leaned against.

"Get you a drink, Fiona?" He circled to the taps, offered me a glass but I shook my head.

"Bit early," I said. "I'm here about business."

"Siobhan?" The name was said with lightness of tone, but his not-so-subtle meaning wasn't lost on me.

"Local thefts," I said, trying to wrangle the conversation into something that didn't make me feel uncomfortably like I was cheating on my dad's trust.

Malcolm's eyes narrowed but he didn't seem surprised, so I figured he already knew. Did that mean he was involved after all? "I'm aware of someone infringing on my territory," he said, answering that question. "And I'm taking steps to uncover who it is thinks they can waltz in and tread on my toes."

I wouldn't want to be the thieves if Malcolm caught them. Which gave me an idea I should have tossed to the wayside the second it crossed my mind. Instead, I spoke up while my heart skipped in wild palpitations in my chest.

"I have information that will help," I said. "If you're willing to let me talk to them when you catch them." Shouldn't I have just trusted Dad? Or let Jill handle it like she said? Except Dad wasn't here and Jill had been hamstrung by Robert. Then again, did I care how the thieves were caught? All I wanted from them was what they knew about the death of Lester Patterson, right?

Um, not exactly, Fee. Dad had been hired to track them down. Well, I was tracking them. Just using unconventional means to do the deed. The fact I was about to tap an illegal source of assistance? That's what my father got for leaving Reading without telling me after giving me the keys to his kingdom.

Malcolm held very still a long moment before nodding, smile returning, eyes narrow and tight. "I think we can be of mutual benefit to one another," he said. "You sure you want to cross the line from the law to my particular vocation, lass?"

"Are you planning to kill anyone?" I really needed to just go. But I couldn't turn to Robert and Jill told me to stay out of it. Dad wasn't here. Neither was Crew. If what I overheard was true, the thieves were going to vanish tonight, once and for all. What choice did I have?

Malcolm laughed, though it was a cold and heartless sound while his boys chuckled in time with him. "Now don't you worry your pretty little red head about that," he said. "You tell me what you've got, and I'll take care of things."

"That's not how this is going to work." I waited for Malcolm to nod before exhaling a barely contained breath of nerves. "I need to talk to them. About Lester Patterson's death."

The Irishman seemed to think about it, though I was confident he'd already made up his mind. When he finally leaned over the bar and tapped the back of one of my hands with a narrow index finger it was hard not to pull away.

"Tell you what," he said. "I'll be happy to bring you along on this little caper on one condition."

Naturally. "What's that?"

He reached under the bar and pulled out a phone, setting it in front of me. The shark-like expression reappeared, though there was a kind of sorrowful eagerness that blunted his fearsome nature. Enough I actually felt a pang of empathy as he spoke.

"You call Siobhan right now," he said, "and you can have anything you want."

I could have rejected his offer. Instead, my heart pounding but the opportunity to act so immediate I couldn't resist, I lifted the receiver, eyes never leaving his. "Number?" Like I needed him to recite it. I knew it by heart, didn't I?

His own gaze widened and for a moment he seemed shocked, even scrambling to pull out a small notebook from his back pocket. Apparently, he hadn't consigned it to rote like I had. He read off an international code before a familiar string of numerals I dutifully typed into the keypad. I held onto the receiver and his gaze while the line rang and rang.

And ended in a message service. "I can't be reached, my love," an older woman's voice said with a cheerful grin behind her words. "Just talk to the machine, why don't you?" Her accent was also Irish, heavier than Malcolm's, and I almost stuttered as the beep turned into waiting silence.

"Ms. Doyle, my name is Fiona Fleming," I said. "Malcolm Murray asked me to call." I left her my number before hanging up, handing the phone over to the staring Irishman. Wait, was that a shine in his pale green eyes, the hint of barely suppressed tears? Just what the hell was my father hiding from me and why? And what could possibly trigger so much sadness in a hardened criminal like Malcolm?

"Thank you, lass," he said, soft, barely audible. He tucked the phone under the counter, shrewd expression returning, that faintly mocking grin back in place. "Now, tell me what you've got on the crew who think I take lightly to poachers."

CHAPTER TWENTY-SEVEN

And that's how I found myself, late that night, crouching in a boat darkened and quiet hovering on the edge of a cottage dock while Malcolm whispered into a cellphone. Still reeling from just how idiotic this decision to join him was, I did my best not to think about how much more efficient his operation was than anything I'd witnessed even when Crew was around being sheriff. If Malcolm wanted to run Reading, he could have from the way he swiftly organized and implemented his plan to use the information I gave him to end the brief but fruitful stretch of thefts the two hooded individuals enjoyed.

All it took was telling him exactly where to find the boat I'd spotted twice now and Malcolm was on the move, a GPS tracker planted on the hidden boat, the pair under surveillance by Malcolm's boys, cameras much clearer and in full color with infrared brilliance showing us their latest journey to head out and make themselves richer at other's expense. The silence broken by their motor puttering as they skimmed off into the darkness was punctuated by the soft hum of the boat Malcolm used, newer and quiet enough to follow without alerting those we pursued.

Ten minutes after we set off after our quarry I hunched low in the prow of the now moored boat and watched with a wince dying to manifest as the two big bullies Malcolm had following by SUV cornered the pair of hoody clad thieves and, with the sort of rough but practiced actions of men who knew what they were doing and had a lot of experience doing it, corralled their prey and cuffed them tight with zip ties. Malcolm lounged next to me in the boat we'd arrived in, a beaming smile on his face, cigar between his lips, casually relaxed enough I knew the pair were in for a terrible time unless I could convince the Irishman to turn them over to the authorities when I was done asking questions.

"Please, don't kill us!" I knew that voice at full volume, even if the whispered version had given me trouble. Though it was shocking to hear so much terror from the hulking form whose head snapped back as one of the towering bullies unmasked him. David Campbell might have looked like a force to be reckoned with all his own, but the way he crumbled in the face of the career criminal seated beside me told me he wasn't nearly as tough as he made out to be.

Then again, if I was facing off with the likes of Malcolm Murray, and not on his good side, either, I'd be pretty scared, too.

"Evening, gents." When the second thief staggered to his knees, his head jerked back by a firm grasp on the ties of his hood, I gaped at the sight of Luke Patterson. Wait, I thought he and Keira's father were enemies...? The whole deception played out in my head with a clarity that had me furious with my own lack of deduction.

Oldest trick in the book, pretending to hate each other on the outside while working together. Great way to misdirect suspicions. I wondered if Luke's girlfriend was in on it, too? Keira's tears had seemed real enough, her worry for her boyfriend's wellbeing. For all I knew, though, she was part of the scam.

Pissed off now by my failure to suspect either of them, I actually considered letting Malcolm do what he wished once I had what I needed, just on principle.

"You two have been naughty," Malcolm said, grinning around his cigar. The pungent smoke reached me, making me cough softly. He glanced my way, shrugged. "And this fair lass has some questions you're going to answer. If you tell her what she wants to know in a way that makes her happy, you just might live to talk about it."

"We don't know anything." Luke shuddered, looked at me, at Malcolm. "About anything."

"Considering she hasn't asked you yet, you might

want to hold off on saying a word, lad." Malcolm's good humor flashed to an evil grin before he gestured to me. "All yours, Fiona, my dear."

He really seemed to be enjoying himself, far too much if I was honest. How much of his delight came from the end of the chase and how much came from me being here with him when both of us knew just how furious Dad would be when he found out?

"You two were caught on tape with Lester Patterson," I said.

"My father," Luke said, snarky enough around the edges I scowled in response. One of the bullies casually smacked him on the back of the head. It looked like a small gesture, but Luke rocked from the blow, cursing a bit before catching himself.

"I'm well aware he was your dad," I said. "I'm not talking about a casual conversation, Luke. I'm talking about the two of you conspiring in the dark with him just before he died. And sneaking onto his boat, too. Within easy reach of his convenient time of death."

Luke and David exchanged a quick look, the young man looking sick.

"I didn't kill my father," he said while David spluttered.

"Neither of us did," the big man said. At least he didn't sound like he was going to burst into tears anytime soon. "We were working for him."

Huh. "Stealing for Lester?" I let enough skepticism sneak into my voice the pair blanched, the bullies leaning in while Malcolm's smile widened.

Right, if I didn't like what I heard, the threat was implicit. I backed off my tone and prodded again while the pair seemed to take me seriously. "Not from him?"

Luke's face darkened. "I would have loved to steal from the old bastard," he said. "Judge me if you want, but I hated my father." He flinched. "But I didn't kill him, I swear. I just wanted to get out from under him." He shrugged, sighed like he had nothing to lose. "He was blackmailing me, his own son. I was stealing from the family. But only because he cut me off from my inheritance."

Good reason to kill him, wasn't it? "What about you?" I looked at David who didn't comment right away despite his proximity to pain and who knew what else Malcolm had in store. "What happened between you and Lester that ended your friendship?"

He hesitated before grunting when a big hand fell on his shoulder and squeezed. I did my best not to flinch in empathetic response as David finally spoke up.

"My past isn't as clean-cut as I've led everyone to believe." David glanced at Malcolm whose eyes narrowed in response. "I have a history of working outside the law. Something I put behind me. For Keira." His daughter made him go clean? Right. So, this wasn't his first kick at the thievery can? "But when I ran into Heather…" he swallowed hard, face twisting into something like longing before he met Malcolm's eyes again. "You know the pull of the con," he said as if the Irishman would understand completely. "It had been years, but I just couldn't resist."

Malcolm did seem to commiserate, though without any kind of empathy behind it. "Go on, mate."

"I knew I could take advantage of certain information I had on her," he said. "Her old dad and me, we had enough of a past I could use it against her." He didn't sound contrite, not at all, and I wished I could change that, feeling for Heather all over again. The sins of the father taken out on the daughter? Despicable. Which made me think about Siobhan and Malcolm and Dad while David went on. "I wasn't greedy, just took a cut of the boats she was selling, keeping it quiet, you know? Easy to hide. Then Lester found out." He grunted, fury flashing awake. "Idiot." Luke seemed to agree with David's assessment. "I don't know how, but he came to me and told me what he knew. Showed me evidence, paperwork that Heather kept, proving I was the one who was embezzling alongside her. Then he cut me out and amped up the fraud. To the point Heather told me he was going to get her caught." He sagged in apparent defeat. "Like Lester cared. He was clean, made sure of that. Heather might have been able to accuse him, but the trail led back to her and me." I didn't feel sorry for him, right? "But he wasn't done." David seemed shocked, at last, like he couldn't believe things had fallen so far, so fast. "He said he knew about my past and threatened both me and Luke with the cops if we didn't steal for him. We didn't have a choice."

Still not convincing me they didn't kill Lester. Considering they were still stealing after the Patterson was dead… "I don't see him holding a gun to your head now, David." He looked guilty enough, at least.

"One last score," he muttered, sounding like an addict. "To make up for everything we handed over to him."

I guess that made a criminally minded kind of sense. But all of this mess? Hard not to see it as a huge motive for murder. Though mention of the boat company rep had my mind turning. Heather's innocence wasn't looking good. "You two were on his boat the night he died," I said. "I have footage proving it."

They both nodded. "We were," David said. "But we left after Heather got there. She was furious, something about her bosses finding out about the skimming. We cut and run so she wouldn't see us."

Luke nodded, swallowed. "But when we were leaving, I heard her threatening my father. That if he didn't give her back what he took from her, she'd make sure he regretted it."

CHAPTER TWENTY-EIGHT

I was sure Jill's discomfort with my appearance at the sheriff's office had more to do with the fact I'd brought in the two suspects and less that I was backed by a pair of bullies and the smirking Malcolm Murray, though perhaps those facts were interchangeable. It was pretty obvious Robert had a lot to say and would get around to saying it when he got over his spluttering and incoherent ranting that turned his face dark red and made him shake like an alcoholic recently coming down from a three-day binge.

Fortunately, Toby had her head on her shoulders. The front desk receptionist surprised me being at the office so late, but she took my appearance and my companions in stride, smiling and gesturing for me to

proceed into the bullpen with the two criminals—
neglecting to remind me the other three were just as
bad, bless her.

"After you, Fee," she said, winking when Robert
wouldn't see. "Nice work. You looking for a new
job?"

I flashed her a big grin, realizing this was the first
time my father's old employee actually mentioned my
affinity for police work. "I'm good," I said. "Dad has
me working cases for him, after all. I think I like
private life better."

She flinched a little, sideways glance at Robert
enough to raise my suspicions. "Your dad makes a
great boss," she said, and dropped it, good humor
gone. Wait, was she implying maybe my father was
trying to poach her out from under the sheriff's
department? That old devil. And Toby loved him
enough if Crew wasn't coming back—stop that,
Fee—she'd likely take his offer and run with it.

"Just what the hell do you think you're doing?"
Robert finally pulled himself together long enough to
speak coherently. Good for him, though I preferred
him silent, thanks.

"Your job," I snarled in return, shoving Luke and
David firmly into the cell, slamming the barred door
shut behind them before turning to Jill, purposely
ignoring the present chain of command. It was only
then I noticed Geoffrey lingering in the doorway to
the sheriff's office, Crew's office. Two thoughts
occurred to me, then. One, that Geoffrey had his
own reasons for wanting Lester dead, didn't he?

Though I hadn't really considered him a suspect, should I? And second, hitting closer to home with more force and anger than it should was the fact Robert hadn't wasted any time moving in. Was that a bad sign or just my cousin's arrogance? Did they know something I didn't?

Jill's strained expression and hands on hips weren't the resounding thanks I was hoping for, though a perfect match for the shocked silence at the other end of the phone when I'd called her to warn her I was bringing in prisoners. I'd hoped she'd have my back, though it was pretty clear she was between a jerk and a slimy councilman at this point so I could hardly blame her for her unhappy attitude.

"We'll take things from here," she said, with a pointed look at Malcolm. The bar owner shrugged, hands in his pockets, that twisted grin on his lean, handsome face not helping matters.

"Just being a helpful citizen, is all, deputy," he said before bobbing a nod at Robert. "*Deputy.*" Oh, he'd called my cousin that on purpose, sure did.

Setting off the acting sheriff exactly as he intended. "I should have you both arrested," Robert snapped, his hands skittering from trying to settle on his waist, his belt, stopping with restless twitches over his shirt sleeves as he crossed his arms like he had no idea how to stand he was so wound up.

"Try it." Malcolm flashed white teeth before turning to me and bowing with a finger touch to his forehead in salute. "A pleasure catching criminals with you, Miss Fleming," he said. "I'll be seeing you again, soon. Say a big hello to Siobhan for me when she gets back to you, won't you, lass?" With that, Malcolm spun and sauntered out, winking at Toby while his two hulking bodyguards marched behind him, silent and scary as always.

I should have been worried that it bothered me less I'd befriended someone who was likely a career criminal than I was by the fact he'd liked working with me. Or maybe both truths should have been equally disturbing? Whatever, I had other issues to deal with, namely a tall, nasty piece of work who glared like he could murder me where I stood just by thinking about it.

As soon as the door closed behind Malcolm, Robert started in on me for real. "Meddling in police business will get you tossed in jail," he began.

Cut short in mid-rant by the soft throat-clearing of the watching councilman. Robert's whole demeanor flinched as he turned, staring with what could only be described as mute impotence while Geoffrey crossed in front of Robert—purposely? Likely—in a visible show of who was the real boss here and held out his hand to me.

I stared at it like it might bite me while Robert muttered something I didn't catch and stomped to Crew's office, slamming the door shut behind him.

"You'll forgive our acting sheriff for not offering his thanks and congratulations on your capture of the thieves that have been evading this office." So smooth and yet so smarmy. I was shocked when Geoffrey's hand settled on my shoulder, his body weight guiding me around and out into reception then to the exit, stopping me on the top step, the door slipping shut behind us. His voice lowered, tone soft as he spoke again, lips near enough to my ear I felt the heat of his breath and almost shuddered in distaste at his proximity. Too much aftershave, dude. Seriously. "It's come to my attention we might be in need of a new sheriff in short order," he said. "Something to do with the FBI and Sheriff Turner's absence?" Was he fishing for answers, or did he know more than I did? Regardless, he fired up my worry all over again, leaving me out of balance and unable to tell him to take his hand off me. Because it was still touching me, now sitting on my shoulder, fingers squeezing with the kind of not-so-subtle pressure that implied intimacy. Gross. "If that were the case, I'd be delighted to forward your name as a possible candidate for the role." Um, what? I wasn't even a police officer. "From what I understand, local laws allow for civilians to take the sheriff's office if the council deems them sufficiently... motivated and naturally talented. As you obviously are. And have proven over and over again." Oh my god, was he leaning closer? It was like watching a slow-motion train wreck coming right toward me down a set of tracks I was tied to and there seemed to be nothing I could do to avoid his nearness. Frozen, stunned and speechless, I gaped up at him while his fingers rose from my shoulder and tucked back a piece of my hair from my cheek, behind one ear, while my skin crawled involuntarily into a mass body rise of goosebumps. "I'm sure you know I'm well on my way to attaining the office of mayor. Having someone of your talents as sheriff would be, shall we say, the sort of partnership that could make me want to come to work every day."

He was lucky I was so surprised and unable to move a muscle because if I had even a heartbeat more to recover? Yeah, he'd be feeling in a personal and physical way that would take him to his knees just what I thought of his idea.

Instead, he spun and left, returning through the door, leaving me on the step with bile burning the back of my throat and the need to scream my horror at his suggestion rising from the depths of my stomach and pushing its way up past my lungs and into my shoulders until, hunched and with the beginning of a tension headache, I stumbled down the steps to the street and practically ran home.

Once there, I immediately got in the shower and scrubbed myself red raw, before tucking into a pair of flannel pajamas—the ugliest I owned—and hugging my pug to me while Petunia whined I was squeezing her too hard. I hadn't even had the wherewithal to question Geoffrey about his possible suspect status, I'd been so creeped out. Sleep didn't come for quite some time and my dreams, when I finally did pass out, were haunted by endlessly chasing Crew in a motorboat while Malcolm laughed at me, and Geoffrey breathed down my neck.

That's why I woke up in such foul humor, why I grumped at my staff, my mother, Daisy—who was avoiding me again—though it was a good thing (or not?) that Rose wasn't around. I was sure if she'd shown her face, I'd have done something she'd regret later and that would likely lose me my best friend until she got over Rose's death and all. I'd help her. She'd be fine. Oh, Fee.

Instead, without Rose as a target, I was left to gather up cleaning supplies and schlump my way through the rooms in the carriage house, scrubbing and fluffing and dusting my way to physical weariness while my mind skirted questions I didn't want to consider, and my heart ached to talk to the one person I couldn't seem to get out of my head.

Why hadn't Crew called me back?

I was on my way back inside when I spotted Heather slipping out. She didn't see me, though from the tight and tear-stained appearance of her she wouldn't have noticed me if I'd walked across her path. Huh, so much for her threat of leaving Petunia's. With the tourist season the way it was, she wouldn't have been able to find a room anywhere close by, no doubt. That meant she was stuck with my snooping. Head down, she headed for the parking lot and the expensive-looking sedan she was driving, peeling out into the street a moment later and almost causing an accident.

Curiosity won, as always, cutting through the angst and concern and anxiety to the point I could think of nothing else. With the pretense of needing to clean her room my excuse, I marched upstairs and through her door, firmly closing it behind me.

I cleaned, I swear. While looking around for something, anything, that might give me a clue as to who she'd been talking to and what her part in this whole thing was. Except, all I came across was her business card, perched on the edge of her briefcase, with the number for her main office typed in heavy text at the bottom.

Yeah, I took it. Maybe I could get information from the donkey's mouth if the horse wasn't talking?

A bit of guilt clouded my actions as I snuck downstairs to my apartment five minutes later and dialed the number, Petunia staring up at me as she always did, though depending on my mood I imagined she knew exactly what I was up to and was judging me for it.

"What?" I nabbed some fresh strawberries from the fridge and tossed them to her to keep her from accusing me of doing exactly what Geoffrey apparently wanted of me. Ew.

"Buckley's Marine Supplies." The gruff man's voice wasn't what I was expecting.

"Good morning," I said, awkward now that I'd taken an action without any idea how to go about getting what I wanted. "I'm looking for Heather Parborough." Okay, Fee, nice save. "Can you get me in touch with her, please?"

The man exhaled heavily and when he spoke again, he sounded furious enough to come through the line at me. "Miss Parborough no longer works for us," he said. "And if you're a client of hers, you'd best know the police will be in touch."

CHAPTER TWENTY-NINE

"I'm actually calling on behalf of Fleming Investigations in Reading, Vermont." Where did that come from? The man grunted faintly in response. "We're looking into Miss Parborough for the town of Reading, Mr...? Buckley, I presume?"

"Yes." He sounded a bit mollified and even slightly eager. Awesome. Eager meant forthcoming, right? "Gordon Buckley, owner."

"Can you tell me how recently Miss Parborough was fired, Mr. Buckley, and the reason for her release?" If I was going to dive headfirst into this opportunity, I might as well see how far he'd let me take it without proof of who I was. But apparently, he'd had it with Heather and was more than willing to spill details. Bless him.

"I told the state troopers everything," he said, "but, in a nutshell, Miss…?"

"Fleming," I said. "Fiona Fleming. Investigative partner." Dad said so, right?

That seemed to give him the confidence to go on. "Miss Fleming," he said. "Say, is your father John Fleming?"

Whoops. Was this an unnecessary repeat conversation? "Have you spoken to him yet?"

Something creaked in the background, a chair spring maybe? "Not recently," Gordon said, though he sounded completely at ease talking to me now. Papers shuffled. "I was going to call him, so thanks for following up."

"My pleasure," I said. "What changed since Dad spoke to you, sir?"

"Heather's whole web of lies unraveled." He exhaled again, though the anger was gone from his voice, settling into what sounded like real regret. "I don't get it. She's worked for us for years. And her father's been one of our best mechanics since I took over from my father. It's been a huge blow to the whole family." He cleared his throat. "We think of ourselves as family here, Miss Fleming."

"What happened?" If he didn't get to the point already, I was going to sigh myself.

"She's been stealing from me, is what happened." There was his anger again. "Hiding it. I didn't notice because we fully trusted her and why wouldn't we? She's been our best salesperson for the last five years." Again the regret. "Turns out she's been processing fraudulent sales."

"As in claiming to sell boats and not?" How would that work? Making money but no product going out? That didn't make sense.

"She's been switching serial numbers from smaller vessels to larger ones." Now he seemed tired, worn out. Compassion simmered as I realized what he was talking about, the small business owner in me wanting to shake my head and commiserate. "Goes back a couple of years, mostly vessels we've taken in as resales, so they didn't get noticed until recently. But her latest switch I caught because I had a buyer who wanted to see the one she swapped out and I couldn't find it anywhere."

Yikes. That was risky of her and not very smart, either. Surely, she had to know she'd get caught eventually? But hadn't David said Lester pushed Heather to frauds she claimed would get her caught? This must have been one of them. "Do you know where the boats ended up, Mr. Buckley?"

He must have nodded because he cleared his throat after a moment's silence and spoke. "Yes. Reading, Vermont. Your town, Miss Fleming."

"You said her father works for you, too? Does he still?" And was he in on it?

"Harry seems utterly shocked by what Heather's been up to." Gordon didn't sound so sure. "I don't have proof he had knowledge, but I had to let him go, too. Poor bastard, but they were family, and I can't have them betraying me like this."

I hung up after another few moments, promising

to have Dad call him right away. Gordon Buckley's emailed proof would be in my father's inbox by now, and as I thought about calling him, Dad read my mind.

The moment I answered I told him what I'd learned about Heather. Dad seemed to take everything I said in stride, sounding almost excited by the prospect.

"She's been my prime suspect," he said.

"Why?" Yes, she'd been rifling through Lester's office, and she was seen on the footage entering his boat the night he died. But for all I knew Dad hadn't seen that videotaped proof.

"She has a record," he said. "That's where I've been, getting the file unsealed."

"Unsealed? She was underage?" And so much for an unrelated case. Good thing Dad had friends in police departments all over the country. One of them must have obliged him.

"Fourteen," he said. "Arrested for murder."

"And they didn't try her as an adult?" That was surprising.

"They wanted to," he said. Ah. Which meant they knew they didn't have enough to convict. "She was sentenced to manslaughter after a plea bargain, tried as a minor. The prosecutor didn't have enough evidence to get a murder charge to stick so they took the best shot they had."

"So, she was hiding it." Made sense. "Who did she kill and why?"

"One of her friend's little sisters. She claimed it

was just an accident, but the state prosecutor thought otherwise. Still, her claim got her a lesser conviction, manslaughter. She was a minor, ultimately, and had her record sealed when she turned eighteen."

Okay, but she had her day in court. Why would that have anything to do with Lester Patterson?

"I have reason to believe Lester was blackmailing her," he said. "That he found out about Heather's past and was going to use it to get her and her father fired from Buckley's." Having a record, even a sealed one, could be motive. Maybe. There had to be more to it, though. But one thing was certain, there was a reason no one liked Lester Patterson. "She might or might not have killed that child in cold blood, Fee, but there's a good chance killing comes easily to her now. This info from Gordon Buckley might be all we need to hand her over to the state troopers." Bypassing the local sheriff's office. I'd be fine with that. "But that's not why I'm calling." Okay, what was with that sudden shift in tone—

Ack. Right. He knew what I'd been up to. I'd gone against his wishes, hadn't I? Well, I was a grown woman and if he was going to leave me with the means to investigate crimes and to my own devices like this, he just had to accept the consequences.

I told him everything without him prompting me for answers, about Luke and David, about Malcolm's assistance—Dad loved that, sure did—and finally about Geoffrey's offer. Though I did leave out the creepy closeness of the conversation. Last thing I needed was my father going full action hero on me and doing something permanent to Geoffrey before I had the chance.

Sigh. Flemings.

Though, when I mentioned Geoffrey Jenkins as a suspect, Dad grunted his unhappy reply.

"He has an alibi," he said. "I need to talk to those boys. Get your butt outside and I'll take you with me to the sheriff's office. You can distract Robert and I'll see what Luke and David have to say."

"How about you distract Robert and I talk to them." Grumpy, Fee? Who, me? But I was already on the move, trotting upstairs, poking my head in the kitchen and gesturing at my phone still against my ear, mouthing "Dad" to Mom who eye-rolled before nodding. She tossed some morsels on the floor, luring my eager pug away, leaving me to dodge out the foyer and the front door.

Wouldn't you know Dad's pickup was parked on the street right outside my place? I hung up as I climbed in the passenger seat, glaring at him while he glared right back.

"We're going to have a talk about who does what," he grumped, putting the truck in gear and heading for the middle of town.

"Just as soon as you stop treating me like a little girl while telling me I have a job to do." So there, Dad.

He held his peace all the way to the sheriff's office, though to be fair it was maybe a sixty-second drive, so he didn't have to be quiet for long. When we entered the doorway and into the reception area, I was relieved to see Jill wasn't at her desk and that, upon peeking, the door to Crew's office was wide open, no Robert in sight.

Toby was on guard duty, apparently, and though I knew she should have sent us both packing she instead stood and hugged Dad then me and gestured for both of us to enter the bullpen, returning her attention to the magazine she'd been reading.

Awesome. "You're totally stealing her, aren't you?"

Dad winked and grinned and I had the obvious answer.

I'd had reason to talk to reticent prisoners in this cell not so long ago, though one had been my friend. Jared hadn't been willing to chat, but David and Luke didn't seem to have the kind of reserve my construction company buddy used to hide his troubles. They both stood immediately, coming to the bars, looking forlorn and more than a little anxious. To my surprise, Keira Campbell stood outside the cell, her face tight and red, wet with tears. She looked embarrassed and angry enough I figured she was just learning what her father and boyfriend had been up to. Good to know she wasn't complicit, though I wondered if the pair would ever live down what they'd done in her eyes.

"The family won't bail me out." That was Luke and the faint wail in his voice was almost comical. So, he'd expected the Pattersons to step up and save his sorry behind? "It's all Dad's fault."

"Your dead father." I didn't mean to use that

particular tone of voice and the carelessness of my words wasn't lost on me, but it was out before I could stop myself. He winced but shrugged.

"They always bail me out." Wow, poor kid. Way to grow up privileged and find out what it's like to be the rest of us.

David looked pissed suddenly like he was about to punch Luke just to shut him up. "Here's the deal," he said. "I talk, you put in a good word. John."

Kiera gasped softly. "Dad," she said, voice catching. "You need a lawyer." That desperation had to be from shock.

He shook his head at her, reaching through the bars to touch her hand. "I'm sorry about this, honey," he said in the same kind of tone my father used on me, sorrow real while she wept. "I'm so sorry I let you down.

Still crying, she pulled her hand free of his and spun, running from the bullpen and out the door. David watched her go, Luke scowling after her like she'd been the one to disappoint him. Patterson, all right.

"Kiera had nothing to do with this," David said, and Dad nodded. That seemed to give the brawny thief the reassurance he needed. He focused on Dad who didn't say a word, all softly stoic small-town sheriff though he wasn't anymore. "Fee." Was that desperation in David's voice? "Please, this was blackmail."

"You started all of it," I said, "when you had Heather rip off the Buckleys." In case he'd forgotten.

David flinched. "I know. And I'll own up to that. But the rest was all Lester."

"Why was someone like Lester Patterson stealing from a small company for money when he was, well, a Patterson?" It didn't make any sense. They were loaded, weren't they?

"Dad was broke." Luke sagged against the bars. "Totally and utterly tapped out. And on the verge of bankruptcy."

Okay, I'd heard that rumor from Chris Nortz, but I hadn't actually believed it. Lester was a Patterson. "How did that happen?" I guess Luke wasn't the only one the family weren't willing to bail out.

"We're all waiting for the old bat to die, okay?" Luke didn't sound all that guilty over it.

"Marie Patterson," Dad said, graveled voice low and deep.

"The matriarch," Luke shrugged, face twisting like the term gave him indigestion. "She controls everything, all the family money. And not just the money, either. There's a lot of stuff around here she's got control of." He shifted uncomfortably, staring at his hands wrapped around the bars while I thought about Olivia and Geoffrey and, for a brief moment, the Reading hoard. Fleeting, that thought, as Dad spoke up. Was it just me or did he sound unsurprised by Luke's suggestion the Patterson matriarch had her hands around Reading's throat?

Something else to talk about.

"You both had reason to kill him," my father said, that smoothed out and practiced tone of voice so familiar I almost grinned.

"We didn't." David finally sounded panicked. "I swear, John. I wanted him ruined, yes. I even considered talking to the troopers myself, despite the fact I was back into the kind of business I left behind when I moved here." He was sweating, a faint film of moisture beading his broad forehead and upper lip. "I couldn't do this anymore."

"I hated my dad," Luke snarled. "But he didn't have anything I wanted. I had no reason to kill him." Though, for an instant, I knew if anything happened to the Patterson matriarch, he'd be at the top of my hit list.

Wasn't family lovely?

"And the insurance policy?" Dad met Luke's eyes finally. "You must stand to benefit from his death, don't you?"

The young man's bark of a laugh almost hurt. "As if," he said. "Go ask the old lady who benefits. And then check her hands for blood while you're at it."

CHAPTER THIRTY

Back at Petunia's, Dad and I huddled over coffee to talk out what we'd learned. Mom did her usual take care of us act while my pug lingered, looking for scraps. Dad's messy eating habits notwithstanding, I wondered how many of his cake crumbs hit the floor because he was actually clumsy or in an effort to hide the truth—he loved feeding Petunia who scrambled with her efficient and noisy snorfling to capture every last molecule.

I was distracted enough by the case to let the tiny bits of doggie contraband slide. "Is there any way the Pattersons are behind Lester's death?" I'd had my suspicions about their influence over Reading for a while now, and the fact one of their own had been dispatched without much sorrow from the family made me wonder. Yes, they'd lost another Patterson not so long ago, but it seemed more of a stink had been kicked up over the death of young Mason despite his distasteful personality than that of who had to have been his uncle.

Money was a powerful motivator for a lot of things, though, wasn't it? And from the way Dad scrunched his nose, munching cake, I knew I wasn't the only one thinking along the lines of the Patterson family guilt.

"I'd love to get a look inside their operation," Dad said, like they were some kind of criminal masterminds or something. But before I could ask him why he phrased his comment in that particular way, he had already moved on. "And I wish this case offered the kind of opportunity I could use to worm my way in. Maybe if Crew was here." A frown deepened between his eyes, his gaze skimming over me like he knew more than he was saying and didn't want to stir the pot. I inhaled to demand he tell me what he knew but Dad was already speaking again. "Doesn't matter, Fee. I don't think the Pattersons had anything to do with Lester's death."

I had to agree, despite myself. "You're thinking Heather," I said. She certainly seemed to be the best suspect thus far, and, as far as I could tell, the last person on the list with motive. "We're counting out Luke and David, right?" Dad grunted, nodded. "Though they were on the boat that night. They could be deflecting."

"Possibly," he said. "Anyone else on your list?"

I thought about it a long moment, sighed. "I know that maybe Chris and Wanda should be at the top, too," I said, "but with the footage they provided, it feels like they're trying to help, not hinder."

"Unless they're showing you what they want you to see." Dad set down his fork, sipped his coffee. "First rule of detecting, Fee, my girl. No one gets a pass until every clue is uncovered."

"Well," I said, "in that case, let's review." I held up one hand, ticking off points on my fingers. "Wanda's business is in jeopardy, but there's no solid connection to Lester that we know of, so unless we find a motive, I'm going to write her out." Dad nodded. "As for Chris, he had a serious hate on for Lester because of the cottages and their constant head butting over the lake. But is it enough to commit murder?"

Dad's turn to muse. "Chris has a temper," he said. "And from what the doc said, Lester had some mild bruising on the backs of his legs and that cord mark around his wrist. It's possible they tussled, and Lester fell, an accident. Manslaughter at the very most."

"Whoever did it had the foresight to eliminate the evidence," I said, "though not in the best location. So smart but panicked?"

Dad grinned. "Now you're talking," he said. "I'll call the forensics folks and see if there are any fingerprints on that string of lights you found. The lab tests should be back by now. But I'm guessing the only DNA and other evidence will be from Lester."

He shrugged. "Here's the scenario I'm considering. Lester and whoever it was, ultimately, got in a fight or argument or pushing match. Lester was either struck or fell overboard, taking the string of lights with him, charging the water long enough to shock his heart and electrocute him before the string shorted out."

"Killing some fish but not leaving any more trace because the power cut when the string died." I had to admit it sounded perfectly plausible. "Considering Lester's money problems, can we also posit that it was a solid motivator for his death?"

Dad stared into his cooling coffee mug. "I hate to discount anything," he said, "but yes, I'm running on that theory, too." He met my eyes, his quiet and calm, that particular look he got when he was close to solving a mystery. I knew it well, had seen it so many times when I was a kid. Admired him for it. Wondered then if I got that same look. Mind you, the times I'd actually stumbled over the truth I'd been rather distracted by near-death experiences and my own shock I'd gotten things right, so maybe not.

"So, if we're working on the money angle," I said, refusing to admit how much I loved this part (loved it!), "we're looking at Luke, David, Chris and Heather, yes?"

Dad didn't move a long moment, gaze far away though his eyes never left mine. "Hmmm," he finally said.

That didn't sound like he agreed completely. "If his son is right and he was broke, Luke's money motivation turns to killing off the old lady." Wow, Fee, that was crass. "Okay, so he's out. That leaves David, Chris and Heather."

"Possible accident," Dad said, "or murder?" He exhaled, grinned suddenly, reaching out to nab Mom and pull her close a moment. He kissed her soundly on the lips, making my mother blush and giggle, smacking his shoulder with the dishcloth she was holding.

"Johnathan Fleming," she said, a bit breathless. "What was that for?"

"We did good, girl," he said, winking at me. "With this one. Didn't we?"

Mom turned her green eyes to me, that loving mom smile making me blush in turn. "We did," she said, reaching forward to pat my hand. "Now let me go and solve this murder, you."

Dad released her after another quick kiss while my heart constricted in what I was shocked to find was jealousy. Would I ever feel that way about someone? Would I ever have the kind of love that lasted through hard times and the best of moments, have someone who would stick by me when I was a jerk and still look at me like I was the only person in the world? Seeing the way they looked into each other's eyes in that last moment before Dad let her go, how Mom leaned into him, how they seemed, for just a heartbeat, to be so much younger, as if the shine of their first love still lingered while a sunbeam emerged through the glass and washed over them gave me goosebumps. Just a coincidence, that timing.

Still, it made my heart ache I'd ever doubted my father's love for my mother and filled me with the sort of longing that woke my renewed worry about Crew.

Sigh. How could love suck so much and be so beautifully awesome at the same time?

The sun scooted back behind a cloud, the warmth of its light and the moment fading but not entirely dissipating as Dad released his hold on Mom and turned his attention back to me. The sparkle never left his eyes and I caught him glancing her way a time or two, my mother returning his attention, while we went on. Enough I actually felt myself choking up over how much they still loved one another. Not to mention the bit of embarrassed discomfort that came with the realization my parents were people, too.

Yikes, Fee. Don't go there. Just don't.

Dad twirled his coffee mug in his big hands, all business again. "I'm going to throw a wrench in the works," he said. "I wasn't sure if you knew, but I don't think you do from what you've brought up."

"That being?" Was this about Crew?

"Just rumors," he said, "but I've heard that there have been discrepancies in the accounting at the club. Enough to make me wonder if Lester was dipping."

"Doreen?" I glanced at Mom who shrugged.

"I don't know, dear," she said. "I was going to ask but John told me not to."

Hmmm. "Dad?"

"It's just a rumor," he said. "Nothing substantiated. And every time I broach it with

Doreen, she seems surprised."

She was treasurer of the club. Surely if someone was skimming, she'd know about it. "Want me to try?"

Dad shook his head. "It's probably nothing." Though, from the crease between his eyes he didn't believe it just yet. "Let me keep digging and you do you."

"Which is what, exactly?" I made a face, not sure where to go from here. "Heather won't talk to me, and David is in custody." That left Chris, I guess, though I really didn't believe he was guilty.

Mom cleared her throat before meeting my eyes. "Did you really ask Malcolm Murray for help?" She didn't seem upset, more curious, though when she glanced sideways at Dad a flicker of concern woke. She knew so much more than she was telling about Dad's history with the Irishman. I wished the two of them would just spill and get it over with. But, since I'd made that fateful phone call to Siobhan, I'd know what I needed to soon enough.

Speaking of which, now that I'd taken the step? Yeah, I wanted her to call me back yesterday.

"Let's talk to Heather together," Dad said, pushing his mug aside. "Thanks for the snack, my love." He smiled at Mom, reaching out to squeeze her hand.

She smiled back. "Have to sweeten you up somehow," she winked. Seriously. My parents.

I followed Dad into the foyer and upstairs, but when we reached Heather's door, I had a sinking feeling at the sight of one of my staff inside, changing the bed.

"She checked out," Megan/Mindy/Cindy said with her usual perky tone (okay, they were all perkyish, so the generalization fit, right?). "I think Rose took care of it."

Snarl. Didn't help Daisy's stepsister was part of the exodus, though obviously, it was a coincidence. Just rubbed me the wrong way, like everything Rose did these days.

Dad and I descended back to the front door where he paused with his hand on the knob. "I'll contact the state troopers," he said, "and get them to track her down as a person of interest. I think we have enough to make them pay attention." His big shoulders straightened, head nodding. "The evidence is certainly piling up against her."

I agreed. "Go get her, Dad," I said. "I have a business to run."

He laughed, hugged me quickly before pausing. "Fee." Dad's hesitation and swift mood reversal made me tense. "I think Crew's gotten himself into trouble he might not be able to get out of."

I swallowed, nodded. "Do you think he's coming back?"

Dad didn't comment which only made things worse. "Try not to worry about it," he said as if he hadn't just given me fodder for picking over in the dark of a sleepless night. And had the nerve to leave me there, in the foyer, one mystery maybe solved but the one close to my heart still burning there.

CHAPTER THIRTY-ONE

An early evening run seemed just the thing to clear my head and give me perspective. Except that, of course, running by the lake made me think about the case and then about Crew and then about the mess and... yeah. Not so clear, right? And perspective? Snort. As if.

I jammed the earbuds deeper and cranked the sound, hoping the pounding beat of the music would shut up my endlessly chattering mind. I'd considered taking up meditation, except every time I tried, I quit after about ten minutes of revolving information that wouldn't stop. Last time I made the effort I somehow went from a recipe for pie dough to what the impact would be on our planet if the crazy scientists who wanted to recreate mammoths actually succeeded to the fact that the baseboards in my apartment really needed a good dusting.

Meh. I guess I just wasn't Zen. Go figure.

Running did help sometimes, but tonight it just added to my frustration. Except, of course, as I rounded the corner near the curve back toward the parking lot, the answers I needed for one mystery fell in my lap, if not the other. There, standing knee-deep in the water of the lake, still dressed in a skirt suit not at all fitting for a swim, stood Heather Parborough.

I stumbled to a halt, pulling the cords of my headphones so the buds bounced against my chest and gaped at her while she sobbed into her shaking hands, her long, dark hair hanging over her shoulder, masking her expression. She didn't seem to know or care I was there, the heartbreaking sound of her crying tearing at me as I finally pushed my feet to approach her, slipping into the water without thought for my sneakers and socks, approaching slowly with dread sitting like a giant fist in my stomach. Because there was only one reason she'd be standing in the water like this.

Heather had a plan to make sure she didn't have to face the music.

She turned toward me, startled when she realized she wasn't alone any longer, and gaped at me, eyes huge, tears real enough, though was she crying because she was afraid or because she was guilty? Or both?

"I figured you'd have left town by now," I said, going for soft but factual.

She shrugged, looked away, staring at the water with hunger. "I have nowhere to go," she whispered, voice hoarse.

That sounded about as final as I expected. "Please, Heather," I said, one hand gentle on her elbow. "Just come back to shore with me. Let's talk about it, okay?" Could I stop her if she decided to kill herself? I formulated a tackle plan to try to overwhelm her physically, not sure if I could manage it if she was dedicated to ending it all, when she turned to me like she finally realized what she was doing.

"Yes, of course," she said, sounding dazed, confused. "I'm trying to pull myself together before I turn myself in."

Sure, she was. I helped her, hand still on her elbow, to the shore, seated her on the bench near the path's exit, shaking so much when I released her, I had to clench my hands in my lap to keep from vibrating. All while my mind accepted she had killed Lester. "I can call my dad," I said. "He'll treat you fairly, take you to the troopers instead of local law enforcement."

Heather fished a tissue out of her bag, shredded the edge with her manicured fingertips, her pretty face blotchy with shed tears and stress. "It doesn't matter," she said, that kind of dull apathy that comes from the depths of surrender hitting me deep inside and making me want to protect her all over again. Sheesh, she was a murderer, and I was feeling sorry for her? "I just wanted a few minutes to get my tears out before I face the music."

Because she hadn't just been contemplating suicide. Whatever she needed to say out loud to make herself feel better. I wasn't about to draw attention to her close call. "Did you want to talk about it?" I did. Forgive me for being ridiculously nosy and awful and an utterly heartless monster considering the fact she'd been this close to drowning her sorrows quite literally, but I really, really did. "Might help you sort things out in your mind." Fee, you liar. This had nothing to do with her state of mind and everything with my own busybody nature.

Still, Heather seemed to buy it, blowing her nose and nodding. "Thanks," she said. "I think I would."

Was it wrong I felt a lifting of my own mood, anticipation burning a hot, bright light in my gut. Yes, yes, it was.

"I don't know how everything went so wrong." Heather met my eyes, hers huge but full of acceptance. "How my life turned into this disaster. But I'm responsible for it, as much as I want to blame Lester."

"You were stealing from your company for him." At least, according to her boss.

Heather gulped, nodded. "It was innocent at first," she said. "I never meant for it to go so far. I believed him when he said he wanted me." Oh, yikes. "That he was leaving his fourth wife for me." Le sigh. When would men stop using that line? When women stopped buying it, I guess. "The affair was an accident, I swear. But I fell in love with Lester. And that was the beginning of the end."

She sighed deeply, sagging into the edge of the bench, staring past me toward the water softly lapping the shore. A speedboat zipped past, sending ripples outward, increasing the slap of waves while Heather went on.

"I tried to break it off with him last year," she said, grim now. "When I realized he wasn't going to leave her after all. And when I found out he was broke." So maybe she wasn't so innocent. "Don't get me wrong, I wasn't after his money. Not at first." She shrugged then like it didn't matter. "I just didn't want to waste more time on someone who obviously didn't love me." Heather's face tightened, her lips a thin line. "I should have realized then how much trouble I was in," she said. "That I'd really stepped in it this time." Bitterness now, beneath the acceptance. "Story of my life."

"You have a history of bad choices," I said, winced inwardly. Is that what I called killing someone now?

Heather didn't take it personally. "Do I," she said. "And I come by it honestly." Right. David mentioned her father, hadn't he? That Heather's dad was one of his old cronies? "But that was behind me. My record was sealed, I paid my dues, I moved on. I thought I had."

"He *was* blackmailing you." That gave me even more assurance she'd murdered Lester. Money and a pressure cooker that threatened the life she'd built? Considering she had a history with manslaughter, it wasn't much of a reach, especially if Dad's assessment was accurate and Lester's death was an accident.

Heather didn't seem to realize the connections I was making in my head. "He used my past against me," she said. "My father's old mistakes. He threatened to tell my boss. And not just about me."

Right, didn't her father work for the same company? "He was going to get your father fired."

She gasped a sob but stilled. "He was going to get my father arrested." Yikes. How? "I didn't care about me, but Lester had information, thanks to David." She sounded bitter about that. "I went to Lester for help, hoping he could convince David to stop blackmailing me. Back when I trusted him, when I believed he might actually love me. Instead, he turned it against me, took the proof Dad used to be a thief and threatened both of us." Anger, so much anger, and desperate horror at what her life had become. "I know I shouldn't defend my father, but he turned his life around, Fiona. He hasn't stolen anything in over a decade." My sense of justice wasn't exactly feeling sympathy for her father, but I did for her, so I kept quiet. Heather seemed to struggle with guilt far more than anything in that moment. "Dad wouldn't just lose his job. He'd go to prison." She sagged against me. "I needed to make sure Dad was safe." Heather leaned forward suddenly, grabbing my hand. I almost cringed at the wet tissue she still clutched but chose to ignore the feeling of it against my skin as she rushed on. "I knew the boats I'd switched out, which of Lester's friends got their deals. I was going to take all the information to the state troopers. In fact, I had a meeting scheduled with your Sheriff Turner to hand over the evidence I had against Lester, but he hasn't come back. And then Lester died." More tears, but silent ones. "I love my father. And I'd do anything for him." Didn't negate any of the suspicions against her, did it? Well, the way I thought about my own father? Yeah, I got her internal battle with self-loathing. "If Lester hadn't threatened Dad, I would have just taken the heat, gone to prison myself for what I did." She was sweating, like she was trying to convince herself. And yet, she hadn't accepted her wrongdoing at any point, had she? Instead, she'd dug herself deeper, to the point she planned to end it all rather than face what she'd done. But it wasn't up to me to make that judgment. I stayed quiet and let her go on. "When he used Dad against me this time, when I refused this last deal, I had to do something."

"You realize that makes you sound guilty." Okay, I hadn't meant to say that out loud. She had to know I knew she'd done it.

Heather grimaced. "I know," she said. "But I didn't kill him. I swear."

I wasn't expecting her to deny it, actually, and found myself floored. "I thought you were going to tell me the truth."

There was enough honest agony on her face I realized she was. "Yes, I was on the boat that night," she said, stumbling over her words as she rushed them past her lips. "He was heartless, laughing at me. Told me he never cared about me, that it was all about the money. We fought and he told me to leave. So, I did." Her eyes narrowed into slits, anger showing all over again. "That was the last straw. I was going to tell Sheriff Turner and the troopers everything." Bitterness and regret? Looked like it to me. She hesitated then, anger ebbing. "I stopped long enough to go looking for the proof he had against my dad," she said, "but I came up empty-handed."

"Is that why you didn't go to the police?"

"How could I?" She flinched. "With Lester dead hopefully, the evidence against my father was lost for good. And the con was over. I would go to jail, not my dad." Unless she ended her own life first.

Still motive, except Lester's death put her directly in the line of fire and without having the evidence against her father in her possession, she'd failed to protect the person she'd gone through this for. I couldn't help but believe her claim. Maybe because she was being so candid about everything else?

Heather's misery was as clear as the blue sky overhead. "I know it sounds bad," she said. "And you have no reason to believe me. But I didn't kill Lester. I just wanted to protect my father."

"Heather," I said, "what happened when you were a teenager? Did you kill that girl?"

She met my eyes with her own full of a mix of so many emotions I couldn't untangle them as her lips parted and she spoke. "Yes," she said.

CHAPTER THIRTY-TWO

No time to judge. Heather wasn't done. Despite my visceral reaction, the gut punch of understanding Heather just might be a murderer after all, she sobbed softly before going on.

"I swear it was an accident," she said, "but I might as well have killed that girl like the courts said I did." She struggled to swallow, her face red, neck and chest mottled from the overabundance of her emotional turmoil. "My friend and I were drinking like we did a lot when we were teens. We were jumping off a bridge, you know? Just a stupid thing to do, especially considering how drunk we were." She shrugged, sniffled, wiped at her nose. "Fourteen is a stupid age sometimes."

I thought back to my teens and winced. I hadn't

drank, per se, if only because my father was sheriff and my mother the principal, but I knew lots of people who had and I'd gotten into trouble a time or two over lack of forethought and sheer idiocy, so I got it.

"Madeline's sister showed up," Heather said, shaking her head as she stared down at her hands, clenched into fists in her lap. "She was young, just twelve. She shouldn't have been there, but Maddy's parents sent her to find her sister, bring her home. We were having so much fun, I didn't want her to go. So, I convinced Bridget to jump into the water."

And now I knew where the guilt came from, where the horror Heather wore and the surety she'd killed someone found purchase inside her. "She drowned?"

"The local cops said I pushed her." She shook like she believed it. "I don't remember pushing her, but some of the other kids there said I did, and I was drunk, so I must have." Heather met my gaze with hers full of agony. "I must have, right?"

I couldn't answer that question. "They tried to try you for murder?"

She shook her head, misery all the more apparent as if she thought she deserved such a charge. "No, they finally ruled it manslaughter. That meant I was tried as a juvenile and my file was sealed when I turned eighteen. But I have to live with it, Fee. "

That she did. I had one last question for her. "Do you know anything about the money missing from the club's accounts?" If Lester was behind the loss of funds, Heather might know about it.

She shook her head, but her brow was creased like she wished she could give me more. "I've heard the rumors," she said. "I wouldn't have put anything past Lester. The man was scum."

She wasn't really making a case for her own innocence at the moment. "You might want to tone down that attitude when the police question you."

She gulped, stiffened. "Right." Her hand found mine, squeezed. "You believe me?"

Maybe I shouldn't have, but I did, despite the evidence. Time to keep digging while she was willing to talk. "You knew Lester was having money problems?"

An eager nod this time. "He was broke," she said. "The man was a total con artist who had everyone fooled. But he complained constantly about the matriarch of the Patterson family, that she'd cut him off years ago."

With no idea why, I couldn't chase down that line of questioning just yet. "Heather," I said, sighing heavily and leaning back against the bench, "you realize you're suspect number one, right?" She flinched but didn't argue. "There's video footage of you boarding Lester's boat just before time of death, but none of you leaving." Yes, I was telling her what was stacked against her. Why? Maybe I really did believe her. "He was electrocuted with a string of decorative lights, pushed overboard." Like the little girl, Bridget had been pushed? Heather's claim the child's death was an accident could easily apply to

Lester as well if she'd shoved him into the water with the string in his hands. Was it manslaughter or murder or just a bad situation turned horrifying? "No matter what happened, Heather, you have to face the truth."

She hesitated, stared at the water. "Why did you stop me?"

I choked on the hurt in her voice, the girl inside her—fourteen and in agony over the guilt of the death on her hands as palpable as the summer air—shining through. "You deserve the chance to forgive yourself," I said. "And dying won't change anything."

Heather was mute a long moment, lower lip quivering, eyes huge and staring until she finally shook, just a little bit, turning toward me one last time. "I'll turn myself in," she said, soft and low. "To your father. If you'll come with me." Her lips tightened to a line. "But I won't be railroaded this time, Fiona. I didn't kill Lester. I didn't push him, I had nothing to do with his death. I've lived with the past far too long to let that happen to me again. To layer more guilt on top of what I already endure every single day."

And despite the evidence against her, I believed her in that moment. Had to. Her emotions were too raw and her truth too apparent for me to accept anything else.

Which left me with the solid fact as I stood and helped her to her feet, walking her back toward the parking lot and my car, that I still had no idea who'd killed Lester Patterson.

CHAPTER THIRTY-THREE

I'd just barely walked through the doors to Dad's office, Heather at my side, ready to hand her over to him and the troopers, when I realized my father wasn't alone. The startled and then hungry look on Robert's face, the sudden tense silence in the room, told me I'd just miscalculated in the kind of massive way that might get the woman beside me incarcerated for something she didn't do. Why I felt so protective of her I had no idea, but I found myself stepping in front of her while Robert lurched toward me, hand reaching for his cuffs at his belt, my father following at a slower pace. The tight, unhappy expression Dad wore told me there was nothing I could do, though it didn't stop me from standing my ground as my cousin came to a huffing halt in front of me.

I glared up at him, positive my disgust showed clearly on my face, while Robert's teeth squeaked from grinding so hard.

"Out of the way, Fanny," he snarled. "I'm arresting Ms. Parborough for the murder of Lester Patterson." His body swayed, like he intended to shove me aside if I didn't move. All the more reason to hold my position. Lucky for him he held himself back while my temper crackled.

"Heather," I said over my shoulder, ignoring my cousin's demand, "don't say a word without a lawyer, you understand?" She grunted faintly, her expression lost to me because my eyes never left Robert's. "Not a word."

I caught Dad's deepening frown over my cousin's shoulder as I finally stepped deliberately aside, hugging myself while Robert roughly cuffed the woman I'd brought in. He had to be a jerk about it, didn't he? He actually looked like he took pleasure from tightening the metal around her wrists. She met my eyes as he turned her toward the door, reading off her rights in a dull voice that barely hid the glee behind the small-minded man he really was.

"Not a word," I repeated. She nodded and didn't resist when he shoved her, hauling her to a stop as he stared down at me for a long, angry moment.

"Careful," he whispered, breath bad enough it could kill a bird in flight, "I'll have you dragged in for impeding a murder investigation."

"Considering I brought you your suspect," I

snarled back, "you can suck it."

Robert twitched, eyes tight, but he didn't comment again, hustling Heather out of Dad's office, the door swinging shut behind him. It was quiet a long moment before my father spoke up, so much so I shivered when he broke the silence.

"You think she's innocent." Not a question.

I turned to Dad. "From the look on your face," I said, taking in his continuing unhappiness, "so do you."

Dad tossed his hands, sighed. "I have no idea, Fee," he said. "But it seems a bit too much like someone made sure Heather's arrival on Lester's boat was a slam dunk. Not to mention all the paperwork with her name on it. David's. But the fact the video cut out right after that makes me wonder what we missed."

Tell me about it. I dialed Crew's number while Dad watched, leaving him a detailed message with everything I'd uncovered. Dad tossed in a few tidbit reminders which I added before I sighed into the phone. "I have no idea if you're even getting these messages," I said. "If you are, I'm going to kick your ass when I see you, Crew. If not..." I didn't want to think about if not. "Just call me. I'm going to keep this up until you do." I hung up then, meeting Dad's troubled eyes, but didn't get to say a word about it. The door to the office banged open, Olivia Walker's angry entrance enough to change the subject.

Or not. "Where is he?" Yeah, not. She glared back and forth between me and Dad, hand shaking as she waved them around like we were hiding Crew from her. "The damned fool is going to lose his job whether we like it or not. If Robert's arrest sticks, Crew is out and there's nothing I can do about it."

Never mind Heather's innocence, I guess. Sigh. Collateral damage meant little to Olivia when she was on a rampage. "I think he's working with the FBI on something." I met Dad's gaze again, caught his subtle agreement. "I have no idea."

Dad opened his mouth to either add fuel to the fire or clarity, only to stay silent when his door opened one more time. Geoffrey strolled through, grinning at me, at Dad, at Olivia, acting like he'd just won the mayoral race by a landslide.

"Well done, you two," he said. "Our acting sheriff is booking our suspect now." Like the councilman had anything to do with Heather's arrest. "I must say, this is turning out better than I expected. Who needs an outsider like Crew Turner when we have the Flemings to save the day?" He made that sound like it was a good thing. Instead, it felt like a knife turning in my stomach. Hadn't Crew told me all along he'd felt like he was being punished for not being my dad? Pressured to include me and my father in his investigations? Bullied, even, into doubting himself in favor of us and, heaven forbid the ridiculousness of the idea, Robert because he was related?

I'd never seen the truth so clearly as I did in that moment, and it made me sick. "You have no idea what you're talking about," I snapped. "None.

Robert is an incompetent ass and you're an idiot if you think otherwise."

Geoffrey's gaze narrowed, smile more shark-like than ever. "I'm fully aware of his failings," he said. "That's why I want you to run for sheriff."

Okay, so that was out in the open now. "You're nuts," I said.

"Am I." Geoffrey seemed to have forgotten Dad and Olivia were there, focusing on me like I was prey. "Perhaps then we should offer the job to Robert permanently?"

"Enough," Dad said in that tone of voice that wasn't angry, wasn't really anything, but held the sort of weight that made people pay attention.

Geoffrey's gaze snapped to my father and for an instant he seemed furious, darkness showing behind the veneer of civility. Worse than Robert's because it had intelligence in it. Though maybe that wasn't accurate. What was more dangerous, an evil man who knew what he was doing or one that had no freaking clue?

I hoped I'd never get the chance to find out. But it stirred a question in me, sure did. "Why did the Patterson matriarch cut off Lester, Geoffrey?"

He looked surprised like he wasn't expecting me to bring that up. "I have no idea what you're talking about," he said.

"And yet," Dad interrupted in his drawling sheriff's voice that demanded attention and got it, "you can't deny it's a possible motive for his death. If he was stirring up trouble for the family...?"

Was Dad going where I thought he was going with his almost accusation? From the fury on Geoffrey's face, he sure was. And I had no qualms joining him in the fray.

"Tell us, Geoffrey," I said in my sweetest tone of voice, "where were you the night Lester was murdered?"

Dad said he had an alibi, but I wasn't above petty smackdowns if I had the chance to deliver. Oh yes, I did go there, asshat. Suck it up.

Geoffrey didn't comment. In fact, he didn't react at all, telling in my opinion. Instead, he spun on his heel and marched out while Dad glared after him, eyes tight around the edges, my own intuition whispering, whispering.

Olivia broke the silence, subdued tone making me shiver. "Did you just accuse him of murder?"

I winked, not sure why I suddenly felt so light and almost giddy. "Someone had to."

Dad laughed. "He has an alibi and neither of us really believe Geoffrey would get his hands dirty," he said, closing the gap between us, big hand falling on my shoulder, "but it raises some interesting questions." About the Patterson family? Dad went on, fingers tightening as if to keep me from asking any of my own despite his statement. "We're trying to get to Crew," he said to the mayor who huffed softly before nodding, looking away with her lower lip between her teeth. "No one wants him back here more than we do." He could say that again.

"If Crew is fired over this," Olivia said, still in

that same soft voice, "and Robert takes his place, I'm done as mayor. I need his ass back here, now." She didn't sound so much like the powerful leader whose persona she'd groomed over the years. Instead, she seemed more fragile than ever. But the very fact she clung to her convictions? I'd give her the benefit of the doubt.

"There's always Dad," I said, looking up at him. "You could take the job again."

But he was shaking his head despite Olivia's sudden flare of hope. "Bad idea," he said. "There are some things coming to light in the next little bit that won't do you any favors if I'm your only backup." What did that mean? I stared at him with fear in my heart while he hugged me against him. "Malcolm Murray is seeing to that." This was about Siobhan? Damn it, what the hell was Dad hiding? "You need someone bulletproof, Olivia. You need Crew Turner."

CHAPTER THIRTY-FOUR

I stepped outside, not wanting to let Dad hear me yell at Crew through yet another futile message. As I stomped to the edge of the sidewalk for the illusion of privacy, however, I had an epiphany. Instead of Crew, I made a different call, internet searching the switchboard for the local FBI office directly and asking, with bated breath, to be connected to Special Agent Elizabeth Michaud. Because Fiona Fleming of Fleming Investigations had urgent business with her.

What do you know? It actually worked. Three rings later and the familiar woman's voice answered. "Michaud."

"This is Fiona Fleming," I said, knowing my words were rushed and running together, practically hearing her tension from the other end of the line.

"Please, don't hang up."

She exhaled softly into the receiver before speaking. "What can I do for you, Miss Fleming?" Was that irritated frustration in her voice? She did not get to be that way with me, nope, uh-uh. Still, I held my temper as best I could as I spoke again.

"Whether you like it or not," I said, "Crew has a responsibility to the town he's been serving as sheriff the last few years." She didn't protest so I went on. "In his absence, a murder investigation is being botched and he's taking a personal and professional hit for not being here to deal with it. Do you understand what I'm staying, Agent Michaud? Your former partner's reputation is being shredded because you refuse to let me talk to him." Yup, I was positive this was all her fault.

She didn't say much to change my mind about that belief, either. If anything, when she finally spoke, her voice low and angry, she gave me the proof I needed she was behind Crew's absence and continuing silence. "While a murder in your little town might feel like the end of the world, Miss Fleming," she said, "Crew understands that his present circumstances carry more weight in the grand scheme."

"He's working a case with you," I said, not a question. "He's not FBI anymore, Agent Michaud."

"Be that as it may," she clipped back, crisp and attempting professional while coming across as bitchy, "his current activities take precedence. Listen," she sighed then as if she knew I wasn't going to let this go, "I realize you two have some kind of personal attachment going on." Was she listening to my messages? The ones I'd been leaving him on his phone? Since she'd answered his cell previously, I could only imagine that was true. Did she think I was some kind of crazy girlfriend who was overacting? Who cared. "That's nice for you." Right, she sounded like that filled her with sunshine and unicorn farts. "But until this situation is resolved, Crew isn't available. And you can take that up with the deputy director of the FBI if you have a problem with it."

"Does he even know his job is at stake?" She didn't answer my question. In other words, nope.

"If I were at liberty to tell you anything, I would have by now." She sounded contrite, to a point. "I can say this has to do with an old case, one Crew felt responsible for." She exhaled heavily. "You might want to blame me for this, Miss Fleming, but it was Crew's case in the first place and he's the one who wanted to see it through when he found out what he'd built was falling apart." Now she sounded worried. "I had to tell him we lost our main witness. He'd never forgive me if I hadn't."

I had a feeling she wasn't supposed to tell me that. But it explained why Crew lit out on Jill in such a hurry and his odd message left on my phone. Blaming Agent Michaud wasn't maybe the right place to settle my aggression. Still, she was all I had. "So, Crew agreed to help you, what? Find another witness? Uncover more evidence?"

Her silence was getting irritating.

"Is he undercover?" At least tell me that much. "Is that why I can't talk to him?" Undercover would explain a lot and notch up my nervousness for him about a hundred times. How safe was he?

Her hesitation filled in the blanks. "I can't discuss the details," she said. "But since the people he'd been working with originally trusted him..." She sounded like she'd gone too far again and finally stopped. "He *had* to go silent. Can you accept that, at least?"

Accept? Fine. Live with it? We'd see.

"You realize he's going to be furious with you when he finds out his new life is falling apart without him here to do something about it." Again, no comment, and a weak argument. This was Crew's choice. If he made it back to Reading with his job and life intact, I was going to kill him myself.

Instead, sounding even testier than before, she tsked. "You do realize you're not helping speed matters by giving me grief, right? Or leaving constant messages for him? You think he'd be out here working this case if he didn't feel responsible?" Yeah, she was turning things back on me, and maybe that was fair, but I wasn't in the mood for her attitude. Apparently, she wasn't in the mood for mine because she ended abruptly. "Was there something else, Miss Fleming? I have work to do. And if you want Crew to stay safe while he's under my care, you might want to stop pestering me."

I could have made a choice comment or two, swore or even told her where she could shove her self-righteousness in the most uncomfortable way possible. Instead, with my teeth firmly clamped shut, I hung up on her. Ever notice how hanging up on someone via cell phone is intensely lacking in satisfaction compared to the hearty slamming that can come from the thud of a landline receiver?

Yeah, me either.

I spun on my heel, heading back inside and to Dad to confirm what we'd both really known all along and almost ran into Jill. She caught me by my upper arms, steadying me and shaking her head at the sight of me. The expression on my face must have told her volumes.

"Crew?" She seemed nervous. No, worried. So, I wasn't the only one? Good.

"His former partner," I snarled. "Come on in, I can tell you what I don't know when I fill Dad in."

She followed without comment, making me think she'd been heading our way initially. And when Dad nodded a greeting to her, I realized I was right in that regard, considering he didn't seem surprised to see her.

I told them both about Agent Michaud and Crew's confirmed missing status thanks to the meddling of the FBI. I was half tempted to contact the deputy director as Crew's old partner had challenged me to do, but I slumped into a chair instead opposite Dad while he took a seat behind his desk, Jill joining us in the same rather defeated posture of a person who'd about reached the end of her rope.

Dad did the honors for the rest of it, filling Jill in on what I'd learned about Heather while the deputy grumbled wordlessly about the details, shaking her head over and over again, blonde ponytail bouncing across her wide shoulders.

"It looks bad," she finally said when Dad finished up. "Considering the footage and how desperate Heather was to protect her father."

"I don't think she did it," I said, though there wasn't much conviction in my tone, I admit. When I heard Dad roll out the evidence against Heather in such a methodical manner, things were rather grim. And without another suspect with so much riding against him or her, there wasn't much I could do to help the young woman, either.

"Thanks for filling me in," Jill said, her frustration bubbling clearly beneath the surface. Her right knee began to bounce, hands clenched in her lap. "I'm getting more from you than my supposed superior right now."

"Robert's not sharing?" Dad's frown deepened. "I guess I shouldn't be surprised."

Jill shrugged, looked away, jaw so tight her lips were white. "This is a mess, John," she said. "Biggest one yet. And without Crew here to sort it and keep Robert in line, I'm worried. Really worried." She met my eyes, hers flat and empty. "If he takes over for the sheriff, I won't be staying on as deputy."

Well, crap. That wasn't news I wanted to hear, though hardly surprising. I wouldn't want to work for Robert, either.

"Let's make sure it doesn't come to that," Dad said, sounding soothing enough but as grim as I'd ever seen him. Was he considering taking Olivia up on her offer to get him back in the sheriff's seat? Maybe. Part of me wished he would, though I knew if Dad said yes, Crew's job would be gone for sure. And I wasn't ready to give up on the guy I'd fallen for just yet.

CHAPTER THIRTY-FIVE

I went home, feeling defeated and out of sorts, leaving Dad at his office and Jill, shoulders bowed, expression darkly worried, heading back to work. I'd hate to lose her, not just as a deputy. I liked her personally, too. Reading would be a smaller, sadder place without Jill in it, certainly on the path to downfall without at least one person in the office to keep Robert in check. Mind you, there was Toby, but I still had my suspicions about the small desk at the front of Dad's new office and the sight of a casually draped fleece vest across the back of the chair behind it. Yeah, screamed defection.

I checked my phone on the way home, stopped at the crosswalk in shock when I realized I had a missed call. A foreign number, one I recognized from earlier, a number Malcolm Murray dialed. But there was no message and when I shakily redialed the number, no one answered. Leaving Siobhan Doyle out of the equation for now, I hung up and tucked my phone away, reactivating the sound on my ringer, though I wasn't so sure I wanted to talk to her right now.

Speaking of difficult conversations, I'd barely set foot in the foyer of Petunia's when I heard Mom's voice calling out to me. I followed her beckoning volume and pushed through the swinging door to the kitchen, finding her sitting at the counter with Daisy beside her, the two huddled over a pot of tea and a tray of fresh-baked cookies.

Relief flooded me at the sight of Daisy's familiar smile, her little wave of welcome. The strained feeling between us seemed to have vanished and the carefree bestie I loved was back in full force. What happened to walking out with Rose? I had to believe her tantrum was just that. She hadn't acted on it, after all. And I was willing to forgive her anything right now. I joined them, hugging her quickly around the shoulders, maybe a bit harder than I'd intended, but her own hands clutched at me a moment like she knew how I felt, the silent conversation of our body language enough to tell me she was as sorry as I was we'd let anything come between us.

Never again.

Famous last words, right?

"We need to talk, ladies." Mom's no-nonsense tone made me feel like I was sixteen again and in a heap of trouble for acting out. Daisy gulped and nodded, all focus on my mother while one of her slim, strong hands held mine like she needed the lifeline. Mom looked back and forth between us, green eyes taking our measure before she leaned forward and patted our joined hands with hers. "This partnership is young, fresh, and we have kinks to hammer out. But we're all in this together. And I want to be sure we're on the same page moving forward."

"Me, too," I said while Daisy nodded with excessive enthusiasm.

"Excellent." Mom whipped out a sheet of paper she'd hidden in the pocket of her apron, smoothing it out in front of her. It was covered in the neat, perfect cursive of her handwriting and looked about as official as any court document in that moment. Gratitude for Mom's efficiency made me grin a crooked smile while she beamed at us and spoke again. "First things first. We rushed forward into this partnership without defining our needs in our roles." She pointed at me. "Yes, we know Fee is in charge of the 'bed' aspect, in the general running of things. And I'm in charge of the 'breakfast' side of the equation." She used air quotes. So adorable. "Miss Daisy, you're our special events and staff coordination section." My best friend nodded again. "But what does that mean, exactly? We've all been crossing paths and bumping into each other as we do." My mother turned to me. "You've been poking your nose into Daisy's work, Fee, and the kitchen. And I've been directing the staff lately." She turned to Daisy again. "As for you, I've noticed you've been taking on a lot of Fee's check-ins and responsibilities that might be taking away from your ability to do your usual job." I did my best not to feel stung at Mom's almost accusation I was slacking. Because I knew exactly where this conversation was heading and why she was addressing things this way. Classic Lucy Fleming. Show a united front as a group while sliding in an option to fix things and, when the time was right, offer up a solution to a problem that the person being pandered to was causing. Namely, Daisy's attachment to Rose.

Brilliant.

"I don't mind," Daisy started saying, but I shook my head, squeezed her hand.

"Mom's right," I said. "You're not our catch-all for everything that needs to be done." And she wasn't, either. I really *was* slacking. Whoops. Murder investigations did that to me. "I don't think there's anything wrong with backing each other up," I nodded to Mom, "but clearly defined responsibilities so we know where we're crossing lines and how to help if one or the other of us feels overwhelmed? That's a great idea, Mom."

Daisy looked thoughtful then perked. "Lucy, you're so smart," she said, right on the edge of a trademark giggle that made me grin.

I am positive things would have been smoothed over, as polished as a freshly washed wineglass, as shiny as a newly buffed teapot. Except, of course, for the wild card who had become such a thorn in my side I had to wonder if she was actually designing her interruptions to create chaos.

This time, when Rose spoke up, startling the three of us, turning us toward the kitchen door where she stood, my immediate reaction was one of utter disgust. Partly tied to the fact Robert hovered at her side, glaring at me, mustache wriggling like an unhappy caterpillar attempting to escape.

"Maybe if you actually focused on your clients instead of each other," she said, whining tone so biting I felt my fingers crush Daisy's for a moment. She meeped and jerked her hand from mine, looking up at me with hurt in her gray eyes while her stepsister went on. "We've been waiting for service for ages."

Right, because I'd only been back here, like, a minute. Snarl. Daisy leaped to her feet, flushing as she rushed forward, the moment between us broken. "The staff should be out there," she said, brushing past Rose and Robert on her way to the dining room. I let her go, crossing my arms over my chest. I'd deal with Daisy later. Right now, the pair of annoyances turning into massive pains in my behind standing in my kitchen? Yeah, they could just take a flying leap into the nearest active volcano.

But before I could cleverly comment on Rose's interference, Robert spoke up.

"Looks like someone should be spending more time at home," he said, "worrying about her own business. And leave the police work to those of us who actually know how to do the job." He sniffed, thumbs hooked in his belt, while Rose looked up at him with adoration.

"You're such a great sheriff, Robbiekins," she said.

Ack. Barf. What? "You'd still be sitting on your hands if I hadn't brought Heather in," I snapped.

His furious eyes locked on me while Rose's disdain made a dent in my already fraying temper. "Your bumbling has made my job all the harder," he shot back. "I had Heather in my sights from the moment I started the investigation. If it wasn't for you poking your nose in, I would have arrested her days ago."

Whatever, creep. "Because of the video footage?" Yikes, I couldn't help myself, could I?

Robert's irritating smugness told me he thought he knew something I didn't. "That circumstantial evidence?" He snorted while Rose preened. "Maybe if you were trained to investigate crime, you'd have found what I did. That Heather was embezzling money from the yacht club coffers and making it look like Lester did it."

I wanted to shake him. "Says who?"

"I've seen the paperwork." He looked away, trying to sound blasé and in control but coming off as arrogantly ignorant. Typical Robert. "Like I owe you an explanation of any kind. But let this be a lesson to you, Fiona Fleming." He jabbed a finger at me. "A little knowledge is dangerous. You run off half-cocked without all the facts and that puts innocent people in danger or under suspicion. If our previous sheriff hadn't been screwing you, you'd be in jail for impeding an investigation. Something I've been seriously considering."

I didn't get to comment. Mom took a firm step forward and spoke up. "You watch your mouth, Robert Carlisle," she snapped. "How dare you malign my daughter? You want to keep that job you're playing at for the time being? You'll show respect, young man."

He actually backed down, though not surprising. Robert was, at heart, a coward. And Mom? Mom had been bossing him around since he was a kid. Still, there was enough defiance in his face, in his posture and in the way Rose paid him attention, I knew courage might find its way into his heart at the least opportune moment. And bravery didn't mean class or good nature, unfortunately. Someone like Robert? If he ever found his spine we'd be in for a whole world of trouble.

"Tell Uncle John I already fetched the treasury paperwork," Robert said, at least using the title Dad was owed. "Lester was the victim here, and Heather the practiced criminal siphoning money and pretending he was blackmailing her." What exactly did the paperwork he mentioned show that he came to that conclusion? I needed to get my hands on it. "Now, I'm officially telling you to back off and that your interference from now on will be met with police retaliation. Are we clear, Fanny?"

There wasn't much I could say to that. All I could do was stand there and fume as Robert left, Rose simpering on his arm while Mom shook her head next to me, looking worried enough I knew I was in trouble.

But it wasn't me my mother was anxious about, apparently. "Poor Doreen," she said. "She must be horrified."

Would have been nice to ask her. Except I'd rather not go to jail, thanks.

Damn, this was turning into one of those days.

CHAPTER THIRTY-SIX

With my chance to make up with Daisy lost, I retreated to my apartment to (sulk) collect myself and (complain) talk over my options with Petunia. The pug, naturally, had very little to say, head tilting comically from side to side as my impassioned pleas for assistance fell on doggy ears either too sensitive to comprehend my patheticness or brilliant to tell me I already knew what I should be doing about Daisy, about Crew, about everything. Starting with dropping the poor Fiona act and doing my best not to worry about things that I couldn't change.

Hush, pug. Way to be smarter than me.

My pacing set Petunia off like my chatter didn't, her soft whining and yawning meows reminiscent more of a cat's protest than a dog's proof of her agitation. I hated upsetting the dear girl, but honestly, I didn't want to be the only one.

"Heather is innocent," I told the tongue-lolling canine as she swiped at her nose fold with one fawn paw before her small, black ears perked in response to my assurance. "I think." Damn it, waffling wasn't helping. "I know, I know," I said, shaking my head at the pug who grunted at me in her oh-so-helpful manner. "The evidence is certainly against her." Was Heather really innocent or was I just being stubborn because I couldn't stand the fact maybe Robert was right, and I was wrong? That thought brought me to a jarring, uncomfortable halt while I swallowed my pride and did a deep breath, shake yourself, put the accused first attempt at collecting myself before I scowled at Petunia like this was her fault. "No way," I shot at her while she whined, her ears dropping, whites of her eyes showing. Whoops, I guess I was angrier about this whole thing than I thought. Guilt over taking it out on my pug sent me to her, crouching to scratch those soft ears. She immediately perked and panted her joy at the attention, groaning in pleasure while she leaned into my hand. "Robert's wrong," I whispered to the silly creature, knowing I was being about as silly, so it was the pot calling the kettle out. "Still." What Robert said about the boat rep stealing from the yacht club just didn't sit right. It made more sense that Lester himself was stealing from the fund, didn't it? So why was Robert determined to pin that on Heather? "I need to see that paperwork, Petunia." Now in my nasty cousin's possession, there wasn't much chance of that happening. Yeah, about an icicle's chance in the bowels of an active volcano.

I hated that my mind immediately betrayed me, carrying my need to talk this out not to my father but the handsome, blue-eyed and dark-haired sheriff I was missing so much these days. No way Crew would be railroading Heather, not without listening to me first. But my option to discuss this with him was long gone, down the rabbit hole of his old case with the FBI that might or might not have him in the kind of danger I really, really didn't want to think too closely about considering the kind of stress I was already under.

On the other hand... I sighed when I sank to the tile floor and hugged my pug, exhaling my anxiety into the quiet of my apartment while the house above me came to life, guests moving around as dinner was being prepared in my mother's capable kitchen. Why was I even bothering? Dad was on the case, after all, helping Olivia. And if Crew wanted to throw his job and the life he'd built here in Reading away, that was his choice. I could sit back, do my thing, really mind my own business for once and let Robert make a fool of himself when the truth of Heather's involvement was proven false.

Then again, what if he bungled things badly enough Heather's arrest stuck and she actually went to prison for something she didn't do? A faint itch woke under my skin, a tingling sensation I couldn't scratch while I squirmed next to the pug who panted up at me with the kind of expression that told me she had utter faith in me no matter what I decided. Good thing one of us did.

I exhaled into the quiet before letting her go and standing, brushing at the seat of my jeans with both hands. "I'm a busybody, pug," I said. "But how much of my need to dig into this is just a way to distract myself from Crew?"

She yipped a soft bark at me, grinning like it was funny. I wasn't getting the joke.

Was I trying to prove something to him? That I didn't need him, could solve the case without him? Or that I had his back, that he could trust me to handle things when he wasn't here? I fought with my ego and all the reasons why I needed to step back, take a breath, mind my own business. All while the sounds of dinner unfolding above prodded me to go upstairs and at least pretend the goings-on in my bed and breakfast had my full attention.

I forced myself to get to work, head down, pug at my feet, mind racing. Normally, I took my time opening my apartment door before hurtling myself into the foyer, but my distracted thoughts betrayed me. It was only the faint gurgling squeak of the woman I ran into that kept me from impacting her in full force and I found myself clutching at Doreen's shoulders with both hands to keep her from falling sideways as I barreled into her.

"Sorry!" I let her go while she flushed bright red, her cardigan askew. When I tried to straighten her out, she shook her head, hugging her sweater to her despite its sideways tilt.

"My fault." She looked like she'd been crying again. "I came to see Lucy, but…" She glanced over her shoulder at the line of guests waiting for the staff to seat them in the dining room, the sound of Mom's voice in the kitchen reaching even through the closed door as she began her bootcamp-like whip-cracking so unlike her normal self it still made me grin and feel a bit afraid of her at the same time. "I lost track of the time." She clutched at my hand, face pinched and still showing grief. "I need to talk to you, Fee," she whispered. "I think Lester was hiding something and I can't go to the sheriff. I know they think Heather killed him and all, but now I'm not so sure they have the right person."

"What was he hiding?" If Doreen could just lead me in the right direction…?

Her distress was pretty clear as she let me go. "I wish I knew. They say that there's paperwork proving Heather was embezzling from the yacht club, but… I do those books, Fee. I'm sure it was Lester." She just said the magic words. "I just remember he always hinted about how he knew more about everyone in town than he should and that even those who seemed above reproach had secrets he kept for his own benefit."

Yikes, that sounded bad. And like more motive for murder. "Why are you telling me? Dad needs to hear this, Doreen."

She nodded, sniffling. "I guess I just got tired of trying to protect someone who wasn't the good person I thought he was."

Poor thing. "How about I tell Dad for you," I said. "If Lester was keeping secrets, my father's the best one to uncover it and protect it." And bring anyone committing wrongdoing to justice.

Doreen hesitated, looking stricken by guilt suddenly. But before I could convince her this was the best course of action, she bobbed a nod and fled, shuffling her comfortable shoes to the door, disappearing between a pair of returning guests and out into the early evening.

The rest of the next two hours passed quickly, more than busy enough to keep me from focusing on Heather, Crew or the murder, and despite how tired I was when it was over, I was grateful for the respite. I hugged Mom on my way out of the kitchen to fetch one last load of dirty dishes, the two girls serving with me tonight pattering past me on sneakered feet. One of them paused as something shiny caught against her toe and went flying and I found myself scrambling to retrieve a set of keys that had somehow slid under one of the tables, lost in the shuffle.

A quick check of the ring told me they belonged to Doreen, a small, engraved panel with her name etched carefully into it giving me the owner. Whoops, I must have knocked them out of her pocket when I ran into her earlier and the keys had traveled under the eager shoes of guests coming to dine. I bounced them in my hand, glancing out the front door glass into the gathering dark. She would have gone home without them, would be missing them. I really needed to return them to her, right? This seemingly serendipitous opportunity woke up my nosiness like I'd been handed an edict from the Universe.

Yes, I'd return Doreen's keys like the good girl I was. Via the yacht club. And a quick check of Lester's office for evidence he was the real thief.

CHAPTER THIRTY-SEVEN

I took care not to slam the top drawer of Lester's desk in sheer frustration, scowling into the dim quiet of his office while my heart beat just a bit too fast and hard for my own good. Sneaking into the club hadn't been that hard, though. A bit of a smile for the two couples boarding their boat for an evening jaunt and acting like I was supposed to be here seemed to do the trick, though I did take care to skirt the view of the camera pointing at the end of the dock just in case. Sure, I might be caught on the one Chris and Wanda had set up, if they were even still filming, but from what I knew they were on my side. Still, there was something about messing around with breaking and entering that left me with that kind of shivery feeling inside that had me on edge and ready to run at a moment's notice.

It didn't help I was left without anything resembling evidence against Lester for my troubles. From what I could tell, the contents of his desk amounted to a couple of legal pads with doodles on them, a stapler empty of staples, some chewed ends of pencils and a giant calculator that an elderly person might need if they had vision problems. It wasn't even that his desk was locked. It was just empty.

Leaving me to believe either Robert had cleared everything out or Lester was about the most incompetent yacht club president in the history of such a position. Mind you, the man was blackmailing everyone he could get his hands on, so I was as inclined to believe my second guess as much as my first one. Not that it made me feel any better, though. But my brain had a funny way of winding through observations at the least opportune moments when I really should have been focusing on keeping myself from getting arrested.

Because I could be absolutely, 100% certain if Robert caught me in Lester's office, he'd throw me in the local lockup just for the satisfaction of doing it. So why was I here, then? Frustration bit deep into my curiosity and finally made me admit I was wasting my time.

I hesitated in the hall outside his door, Doreen's keys in my hand. Maybe he wasn't in possession any longer of anything of help, but she was the treasurer, right? Hadn't she said she knew the books intimately?

I almost kicked myself for being so slow, crossing to her door with renewed waves of giddy excitement mixed with what the hell are you doing, Fiona. Her key was a match to his, marked carefully with a strip of white plastic from some kind of label maker. Bless her for making my life easier. Unlike Lester's office, hers was full of goodies and I found myself quickly rooting through piles of neatly stacked paperwork, rifling the filing cabinet thanks to yet another nicely labeled key, and even sorting through her trash can just in case something might have been missed. Her computer was on, at least, and a quick glance at her desktop finally gave me the gleeful moment of "Yes!" I'd been hoping for. My butt hit her seat and, with a quick glance toward her closed door, I wiggled her mouse to life and clicked the file folder marked "Accounts."

Now, I was no accountant or anything, but I ran my own business and I figured I knew what to look for if someone was embezzling. Never mind Doreen's bookkeeping was leaps and bounds ahead of my own apparently feeble attempts to track the financial comings and goings through Petunia's and the annex. It was quickly obvious I was sadly lacking in the skills required to make any sense of the numbers and categories I scrolled through.

Well, wasn't that craptastic? Here was the information I'd been seeking, and I couldn't even figure out what it said. More frustration, this time audible, as I sighed deeply and sat back, fingers drumming on the arms of Doreen's chair, my right knee bouncing up and down in a rapid-fire protest of failure.

I did a half-hearted rifle through her top drawer and, with shock burning away my self-judgment, I found myself in possession of a new key. This one labeled "Lester's Boat." Even as my heart leaped. Because where, oh where, would he keep his most important secrets if not his floating palace?

Refusing to look a gift horse in the mouth, I leaped to my feet and headed for the scene of the crime. As I passed under the camera over the door, whispering a soft curse at my clumsiness, I hesitated, key in hand. Well, I could always just go back inside the club and erase the tape, right? That decision made, I hurried to the end of the dock and trotted up the steps to the side of Lester's boat, surprised to find not a scrap of police tape or even a barricade of any kind preventing me from entering. Robert's spectacular police work, no doubt. Still, at least it gave me free access and, as I slipped the key into the lock keeping me from entering the main cabin, I thanked him with a grin for his incompetence.

The wood panel door slipped silently shut behind me while I breathed into the dark interior of the boat, the slapping sound of soft waves against the hull outside muted but audible, the gentle rocking triggering the slight bend of my knees to keep my balance. I'd never really liked boats, tended toward seasickness and thoughts of sinking, sharks and watery graves, but this particular boat was docked, firmly tied to the pier and I had evidence to dig for.

The scent of Lester's particular brand of aftershave still hung in the air, permeating everything. I resisted the urge to sneeze, skirting the coffee table bolted to the floor, admiring the beautiful décor even as I realized the only reason the man had possession of this vessel was because of Heather. That soured my appreciation pretty quickly.

I took my time going through the space, pulling at cushions, lifting bench seats to test for hideaways. I even rummaged through the fridge and freezer, just in case, though stumbling over a new bottle of coffee-flavored tequila in the icebox made me thirsty. But it was a search of the cupboards that finally gave me what I was looking for. When I opened the last door, pushing at the box of cereal he'd tucked into the corner, the unusual weight of it sent it toppling to its side with a soft thud. Huh. Curiosity now at full burn, I tugged it loose, and flipped open the top flap, peeking within.

Tucked inside, between the plastic sleeve holding the remains of the sugary breakfast treat and the cardboard container, was a large yellow envelope. Fingers trembling, I pulled free the contents and flipped through the pages of documents, photos and news articles, the stack about as damning as any police file. I recognized a few names, faces but knew if I stood there too long trying to sort out all the truths Lester dug up, I would likely get caught. Instead, vibrating with the need to take his treasure home and catalog every single scrap of information, I stopped at the final photo.

I recognized David Campbell, younger then, but still himself. And, beside him, a man who looked enough like Heather he had to be her father. Here was the evidence of his wrongdoing Lester held. The news article clipped to it mentioned both men, though their names were different. Still thinking about how to help Heather—this discovery might just make things worse for her, after all—I turned over to the last few pages.

Bank statements, four of them, a list of deposits. My mind stuttered over the details as I read them over, eyes widening while my heart actually skipped a beat before hammering back to life in one huge, painful thud.

Even as I realized we'd all been looking in the wrong place. I had to get this evidence to my dad.

Hurrying had always been my downfall and tonight was no different. I took the time to bag the evidence in a zipper freezer bag I found in the cupboard, the thumb drive at the bottom of the envelope surely holding even more blackmail information. I knew my fingers all over the envelope and pages likely negated any evidence that might have been helpful, but I had to at least try to preserve whatever trace might linger.

Job done, I dodged out onto the deck and headed for the steps and the pier, realizing at the last moment I'd exited the opposite door I'd come in. Cursing softly at my own lack of attention, hands tucking the envelope into my back pocket, I spun to go back inside rather than circle the deck.

Only to feel something impact with a harsh thud between my shoulder blades. Hard enough to send me over the rail.

CHAPTER THIRTY-EIGHT

I grasped for the rail as I hit it, fingers sliding over the slippery wood, my equilibrium already a mess thanks to my dislike of the rocking motion. I caught at the thin metal under railing and hung on, whoofing out a breath as my full body weight impacted the side of the boat. Sneaker rubber squeaked on fiberglass as I fought for purchase, panting and staring up at my assailant who peeked over the edge.

Doreen's curly head looked oddly innocuous, her glasses catching the light. As I drew a breath to scream for help, one of her small, wrinkled hands dropped a long string of decorative lights over me, the end landing with a splash in the water. At the exact moment her foot stepped against my fingers and the pain made me reflexively release my grasp, sending me over into the water.

But not before, in a final desperate grab, I latched onto her ankle and, with my body weight behind my momentum, jerked her into the water after me.

I plunged under the surface, feeling something tingle against my leg, terror seizing me as I realized I was about to die from electrocution. It didn't happen, though, the light string blinking out the same moment I passed beneath the surface, Doreen's weight on top of me more of a concern in that instant than my heart stopping. While I might have been spared the fate Lester suffered, when the old woman's feet struck me full in the chest and drove me further under the water, I not only lost my hold on her, I lost all of the air keeping me buoyant and, frankly, without enough oxygen in my system to survive returning to the surface.

My hands lunged outward, caught for something, anything to save me, tangling in the line of lights now anchored to an extension cord, sinking slowly down after me, the end no longer plugged into anything. Saved and killed in the same attempt to survive. Doreen's downward plunge wasn't nearly as dramatic as mine and, as I felt my body sink, my resistance failing while my brain screamed at me to inhale, inhale, inhale, I watched her bob to the surface.

The cord of lights pulled tight, the other end snared in her clothing. I jerked on it with all my might, panic bursting inside me, clawing and thrashing for safety above me, light reflecting on the shimmering surface above while I felt my need for air overwhelm my knowledge breathing would kill me.

Blackness closed in around the edges of my vision, my last memory in that moment of the faint image of a compass etched into the rock of the pier, an image I knew well, one I'd seen before, many times, in a book in my kitchen, on a scrap of paper in my music box. The same image I'd spotted when I'd rescued Petunia and one that tied me to Crew Turner in ways I had as yet to understand.

And would never get a chance to, it seemed. Because darkness, the black, thick, heaviness of the end of everything, washed over my consciousness as agony seared through my chest, water filling my lungs while my body betrayed me with a spasmodic inhale of dirty lake water.

Then I was spluttering, choking, coughing out water onto the dock while Dad pounded on my back, shouting for an ambulance while Jill wrestled Doreen into handcuffs and I gasped for air, my father's strong arms around me.

"Fee," he whispered. "Damn it, Fiona Fleming. I didn't make you part of my work to lose you."

I gaped up at him, unable to speak, while Doreen, her guilt now obvious, screamed at me.

"Lester's death was an accident!" She jerked at the cuffs on her wrists.

Dad spun and snarled. "And my daughter?"

Doreen stilled then, head dropping, shoulders rounding forward as the fight went out of her. Jill's grim expression was nothing on Dad's flicker of rage and, I think if he'd had the woman in cuffs in that moment, she'd be back in the water with the extension cord she'd tried to kill me with wrapped around her neck.

"He was going to turn me in," she sobbed then like I cared. I struggled to sit up, Dad supporting me, lungs burning and my head light but needing to hear what she had to say. After everything I'd been through? Yeah, I was getting the end of the story, thanks. "At least, I thought so. Turned out he just wanted to blackmail me for a cut of the money."

"Why, Doreen?" Dad's cold tone was nothing like the usual stoic one he used with most suspects. "Why were you stealing?"

She grunted, shrugged, tears suddenly forgotten. "Because I could," she whispered. Giggled. Met his eyes with her own full of a sort of giddy madness that made me cringe, sobs long vanished like a crazy switch got flipped. "It was fun."

Holy crap. How had no one noticed she'd fallen off her rocker and into la-la-nutsoland?

"Lester's blackmail evidence. He had bank statements." I coughed, voice hoarse, barely able to speak as I fished out the envelope—still safe in the plastic baggie I'd used to protect it—from my back pocket, handing it to Dad. "You were taking from more than the yacht club."

Doreen's flash of a smile cracked at the edges. "Of course," she said. "I don't just do the books for this rat hole, do I?" Yikes. "Cottagers, the White Valley Lodge, the equestrian center." She giggled again, sighed. "I had a great scam going."

"And the money?" Jill sounded disgusted and more than a little surprised. I only then noted the gathering of people standing back, watching, whispering. Word would be out in no time. And from the scowl on Chris's face, the way Wanda huffed, they used Doreen's services themselves. "What were you going to do with it?"

Doreen tossed her head, water droplets flying from her heavy, short curls. "Nothing," she said. "It wasn't about the money."

Yup, cracked.

"So, Lester found out and tried to extort it from you." Dad didn't sound even a bit sorry for her.

She snarled, lunged, almost got free of Jill who caught at her with a shocked expression, like she was caught off guard. "I underestimated him, imagine." She seemed surprised by that. "He was going to ruin everything," she said. "How he found out about my secret bank account, I have no idea. But he made it plain that he planned to use it against me. I tried to talk him out of blackmailing me, but he wouldn't listen." The singsong tone of her voice made my skin crawl. "So, I came to see him that night, to reason with him." Sure, she did. "And when he wouldn't listen, well." Her grin reminded me of the flash of a skeleton's creepy remains. "I had no choice, did I?" She shook Jill's hard hold off, squared her old shoulders inside her dripping cardigan. "I meant to strangle him with the lights," she said. "The electrocution was rather anti-climactic when I really wanted to watch him die in my hands."

Wow. Just wow.

"You just had to show up and find the body." She glared at me like this was all my fault. "Before I could locate the bank statements he stole from me. The only evidence against me." She wrinkled her nose. "Smart girl," she said. "I had you fooled. Did you like my acting job?" In an instant, a flicker of emotion, she was sobbing, wracked with grief before a hideous laugh won through and she winked at me. "I almost had you, too. Dropped that hint that got you down here to snoop on my behalf. Even left you my keys so you'd have a way to do my dirty work." Her appearance at Petunia's tonight was a setup? My intuition clearly failed me, my nosiness almost paying off in her favor. "Owed you, I figure." She grew still, glaring before bursting into another peal of laughter. "She does, too, and was happy to supply me everything I needed to continue our little operation in her absence." Before I could ask Doreen who she was talking about, she stilled and stared, creep factor upping by about a million. "Peggy says hello, Fiona Fleming."

Chill that had nothing to do with the water or my near-death experience made me shudder as Jill pushed Doreen forward, dragging her away, my dad's arms tightening around me while memory flashed to the photo in Doreen's office, the image I'd seen of four smiling young women. One of whom was Doreen, another my Grandmother Iris and the third, the familiar one on the left I'd failed to place? None other than Peggy herself. As for the fourth, I had no idea, though I needed to find out. Because I couldn't help but wonder if Peggy Munroe, the first person to try to kill me, could reach me from inside her prison cell.

I wasn't getting an answer for that tonight. But I was going to see the resolution of another issue pending. I huddled in Dad's arms, waiting for the paramedics to check me over when a dark sedan beat a deputy's car into the parking lot and two men hurried our way.

CHAPTER THIRTY-NINE

Crew looked good, too good for someone who should at least have suffered somewhat for the agony he put me through. I couldn't bring myself to be angry with him, though, not when his long, fast strides carried him toward me. A third car ground to a halt as Robert tried to catch up with his boss, my cousin's expression one of utter loathing, aimed at Crew's back. I needed to warn the handsome sheriff what he was getting himself into, but I couldn't seem to breathe properly just then.

The water in my lungs or the sight of tall, dark and handsome home again? I'll let you decide what made talking impossible. But Crew didn't reach me before Olivia's strident voice broke his pace.

"Sheriff Turner!" He spun abruptly, cowboy

boots digging into the asphalt, expression grim, shoulders set. I half expected Dad to leave me, to go back up Crew, but instead, he stayed put, holding me close, watching in silence as I did, while the drama of the Reading Sheriff's Department unfolded in front of everyone.

"Mayor Walker." Crew sounded pissed. "I'll be right with you." She spluttered before he turned his back on her, on the glaring Robert, on the not-so-subtly smiling Geoffrey Jenkins, and finished his journey all the way to me. He crouched beside me, eyes meeting mine, then Dad's, before his gaze fell to me again. "Fee," he whispered, voice cracking. "Please stop almost dying, okay?" I managed to smile, if faintly, unable to be angry with him anymore. "You came back."

He flinched, like what I said actually hurt. Crew didn't comment on his return, but one big hand settled over mine, squeezed just enough. "John, she needs to go to the hospital."

No way was I leaving now. But Dad nodded agreement while Crew stood, turning back to face the music. Alone. I fought against my father, the two paramedics who lifted me onto a gurney, slipping off a heartbeat later, legs shaky from my ordeal but refusing to abandon Crew when he needed my support.

Dad didn't fight me then, joining me with one hand on my shoulder, both of us firmly behind the sheriff as Robert closed ranks with Geoffrey and Olivia, her anger visible despite her usual polish, crossed her arms over her chest and glared. I felt Jill's hand close on mine a moment as the mayor spoke, nodded to the deputy who nodded back.

"Where have you been, Sheriff Turner?" Olivia's tone told me she was ready to throw him under the bus if it would keep her in the mayor's seat. Good to know where she stood.

"Upholding an old responsibility," he said, voice low, level, completely reasonable. "I was assured, Mayor Walker, the selection of Deputy Carlisle was the right choice in my absence." My insides quivered and zinged as I realized what he was up to. What his plan was. And I almost ruined it by squealing in delight at his cleverness.

Robert didn't seem to get it, grunting as he thrust out his chest, thumbs hooked in his belt. "That's right," he shot at Crew. "I handled this murder—and those meddling Flemings—better than you ever could." Was it possible Robert had no idea what had just happened here? That he had zero clue who Jill had in the back of her cruiser and why? If so, he was even more of an idiot than I thought.

"Except," Crew said softly, faint amusement in his voice, correcting my cousin in the best possible power play, "I understand you're holding the wrong person in custody." Wait, how did he know? I caught Jill's smirk. She'd called him, caught him up? Even more clever. And perfect.

Robert's confusion? A beautiful thing to behold.

"Suffice it to say," Crew went on in that smoothly reasonable tone, "your choice for acting sheriff appears to have been misguided. And those meddling Flemings as you call them have once again handed over the real perpetrator."

I wished for a brief moment I could have videotaped Robert's expression, caught it for posterity so I could watch the pale comprehension and utter fury wash over him in that instant. The moment he realized Crew Turner won again. Except, of course, my fears about my cousin's state of mind roared back to life when the acting sheriff glared at his boss. Dad and I weren't Robert's only targets.

Crew shifted from one foot to the other, though not out of restlessness. If anything, his move seemed to ground him further, give his power stance more weight. "I'm disappointed to discover my deputy failed in his duties," he said. "We'll be discussing the case at length, I assure you. Knowing I have staff I can count on, trust to carry out competent investigations, is an absolute necessity if I intend to remain in Reading as sheriff."

Enough gasps from the crowd told me he'd won public opinion if not the love of Geoffrey and Robert. Still, I could see the evolution of acceptance and grudging admiration in Olivia as she absorbed Crew's cleverness, noted he'd taken the upper hand without a fight, made her choice and took sides.

The right one, in my opinion.

"We'd hate to lose you, Sheriff Turner," she said. "I'm happy to take part in a conversation about moving forward from this unfortunate event."

And, just like that, the incredible and delicious

Crew Turner was her golden boy again. Naturally.

I coughed painfully, chest on fire, the heaviness like someone sat on my chest waking a vaguely panicked feeling I had to fight off to keep from coughing harder. Dr. Aberstock listened carefully with his stethoscope pressed firmly to my back, his free hand soft on my shoulder. I felt the now warm circle of metal and rubber slide sideways under my t-shirt and inhaled slowly so he could listen to the other side while my head pounded from fighting the urge to hack up a lung and show him what it looked like in person.

"Definitely pneumonia," he said, sighing as he leaned back, shaking his head, the black rubber of the instrument tucked around his neck. He tsked softly at me, patting my hand as I leaned back into the headboard, Mom hovering next to me, hands wringing, face tight with worry. "You're going to be in bed for a bit, I'm afraid, Fiona. Might I recommend next time not breathing in lake water?" He shuddered faintly, sweet Santa face scrunching at the teasing. "It's filthy."

"Yeah, thanks for that." My voice rasped from my throat, breathy as my lungs contracted in protest. "I'll do my best from now on."

His warm, steady hand touched my forehead, my cheeks. "And running a fever," he said, looking up to meet Mom's eyes. "She's staying in bed, Lucy?"

A solid twenty-four hours of it, thank you very much. "You can ask me, you know," I snapped, grumpy feeling making me petulant. Yes, I clearly recognized the cranky little girl I was being. Thankfully, Mom had the patience of a saint.

"We're doing our best," she said. "We could move her to the hospital." That particular threat made me want to cough my lungs out so that pair of traitor organs could go and leave me here to die in peace and quiet.

"I'll be good," I said. "I promise." But Petunia's was packed, wasn't it? And Daisy's old request to have Rose help made me nervous. I had to get out of bed. Just as soon as the doc left.

"How long will she be out of commission?" Dad didn't sound as worried as Mom as he darkened the doorway to my bedroom. Then again, he was better at hiding his concern than my mother. Was he actually anxious about my well-being or was he wondering when I'd be up and able to help him with his cases? Made me wonder if Mom knew about him adding me without my permission to his business roster.

"Another couple of days of quiet should put you to rights." At least Dr. Aberstock was talking directly to me again and not my parents like I was six. Come to think of it, though, I'd caught this very illness when I was that age, so maybe he was having flashbacks. He tucked his stethoscope into his bag, squeezing my fingers once again, his chubby ones soft and comforting on the surface of the quilt covering me. "Might I congratulate you once again on another case solved, Fiona?" His eyes twinkled and I swear he looked far too pleased with this whole situation. "And may I offer my support if things head in the direction everyone is thinking they might?"

"What direction is that, Doc?" Dad sounded calm and rational enough, but Mom's flicker of nerves made me pause.

Dr. Aberstock stood, medical bag in his hand as he half turned and leveled Dad with a sterner expression than I was expecting. "You know very well what I'm talking about, John." The doc winked at me. "Another Fleming sheriff would be welcome in Reading."

He left without another word, leaving me gaping after him, though the suggestion wasn't exactly a shocker. Still, if even the mild-mannered doctor was willing to put voice to the fact maybe Crew wasn't going to be running the show any longer and that I was the town's choice for replacement...? But, what about his recovery last night at the yacht club? Surely that put things to rights? If not, if Crew's position was still precarious, I had to help turn things around for him.

Yikes. I didn't want to be part of the Fiona Fleming for sheriff conversation with the current one. Oh, wait. I was dating him. That meant the talk was pretty much inevitable if he caught wind of it.

Yeah, this was going to go well.

CHAPTER FORTY

Dad didn't say anything while Mom sighed, bending to kiss my cheek before brushing past him on her way out. I let her go, not willing to think about what Dr. Aberstock said.

My father, instead of dwelling on such a future, filled me in on the past. "Thankfully I was with Chris and Wanda looking at the live feed of their surveillance when you showed up tonight." That's how he knew where I was? "We watched Doreen follow you on board." He sounded a bit bemused. "She didn't look happy, so I went to check on you."

"I'm glad you did," I said.

He nodded, swallowed like he didn't want to think about the alternative. "I got a look at the paperwork Doreen gave Robert. She did a great job setting up Heather. Then again, she didn't have to do much. Lester was pretty thorough, kept everything nice and neat so he could pin her and David for the scheme. Heather's going down for fraud and embezzling." She was guilty, so I couldn't feel too sorry for her. "But her father's employers are paying for her legal fees. I guess they take the idea of family seriously, especially when they were able to recover the missing boats Lester forced Heather to sell illegally." Huh. Well, good for Gordon Buckley. Sounded like he was a better person than most. "They never recovered the evidence against her father, so he's in the clear." Because that evidence was in Dad's possession. Did that mean he had no plans to hand it over to the state troopers or Crew? Interesting. Heather would be happy about that, at least. "A handful of boat owners are being investigated for dumping, thanks to Wanda and Chris. I convinced Olivia to step in when Robert wanted to charge them with illegal surveillance. None of what they filmed is usable in court, but it's enough to trigger a look into dumping violations." Good to know. Our lake needed to be protected. Dad continued his litany for my benefit, without prompting. Nice of him to fill me in when I couldn't get out of bed to get my own information. "Doreen admitted she found the camera they set up at the club and shut off the feed when Heather went on Lester's boat the night of his death. She then waited until Heather left before going on board herself." Far cleverer than I gave her credit for and reminiscent of

Peggy Munroe's deceptions. Considering my own Grandmother Iris had her secrets, I couldn't help but wonder who the fourth woman in the photo in Doreen's office was and if I had one more old lady to worry about. "David and Luke are both going away for the thefts and Doreen's been taken by the troopers. I hear they're going to try to charge her with murder and not manslaughter, but with your attempted murder on the docket, too, I'm not sure they need to push things. She'll be going away for her own fraud."

"Dad, what about Peggy?" I didn't want to think about the old woman's ability to reach me beyond her prison cell.

My father looked like he found her involvement about as concerning as I did, but when he spoke his tone was soft and supportive. "Don't you worry about Peggy Munroe. I'll have a chat with an old friend in the prison system. He'll keep an eye on her."

I was going to mention the fourth woman, the other three identified from the photo, but didn't get a chance. Dad looked like he wanted to leave and, with Daisy's slow, hesitant appearance he used that interruption to shut down. He offered her a small, grim smile before waving at me and disappearing through the door into my living room, leaving me alone with my best friend.

She looked upset, though when she didn't rush to my side to hug me or hold my hands like my old bestie would have, I realized it wasn't my physical distress that was causing her pain. And when she opened her mouth to speak, I had a horrible feeling in the pit of my stomach that had nothing to do with my latest near-death experience.

"I had to, Fee." She blurted those words like I'd accused her of something instead of just sat there in my bed, slowly dying from being too hot and too cold and coughing all at the same time. "I didn't have a choice."

Whoa, hang on a second, sister. "Daisy, maybe if you started at the beginning." There, that was calm and rational despite my lack of ability to really focus closely. The heavy dose of antibiotics Dr. Aberstock gave me muddied my mind.

She stopped suddenly, hands clasped in front of her while she flinched, facing me with so much worry and stress on her face I wanted to hug her while I shook her hard enough to cause permanent damage. Because the only reason Daisy would be that upset had to do with me and Rose and maybe Petunia's and I just wasn't sure I was in a position to accept any excuses she might have.

"Tell me," I growled, partly from my raw throat and lungs and partly from growing anger over something I was only guessing at.

"I asked Rose to help us." She swallowed, hurried on. "Just while you're sick."

Yes, I was going to shake her after all. And shake her and shake her and shake her. "Did you talk to Mom about it first?" From the look on her face, that question was hitting a big, fat nope. "Jeeze, Daisy, this is *our* business. *All* of ours. Where in our partnership does it say you can make arbitrary decisions for the three of us?"

She spluttered a moment before her cheeks pinked and her gray eyes flattened. For the first time ever, I saw the kind of meanness in Daisy that I'd seen regularly in Rose, and it scared the crap out of me. "You would both have said no," she told me, voice cold like she was repeating something she'd heard a million times and only now had it beaten into her long enough to say it out loud like it was her own personal thought. "And I need the help. So, I asked her."

"You know how I feel about her," I said. "I don't want her having anything to do with Petunia's." Yes, I was being harsh and not pulling back like maybe I would have if I was healthy. Wait, who was I kidding? I never pulled back.

"Then maybe you don't want me to have anything to do with this place, either." Wait, what? That was the second time she used a line like that, and I was about done with it. She bobbed a nod like she was making a decision. "If Rose isn't welcome, I'm going, too." And, with that, she stormed out of my room, as if that was the last word on the matter.

While my heart stuttered, and my chest tightened around my too-fast pulse as I tried to comprehend what the hell just happened.

Even as tall, dark and handsome walked through my door.

CHAPTER FORTY-ONE

Maybe I should have been happy to see him, or at least offered up an attempt at a smile, a welcome, a "Hey, Crew, you're alive and not murdered by who knows what gang of imagined thugs who took your undercover self and turned you into a flayed piece of flotsam for the FBI to find in ten years." Yeah, maybe.

I'm not good at maybe.

But he beat me to the resounding ass-kicking he had coming, sinking to the edge of the bed and kissing me like he'd actually missed me. He'd been home for a whole day, and this was the first time I'd seen him since his appearance at the club. Sure, he was probably busy saving his job and dealing with Doreen and Robert and Olivia all, but seriously.

Priorities. Still, I let him kiss me, grumbling around his delicious lips, refusing to let my hands slide through his thick, dark hair or trace over the stubble on his cheek—

Hey. Traitor hands. What the actual…?

I pulled away only because I had to cough, Crew cradling me against his chest ever so gently while I fought for a clear breath. When I finally sagged, sweating and pale and wanting to die, back onto my pile of pillows, the misery on his handsome face cut off the sharp anger I'd been harboring for his absence and instead distilled everything I'd been feeling down into the kind of disappointment that shattered relationships.

At least, I worried that was inevitable.

Crew wasn't ever in the habit of taking what I dished out, so I was pretty sure the moment I said a word he'd be out of there, gonzo, see ya, Fee, nice knowing you. He looked tired, worn out, stressed, still with the short haircut that made him look more FBI than the sheriff I loved. Was it a foreshadowing of the end of what we could have been?

To my utter shock, as he squeezed my hand with one of his the other ruffled his already messed hair while he met my eyes without a trace of argument.

"I screwed up," he said. "Fee, I'm sorry."

Whoa. An apology was the last thing I'd been expecting. And saved us, I think.

Did he know it? There was that maybe again. Okay, so I might be good at maybes after all.

"You're okay." I croaked that, choked on the

tears behind it. Clasped his fingers a bit too tight.

He nodded, squeezed back. "I can say I didn't have a choice," he whispered to me, shaking his head. "I can tell you that I owed it to the FBI, to the people who trusted me with the case originally. But I'd be full of crap."

"Then why?" I held on while he went on.

"For Liz." He swallowed hard, shrugged. "I owed her, Fee. My life. And she needed me."

I didn't ask the obvious, but it must have been written all over my face because he instantly paled, stammered, shook his head.

"No," he said. "It's not like that. Liz was my best friend at Quantico. We'd been partners for years."

I'd take his word for it. "She wouldn't let me talk to you." Petulant, much?

He leaned in, stroking hair from my forehead, concern so deep and true and authentic I wanted to cry, to hug him tight and never let him go instead of sitting here, staring at him like I'd rather he just left already. "It's not her fault," he said. "It was my responsibility, and I chose to stay quiet." Crew's blue eyes shone with regret, enough I finally relented and nodded. The compass tattoo on his wrist hit me like a freight train, the memory of what I'd seen under the water gurgling up from the depths of my subconscious. It took me over so hard I missed half of what he'd said until I jerked abruptly at the sound of his voice, cluing in again. "—known you'd be in the middle of a murder when I got back." Was that amusement in his voice? He hadn't earned back the right to tease me just yet.

Still. The softening between us? I'd take it.

"It was only supposed to take a few hours," he said, sighing, rubbing at his face with his free hand, never letting me go all the while. Like he fully planned to keep my fingers clasped in his forever. Not complaining or anything. "And turned out to be far more complicated than it should have been." His lips parted as he started to go on, paused, started again, and finally shrugged with a rueful grin, boyish, sweet. "I promise," he said, "I'll never do it again."

"This isn't funny," I said. "Olivia says you're this close to losing your job." I pinched my fingers together to show him just how precarious his situation was.

But Crew didn't seem worried. "I'm more concerned about you," he said. "The doc said it's pneumonia but no lasting harm?" More guilt as he stroked my forearm like that action could heal me with such a simple touch. Well, I was feeling better, so maybe he was that powerful.

"Fee." Crew cleared his throat before leaning in and kissing my forehead. "We can talk about this when you're better. But I'm not so sure I want to keep my job."

He said what? "Are you going back to the FBI?" Such misery, Fee. Way to whine and everything.

But Crew shook his head, a frown pulling his dark brows together, that firm grip on me not relenting. "Olivia's on her way out," he said. "And without her, I won't be far behind. But I've grown attached to a few things about Reading." His wink was soft, without anger or regret. "And there's always the Fleming Investigation agency. I hear the boss is hiring."

Oh my god. Dad. Poaching my sorta boyfriend? Seriously.

I should have told him over my dead body. Except I'd almost died, so the joke didn't have the same sort of humor to it that might be required. Besides, it was hard to argue with Crew Turner when he was kissing me.

CHAPTER FORTY-TWO

It wasn't until Crew was long gone after a lovely interlude of lips and hugging and more apologizing—enough to last me until the next time, I guess—that I realized I'd failed to mention my underwater discovery. But before I could text him to come back, my phone rang in my hand, the vibration and sound making me jump and squeal a squeak of hoarse surprise. I answered it instantly, by habit. And held my breath in my tight and weighted chest as a woman's voice spoke in an Irish accent.

"Fiona." She almost breathed my name into my ear, sounding so sad I shivered and teared up from that single word. "Dear God in Heaven, is it really you at last?" I had trouble making out her words at times, her thick accent garbling what I heard, though

I was able to piece it together enough I knew exactly who was speaking on the other end of the line. "I've waited ever so long for you to reach out to me, lass."

"Siobhan," I whispered back. I didn't know her, only had guesses and suppositions and scraps of maybes to go on. But as she sobbed once from the other side of the Atlantic, I felt my entire heart go out to her as if she were a loved one I'd missed desperately for years.

"Dear Fiona," she finally said after pulling herself together, "forgive me for being a daft old woman. For letting this go on so very long without talking to you myself. Malcolm," she choked on his name before rushing on, "Malcolm said you'd be in touch when the time was right. But I never believed John would tell you about me or let you call yourself."

I inhaled slowly, forcing air into my sore lungs, feeling even more feverish despite the fact I was on the mend. This had nothing to do with pneumonia and everything to do with the mix of fear and anticipation that fought a pitched battle inside me. "Siobhan," I said, coughed softly to clear my throat. "I don't know anything. I need you to tell me what's going on." Another cough escaped me, without my consent. "Please, what happened? Who are you?"

She didn't speak for a long moment, the quiet sound of crying telling me she struggled with her own inner demons. "My sweet," she said then, exhaling audibly into the phone, "this isn't a conversation to have anything but face-to-face."

She wasn't going to leave me hanging, was she?

"But—"

"It's been over thirty years since I set foot in Reading," she said, voice firm now, the sound of movement in the background as she clearly rose from wherever it was she sat. "I've been hiding at home, Fiona, back here in Ireland. But the truth has to come out. And if Malcolm is right, if you're the girl he thinks you are, we'll uncover what needs to be told together."

I wanted to argue but I honestly didn't have the strength. "When are you coming?"

"I don't know," she said. "I'll do my best. But it may take some time to put my affairs in order."

That sounded kind of permanent. "Siobhan," I said, "are you okay?"

She paused, laughed softly, breathy and quiet. "My darling dear," she said, "I will be. I'll see you soon." And hung up.

I hit end on my cell, dropping it to my chest, forcing myself to relax after a bout of coughing took my breath away and left me drained. I stared at the ceiling for a long moment before turning on my WiFi and doing a search for her name. Came up empty— no cases, no anything. Over thirty years ago, huh? There were records in the library that might give me information.

Then again, I'd waited this long. And did I want to hear anything about what she had to say from anyone but her? Well, the point was moot at the moment. I was bedridden at least the next little while. But my curiosity was winning at last and with my trust in my father renewed, I vowed to find out what I could before the mysterious woman who felt like an old friend landed in my life. Likely with the power to shake everything I knew to the core.

Considering how often the snow globe of my life was shaken the last few years? Yeah, I was ready.

Sure, I was. One thing was certain, though, I was done stepping back and worrying about what people thought. I cared about my town, about the folks in it. The Pattersons, Blackstone, my friends, my family, the council issues? Time to step up and see if I could really make a difference.

I dragged my laptop toward me, glaring at the screen and the blinking cursor, the blank page with my byline written beneath it. And started typing.

Reading Reflections by Fiona Fleming

Welcome to Reading, Vermont, the cutest town in America.

That's us, right? Who we've been branded to be, thanks to the hard work—may I say tireless effort—of our mayor, Olivia Walker. Adorable, quaint, picturesque, the kind of place everyone in the world wants to not only visit but call home because we're just so lovely.

Right?

I'm as proud of our town as the next resident. Proud of what we're building, what we've already accomplished. With the right leadership, who knows where our ambitions and natural talents can take us?

The right leadership. Progressive, attentive to detail. Supported by well-educated and intuitive law enforcement with our safety and progress in mind. We're all in this together, after all, from the baristas at Sammy's Coffee to the chambermaids at the White Valley Lodge to the owners and operators of our most viable and successful businesses. We are responsible, as a town, all of us.

Division serves no one. Allowing division to come between us creates chaos and brings us all down. The choices we make now, either in the passion of the moment or the cold calculation of logic will decide our future as a whole.

So, tell me, Reading residents. Are we falling back into who we used to be? Or are we moving on?

FRENCH'S
Handmade Bakery
(555)555-5551

MARIE PATTERSON
Olympic Equestrian
Center
(555)555-5555

MARIE PATTERSON
Olympic Equestrian

The Reading Reader Gazette

VOLUME 1 ISSUE 1   AUG 16TH, 2019   WWW.RRGAZETTE.COM

News Briefs

1 **Equestrian Center fundraiser:** All Reading residents are invited to the first annual Marie Patterson Olympic Equestrian Center fundraiser, being held on September 25th. Join local riders, horse enthusiasts and breeders as we celebrate our new facility!

2 **Parking Violations:** Your town council would like to remind you that parking restrictions are ongoing this summer. Due to increased tourist activity, a year-round ban on street parking will be firmly enforced. Please note, violators have been ticketed and fines will be pursued. Any Reading resident whose vehicle is found parked outside their driveway will be towed at their expense. The sheriff's department asks you to please park responsibly. Let's keep Reading's streets safe!

3 **Family Fun:** Come one, come all to the Reading Family Fun Day - rain or shine - in the main town plaza on Saturday, Aug 21st. Dress in your favorite pirate costume and have fun getting your face painted, sampling local products and enjoy the theatrical re-enactment of the arrival of Captain Reading and his cabin boy, Patterson, as they choose our fair town for their very own.

4 **Vandalism Costumes:** We know you think you're clever, circumventing the curfews we've set up to protect the statue of Captain Reading. We also know you're using pearls purchased from Campbell's Hardware. We're tracking you now. And we will find you.

Winner of this week's Fire Hall 50/50 is our Lily Myers. Congratulations, Lily!

Please send any pressing community notices to pamela@rrgazette.com before 4PM.

Blood in the Water: Cutter Lake

Doreen Douglas, 74, of Reading, is in police custody for the murder of local yacht club president, Gerald Patterson.

Bookkeeper Bilks Businesses, Brought to Bench

By Pamela Shard

In a shocking turn of events, well-known and respected book keeper and Reading Yacht Club treasurer, Doreen Douglas, has been arrested in connection with the murder of president Gerald Patterson, 58.

With the vital assistance of local private investigators John and Fiona Fleming of Fleming Investigations, Douglas was apprehended for her crime. The pair also uncovered a slew of criminal activity until now either missed or ignored by local law enforcement.

Among those charged with a variety of crimes are Patterson's own son, Luke Patterson, 18, of theft along with his partner in crime, David Campbell, 51. Responsible for the rash of thefts from local cottages, the thieves were captured due to the diligence and detective skills of Fiona Fleming.

Also being held for illegal activity is Buckley Marine sales rep, Heather Parborough, on charges of fraud and embezzlement.

It should be noted that our own Fiona Fleming was yet again instrumental in not only uncovering the murder victim but in revealing the identity of multiple perpetrators, putting her very life at risk for our town once again in her pursuit of justice.

As usual, Mayor Olivia Walker refuses to comment on anything to do with this incident, though the Gazette has been assured that local accountant and Patterson son-in-law Geoffrey Jenkins continues his bid to run for mayor in the coming fall election.

The notable absence of our sheriff, Crew Turner, during this dark time has not gone unnoticed. His return after the fact leaves this reporter wondering where his priorities lie. Meanwhile, Deputy Robert Carlisle previously acting sheriff, insists his ability to solve the crime was thwarted by the interference of the Fleming investigation.

"The next time they try to poke their nose into a case," Carlisle stated with great heat, "I'll make sure they let the lockup so fast they'll wish they'd minded their own business."

Looking for more Fiona Fleming?
Book eight, *Guns and Ammo and Murder*,
is available now!

AUTHOR NOTES

My darling reader:

Thank you for your patience in waiting for the release of ***Anchors Away and Murder***. I don't often take time for myself, but the last few months of rest and rejuvenation have been a blessing and I'm grateful for the chance to fill myself up again so I can dive back into the work I love so much.

I adore how Fiona has been dribbling information to me the last few books, namely the bigger picture details that are dictating how her overarching story is developing along with the murders she solves. For instance, I had no idea starting out she'd be working with her father in his P.I. firm, nor that Peggy Munroe would peek out of the shadows at Fee seven books in. All the connections and evolution of meaning are so exciting to me—I can't wait for you to read what she has in store.

Change and progress are a good thing, right?

Happy reading in Reading,

Patti

ABOUT THE AUTHOR

EVERYTHING YOU NEED TO know about me is in this one statement: I've wanted to be a writer since I was a little girl, and now I'm doing it. How cool is that, being able to follow your dream and make it reality? I've tried everything from university to college, graduating the second with a journalism diploma (I sucked at telling real stories), am an enthusiastic member of an all-girl improv troupe (if you've never tried it, I highly recommend making things up as you go along as often as possible) and I get to teach and perform with an amazing group of women I adore. I've even been in a Celtic girl band (some of our stuff is on YouTube!) and was an independent film maker (go check out the Lovely Witches Club at www.lovelywitchesclub.com). My life has been one creative thing after another—all leading me here, to writing books for a living.

Now with multiple series in happy publication, I live on beautiful and magical Prince Edward Island (I know you've heard of Anne of Green Gables) with my multitude of pets.

I love-love-love hearing from you! You can reach me (and I promise I'll message back) at patti@pattilarsen.com. And if you're eager for your next dose of Patti Larsen books (usually about one release a month) come join my mailing list! All the best up and coming, giveaways, contests and, of course, my observations on the world (aren't you just dying to know what I think about everything?) all in one place: http://smarturl.it/PattiLarsenEmail.

Last—but not least!—I hope you enjoyed what you read! Your happiness is my happiness. And I'd love to hear just what you thought. A review where you found this book would mean the world to me— reviews feed writers more than you will ever know. So, loved it (or not so much), your honest review would make my day. Thank you!

Made in United States
North Haven, CT
29 August 2024

56708159R00172